MUCKERS

Inspired by a true story . . .

MUCKERS

**WHEN YOUR TOWN'S ABOUT TO CRUMBLE,
YOU DIG DEEPER INTO THE MUCK AND FIND A WAY TO WIN.**

SANDRA NEIL WALLACE

EMBER

Text copyright © 2013 by Sandra Neil Wallace
Cover art copyright © 2013 by Alfred A. Knopf
Photograph reproduced on the cover is of the actual Jerome Muckers team.
Map copyright © 2013 by Graham Evernden

All rights reserved. Published in the United States by Ember, an imprint of Random House Children's Books, a division of Random House LLC, a Penguin Random House Company, New York. Originally published in hardcover in the United States by Alfred A. Knopf, an imprint of Random House Children's Books, New York, in 2013.

Ember and the E colophon are registered trademarks of Random House LLC.

Visit us on the Web! randomhouseteens.com

Educators and librarians, for a variety of teaching tools, visit us at
RHTeachersLibrarians.com

The Library of Congress has cataloged the hardcover edition of this work as follows:
Wallace, Sandra Neil.
Muckers / Sandra Neil Wallace. — First edition.
pages cm.
"Inspired by a true story."
Summary: "Felix O'Sullivan, standing in the shadow of his dead brother, an angry, distant father, and racial tension, must lead the last-ever Muckers high school football team to the state championship before a mine closing shuts down his entire town."—Provided by publisher
ISBN 978-0-375-86754-5 (trade) — ISBN 978-0-375-96754-2 (lib. bdg) —
ISBN 978-0-307-98238-4 (ebook)
[1. Football—Fiction. 2. High schools—Fiction. 3. Schools—Fiction. 4. Fathers and sons—Fiction.
5. Copper mines and mining—Fiction. 6. Grief—Fiction. 7. Race relations—Fiction.
8. Mexican Americans—Fiction. 9. Arizona—History—20th century—Fiction.] I. Title.
PZ7.W15879Muc 2013 [Fic]—dc23 2013003537
ISBN 978-0-375-86526-8 (tr. pbk.)

Printed in the United States of America
10 9 8 7 6 5 4 3 2 1
First Ember Edition 2015

To the 1950 Jerome Muckers football team, their beloved coach Homer Brown, and Principal Lewis McDonald, for those letters.

And to the Arizona mining town itself, for putting up such a howl.

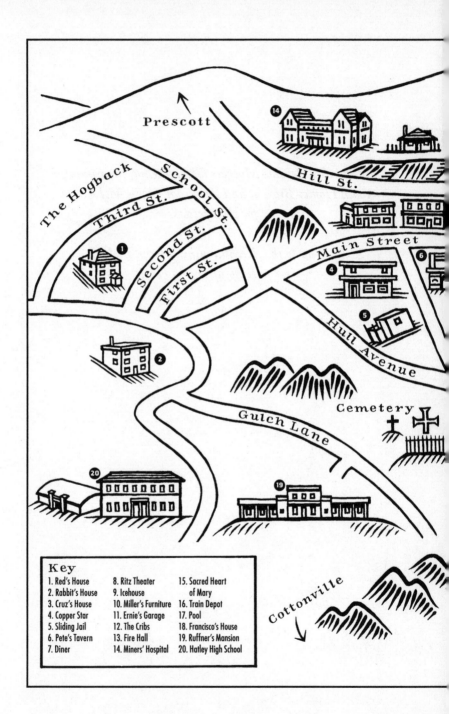

Prescott

The Hogback

Third St.

School St.

Second St.

First St.

Hill St.

Main Street

Hull Avenue

Gulch Lane

Cemetery

Cottonville

Key

1. Red's House
2. Rabbit's House
3. Cruz's House
4. Copper Star
5. Sliding Jail
6. Pete's Tavern
7. Diner
8. Ritz Theater
9. Icehouse
10. Miller's Furniture
11. Ernie's Garage
12. The Cribs
13. Fire Hall
14. Miners' Hospital
15. Sacred Heart
    of Mary
16. Train Depot
17. Pool
18. Francisco's House
19. Ruffner's Mansion
20. Hatley High School

mucker (*noun*)**:**
1. one who shovels loose rock or muck into the mine core, sorting the ore from waste.
2. a vulgar, ill-bred person.
3. the name of our team.

SUNDAY, OCTOBER 22, 1950
BEFORE DAYBREAK

I COME TO THE SHANTY in the Barrio from behind, dipping under the broken shutters so the late-October moon won't cast a shadow and wake up Cruz. Then I suck in my breath—there can't be more than two feet between us—and tread lightly onto the porch. What I'm holding belongs to him, but Cruz is too stubborn for me to do this face to face. *And persuasive.* I admit he almost had me convinced about the mine. But there were things Cruz believed in all along that he shouldn't have and ones that I should have and didn't. Like the football season. Cruz sure was right about that. He knew it before we even started, back in August, when Rabbit and Coach and Angie were still here and only a miracle could make winning possible. It was so hot and dry in Arizona then, you could watch the dust and the smelter smoke fighting each other just to get to the top of the mountain.

1

We were fighting, too, down in the slag below like all Muckers do. Not against the Commies in Korea or the ones that Sims and Superintendent Menary were hoping to find in Hatley. We were fighting to win football games—Mexicans, Slavs, and Anglos like me.

Sounds pretty simple, doesn't it? Win six games in seven weeks, going undefeated against teams bigger and better than we were, and make it to the state championship game. Teams with real uniforms and grass fields. Every one of those quarterbacks was better than me. That's what I thought. And I sure knew my brother, Bobby, was better when he played for Hatley High. But that's not what Cruz or Coach or even the town believed, though I wanted no part of their praise. Looking back, we all had different reasons for winning. But once we found out about the mine, what we wanted more than anything was not to lose. Because the only thing worse than losing is being forgotten.

1950 HATLEY MUCKERS FOOTBALL SCHEDULE

Friday Aug 25	RIM VALLEY	HERE
Friday Sept 1	PRESCOTT	THERE
Friday Sept 15	COLDBROOK	HERE
Friday Sept 22	COTTONVILLE	HERE
Friday Sept 29	KINGMAN	THERE
Friday Oct 13	FLAGSTAFF	THERE

Chapter 1
HATLEY'S BODY PARTS

THURSDAY, AUGUST 10

4:32 P.M.

IN THE DISTANCE, AS WE drive up from Cottonville, she looks like a pair of tanned knees. Sunburned and gnarled. Scraped bare from millions of years of abuse by the desert sun and now us.

But Cruz says the mountain above our town looks more like a woman lying down, tits up. One spread out, the other firm and pointy. I wouldn't know. I've never even seen tits up close. Well, maybe once. But that was by mistake during Mexican pool hours, looking for Angie. And I've certainly never felt them.

Anyway, the old prospectors christened her Nefertiti, after the Egyptian queen. And the mountain must have been beautiful once, back when she was covered in pine. That was some time ago, and none of us call her that anymore since Cruz came up with the nickname Nefer-*titty*.

Cruz pulls the Lucky Strike from behind his ear and lights it, nursing the convertible wheel with his knees and blaming Nefertitty's sagging on old age instead of the mine cave-ins. He points to the taller, perkier tit, in case me and Rabbit couldn't tell the difference.

We've been calling Sal "Rabbit" since second grade. Not that he's fast. No one's quicker than Cruz. Or because Rabbit's ever been with a girl either. (You know how rabbits can breed.) It's because of the harelip, which is why Rabbit can never look angry. It's as if the deformity's given him a moral compass somehow that stops him from doing anything half-way mean. Not even when he writes about our games in the *Pick & Shovel*.

Rabbit stretches for Cruz's cigarette from the backseat, but there's no way he'd smoke it. Instead, he makes a branding motion with the lit end toward the mountain, as if he's about to mark a steer. Because the other tit—the lopsided one—has a stone tattoo on it forming the letter *H*. We can take the blame for that. It's been a school tradition since '24 to brand the mountain with the spirit of good ol' Hatley High. That's when Principal Mackenzie led the Muckers to the Northern Crown. They nearly took the state, too, but those Phoenix refs had other ideas. Now we paint the H once a year no matter how we play, to keep the spirit of the town alive.

The stones get blasted out from the mine all day across Nefertitty's shoulder. Cut into stomach-sized chunks in the open pit by miners like Santiago, Cruz's father. That's how I know Hatley's problems have nothing to do with old age or one sagging boob.

It's because of what our fathers and their fathers before that have done to the mountain, poking a shaft into her seventy years ago and finding enough copper to fill her belly up with smoke. The way my pop still makes others do, shouting orders at Santiago and the powder monkeys to blast her skin off layer by layer until they get to the insides.

Rabbit's been watching the cigarette burn. He waits till there's about an inch of graying embers, then blows at it, spreading ashes all over the upholstery.

"You idiot! I just washed the car," Cruz says, snatching the cigarette back.

You'd think it was a diamond the way Cruz treats this old car since he won it off a miner. He puts up a howl and tries to smack Rabbit, but Rabbit leans far enough away and Cruz misses. That's the end of it. The light by the Tumbleweed gas station's up ahead, and Cruz slows down, not wanting to stop completely. We're in the middle of enemy territory: straddling both sides of us is Cottonville—the flat-chested community they built at the bottom of the mountain to process what we mine, and who we plan on beating the crap out of in football this year. Practice starts on Monday.

"Hang on," I tell Cruz, and get out of the car. I run up to the filling station and grab a newspaper off the top of the gas pump. The ones with two rocks on them are a couple days old and cost a penny instead of five cents. Benny from the diner lets me have them for nothing after game days, but that's still two weeks from now.

"What is it with you always wanting to read?" Cruz says, poking the *Verde Miner* with his elbow.

"That's how you find out things," I tell him.

"Oh yeah? Like what? Tell me something I don't already know."

"Well, it says here Ty's chickens are as tender as a mother's love. And that Peach Kellerman's been irrigating with the runoff. Says the cyanide helps his melons grow. He lost his wallet, too, walking into town."

"Again?" Cruz laughs. The slick's coming out of his hair. He smooths a hand over the black ends (which are brownish-black, really, like the feathers of a golden eagle caught by the morning sun). "And I bet Peaches can tell you what's in the wallet, no?" Cruz rubs a thumb and two fingers together. "Dollar bills." He smirks.

"There's houses for rent, too," I say, folding the paper and turning to face him. "Nine of them . . . *up on Company Ridge.*" To me, that's a sure sign the mine really is going to close, but I can already tell Cruz isn't buying it. He takes a long drag, making the Lucky smolder red then a flickering orange before tossing it into the Cottonville dirt. And he still won't look at me.

"What?" Cruz finally mumbles. "Don't mean anything except higher-ups getting on Ruffner's bad side. And they always lose muckers on quits. What is it with you Anglos? Never staying in one place for too long."

"How much are the chickens?" Rabbit asks.

"What do you care, Rabbit? Your mom raises them," Cruz says.

"Yeah, and she only charges forty-three cents for a pound."

I tell Rabbit there's a number to call and find out how much, then give him the paper. Cruz hangs a left onto the switchback that takes us up to Hatley. Now the tits have become one. All we see is the H we're headed for. Cruz puts the Ford Deluxe in low gear, flooring the gas pedal to make it up the steep pitch. The revs reach into our guts and Cruz grins, nodding at the radio on the dash—his signal for me to turn it up.

You've broken your vow, and it's all over now
So I'm movin' on.

Hank Snow's on the radio and it's all over now for me and Rabbit. It's Cruz's favorite song, only he can't sing.

"I bet he's got those rhinestones on right now, playing that song on the guitar!" Rabbit hollers from the back.

"They're not playing it right now while we're listening to it, stupid." Cruz blows a smoke ring at the rearview mirror. "It's a record. Huh, Red?"

"It's a recording," I say, not certain who to look at. "But it was done live. You know, like in the studio or on television or something."

I don't want to get into it or start an argument, so I look past Cruz's profile over to Deception Gulch. It cuts deep and red to the left of us three hundred feet below, where cactus are still blooming, even though it's nearly halfway through August and there's been no monsoon.

Cruz is too busy crooning along with "The Singing Ranger" and Rabbit's probably too hung up on imagining the sparkles on Hank's shirt for either of them to notice that slowly, in small ways, the mountain's beginning to heal. Like hair that grows back on a scar somehow. But it's too late; at least that's how I feel. Besides, the mountain may be healing from the outside, but inside she's dying. Been hollowed, cleaned out, and scraped bare. Eureka Copper keeps cutting back shifts, forcing people to leave and slicing Hatley's population in half. Since those miners got killed in the blast last month, we're two short of a thousand.

The E.C. says there's not enough copper to make bullets and motors like they did in the Second World War. And I suppose we'll have to drop the A-bomb over in Korea.

"Can you smell it?" Cruz's face lights into a goofy grin. "Rainbow bread."

Sure smells like the Palermos got the brick ovens going. It's picture-show night, and the bakery's gonna be jammed.

We make a hard right, turning onto the final switchback, and see the Mexican-tiled roof of our school. That's when Cruz stops singing, and Rabbit's not tapping on the back of the flip-top anymore. They follow my gaze beyond the roof, up to the H. But really, I'm eyeing the mining hospital just below and the balcony that leads to Maw's room.

I wonder if we'll heal. We've been hollowed out, too. Our families exhausted by the mine and the war that took my brother, Bobby. They're even closing down the school. *Bobby's school*. That's how I'll always think of it, especially with football starting. Bobby put Hatley back on the map in one season of football, winning that second Northern Crown. But there's only sixty people left in high school, and that's not enough to keep it going, though I sure hope it's enough to win. That's what I'll focus on—winning. Nothing beyond that.

"Seniors of fifty-one," Cruz murmurs, eyeing the steps of the school. "All frickin' twenty-four of us."

We're the last graduating class of Hatley High. Our motto is "Try, it's worth it." And I really want to believe that. But to me, the town and the team just haven't been the same since Bobby died.

We round the Hogback and Mrs. Palermo calls out, *"Andiamo, Salvatore,"* the braid above her head looking even whiter with all that flour.

Cruz pulls up in front of the ovens, and Rabbit's father hauls a giant, wood-handled slab from one, with a steaming loaf of bread on it the colors of a rainbow. Balancing it in the air, he slides it into a flour sack. Mrs. Palermo rushes over to Cruz's car and slips the bagged loaf into Rabbit's lap.

"Mangia, mio piccolo," she says, gripping Rabbit's chin. I

know that means "eat" in Italian—Mrs. Palermo stuffs Rabbit all the time since he weighs ninety-eight pounds soaking wet on the P.E. scale next to the showers. (We may only have twenty-six boys in high school, but there's no way Coach would let a guy like Rabbit play.)

Cruz leans back and rips a steaming hunk off the green part of the bread, sucking in his breath while he proceeds to burn his fingers, then his tongue.

Brushing the sweat of baking from her hollow cheek, Mrs. Palermo gives Rabbit a golden smile—eighteen karats' worth covering the left front tooth. Rabbit thinks that's the reason his mother smiles, but he's dead wrong. Whenever Mrs. Palermo sees Rabbit, her eyes light up the way the sunset does, exploding with color behind the mountain then lingering awhile, not wanting to give up the day.

She must have been over forty when she had Rabbit, which just about killed her, so he's the only one. "A miracle baby" is what Cruz likes to say—the *bambino milagro*—with a scar above Rabbit's sutured lip to prove it.

Mrs. Palermo pinches the fleshy part inside one of Rabbit's chicken-skinned elbows, but she can't get her fingers on much. And it's at times like this that I find it hard to breathe normal. Something gets caught in my throat and my eyes start to sting.

Maw used to do that—touch me in a caring way. But that was before everything changed.

"Hush now, Reddy," she'd whisper so only I could hear. It was after I'd fallen into Bitter Creek Gulch and nearly gotten myself killed. They'd had to stitch up both knees once they took all the mud and the prickers out. I didn't mind the mud. I never do. I was born in it, halfway down that gulch when Maw went looking for Pop. Loco Francisco caught me.

Doused us with his holy water so many times Bobby said I arrived home cleaner than anything coming out of the miners' hospital. Maw had Francisco baptize me right then and there. *Felix Francis.* I suppose that's when Pop's loathing for me started, since I'd gotten a middle name that had nothing to do with him.

I try to remember the sound of Maw's voice. I know it's much softer than Mrs. Palermo's and that the accent's all Antrim, as if Maw just rode off the Irish Glens and hopped on a train to Hatley. She used to smile like Mrs. Palermo, though. And bake bread, too. I'm hoping I can do something to bring that all back.

Chapter 2
FIGHTING THE SCHOOL BUS

MONDAY, AUGUST 14
3:17 P.M.

IF I HAD A DIME in my pocket right now, I'd ride up to the
soda fountain and have Benny make me a Horse's Neck with
a squirt of chocolate on that dip of ice cream. That would
give my stomach something to work on. But Coach would
tear my head off, and I don't get paid by Ernie till Friday.
So I keep walking my bike up Second Street, guiding it over
the cobblestones as I climb the concrete steps—all fifty of
them—next to our house in the Hogback.

"You know what you gotta do this year, Red. Nine years
is a long time!"

That's Cussie Rakovich's dad from next door. Already
he's hollering at me and we haven't even had our first
practice yet. I'm nowhere near his driveway to respond, so
I nod.

School starts next Monday, but there's only one thing
around here the town cares about besides mining, and
that's football. (Just because we've only made it to the state

11

championships twice in twenty-six years doesn't mean you give up hoping.)

There's really sixty-two steps from our house at the Rakoviches' driveway to the top of the hill, in case you're thinking it's no big sweat hauling a bike up this pitch in August when Benny could fry an egg on the lunch counter. But I avoid the first dozen steps if I take the back porch. All our houses are stacked in rows up the side of the mountain: three stories in front, two out back, with a street on either end. Cruz says we Anglos must like living in a fishbowl since there's plenty of opportunity to look inside. But I can't see being stuck in a gulch like he is as a whole lot more private when you've got nine brothers and sisters around.

It's good to have on the orange-and-black uniform again. Feel the heavy stitching of number 7 across my back, same as Bobby's. He won Hatley the Northern title in '41 as quarterback, but they lost to Tucson in the state championship. Hatley's never come close since. The town's aiming for me to change that and I sure want to. They say it's finally my turn. No more backup QB. I start now, since Winslow's graduated. And it's my last shot.

Things level off when I make it up the hill to School Street, so I hop on my bike and ride to the other end of town where the field is. Rabbit's dad's on his burro delivering bread, hollering, "Give 'em _ell down in . . . Go _uckers!"

I know he must've said "Muckers" and that we give it to Cottonville, but the afternoon wind's found a way into my helmet so I can hardly hear through the leather. And I'll blame the sweat dripping down my jersey on the desert sun. I promised myself I wouldn't get nervous this year, but I won't have the bench to lean on. And the truth is, I don't know if I'm all that good on my own, and I've got to be. It's the town's last shot, too. All they have left is this season and me to get it right. But they think I'm as good as Bobby was. In two weeks they'll find out I'm not.

Upper Main's about to run out when I get to Gibby, who gives me a wave from the icehouse. It's where the pavement ends and our field begins—on the only hundred yards of even ground in Hatley, hanging over the pit at slag level like a chin—and where Coach Hansen is standing, lit up by the sun.

I press the brakes and watch the silent picture show Coach is giving, his lips opening and closing like a furious drill sergeant's as the shovels grind out ore behind him and drown out the commands. Coach is weaving his body side to side, forgetting all about that scar and pumping his legs so fast you'd think he'd fall right into the pit.

I yank off my helmet, but I still can't hear him until I start pedaling again and get deep into slag level, too. We don't measure our town in feet but in pit levels, according to where they dig. Slag level is where we begin, going up or downhill from there. Below slag it's ten cuts down the mountain to the 1400 level, but they've already gone underground by then. Above slag there's five ledges blasted through a stubborn rock face of diorite towering above our field. And then the mountain runs out.

"You guys did nothing but sit on your butts all summer, didn't you?" Coach starts yelling. "And drink and smoke and stuff your faces with tamales. Well, we're gonna squeeze the living Schlitz out of you boys by the twenty-fifth!"

Coach looks way too fit up this close, his white T-shirt stretching tight across his chest, which is thick from those years in the service. And I know he's got it in store for us. There's a *W* wedged in between the names Ben and Hansen.

The old players say it means "Wild" because of the crazy things Coach cooks up for us in order to win.

It's been a while since I rode my bike across the field. If you're not careful, that's just asking for flats. Our field is made from that slag—basically, mushed-up gravel that the Cottonville smelter belches out after digesting all the good stuff. There's no such thing as lawn in Hatley. Nothing without skin sharp as barbed wire has a shot here. When they first made the field, they dumped a layer of dirt on top of the slag, but it didn't take long for the rocks to work their way back up. They were at the surface by the next season, so folks just gave up.

"O'Sullivan, get your skinny red butt over here," Coach yells. "I hope to God there's still some muscle under all those freckles."

So I'm the only red-hair on the squad. *Big deal.* That doesn't mean my butt's red. Everybody's got a nickname. Mine's Red. Everyone calls me that.

"Hey, Ugly Red Butt. Hurry up. It's comin'!"

Except for Cruz, who makes a habit of sticking "Ugly" in front of everything else he calls me, especially when he's steamed. But he'll use it when he's happy, too. And it's hard to tell the difference if he won't show you his eyes.

I can't believe Cruz is here before me. He's never early. Usually it's just the freshmen at this hour and Melvin Sneep, the puny junior who can't seem to grow. Coach asked some of us seniors to demonstrate drills and I thought I'd be the first one here. I lean my bike against the bleachers, knowing what comes next, but the new kids have no idea.

The train whistle signals the start and it still scares me every time. I should know it's coming and Coach Hansen knows it's coming, timing his verbal assaults in between the shrill sounds. He's laying it on real thick for the rookies like we're in boot camp or something. But I don't mind. Cruz and I are racing the train that's headed for the depot next to the pit beside us, only we're really racing each other as we jump through two rows of tires thrown on the slag.

The new kids are yelling their faces off, thinking that one of us can actually beat the rumbling machine, but the train always wins. This time, though, the cockiness of being seniors makes it real close. Cruz is a wingback and a faster runner than me at any distance, but somehow my foot pops out of the tire before his. Then I lunge toward the goalpost to make sure I beat him.

"Hey, Ugly, maybe we should trade places and *you* carry the ball."

"Nah, too small." I can't say much else—I'm awful winded—and my legs feel like they're still pumping even though we've stopped. "They'd tackle my red butt in two seconds flat," I finally gasp out.

"One second." Cruz laughs.

"Hey, boys!" Coach yells. "Time to show the bus who's boss."

Whenever the school bus is available for practice, Coach drives it over and uses it as a piece of equipment. We don't have a blocking sled so we push the bus around the field. And Coach won't let up just because you're a quarterback.

He goes over to Wallinger, his assistant, who's working with the new guys to see how they'll do, though I doubt anyone's gonna get cut—I count seventeen of us on the field. Coach points to a doughy freshman, then picks out three of us, the whistle slung around his neck bouncing from one pec to the other as he demonstrates the move.

And I wish Coach could play for our team like he did for Missouri State. From what I can see, he's the only one on the field with muscle that's meaty—the kind we're gonna need to take the state and finally win the Yavapai Cup. The only one who comes close is Tony Casillas, our guard (he made All-State last year). The rest of us—even the new senior, Rudy Kovacs, who gives us some height—can't be thirty-five pounds more than Rabbit, tops. Can you win a championship with that?

Coach grabs the wheel to control the steering while we push. It usually takes four of us to get it moving. This time it's me, Cruz, Tony, and that freshman who's more fat than scrawn.

The three of us make like we're heaving pretty hard, only we're not, and the poor freshman's face turns bright red as he tries to move the load on his own. You can see the blood vessels popping out of his neck, and then his knees buckle and he crumbles under the bus.

"What's going on back there? Did we lose the kid already?" Coach looks peed off at us through the rearview mirror.

The knees of the wobbly freshman are dripping blood onto the slag and I don't think he'll make it. I want to tell him to keep going, that if you don't you're sunk. But he'll have to learn for himself. We're hanging off the side of a mountain exposed to the desert's blazing sun with the heart of our town ripped open, churned up, and processed into copper. We play football on the discarded part—the gunk that gets delivered back to us from Cottonville—so what do you expect . . . a carpet of rose petals?

I motion for Cruz and Tony to pick the kid up and try it again for real. By the time we get the bus going, the brake light comes on, which is annoying since we still have to push until Coach blows the whistle. And I don't like the feeling of futility, or somebody jerking me around. But you have to play by the rules. And all you can do is learn to work around the slag. Discover where the worst parts are—like Hell's Corner—and how to push your opponents into that ground.

"Keep goin', Ugly," Cruz grunts at me. "Can't win if we don't push."

With every useless heave, Cruz also reminds me we're one step closer to winning the championship. And I know Coach has been through a lot. Got cut up pretty bad in the war and it left an ugly scar on his head.

The whistle finally blows and we collapse against the wheels, wondering how we're going to make it through the rest of practice. Our starting eleven is now all here, the guys who will grind through this gravel every day for the next two months, no matter what. Nick Managlia, our fullback, runs over and hands the freshman a towel for his bloody knees. Managlia's eye looks even worse. It's dark as a blackberry.

"Stairs get you again?" Cruz growls.

"Lay off," I tell him. Cruz doesn't understand.

Coach climbs down from the bus and looks at Managlia. "What happened to you?" he asks.

"Took a tumble on my bike." But Managlia won't look up at anybody, especially Coach.

"Starting tomorrow, we all walk to practice," Coach barks. "I can't afford to lose any of you. Not one. I need everybody for the entire season."

My arm's already aching, even though I've been throwing all summer with Cruz. Guess it's not the same without the bus and Coach Hansen yelling in your face.

THE VERDE MINER

Twice-Weekly News of the Mountain

HATLEY, ARIZONA   WEDNESDAY, AUGUST 16, 1950   FIVE CENTS A COPY

MID-WEEK EDITION

Muckers Coach Rallies Players with Game Film

The Hatley Muckers football team took to Ruffner Field this week in preparation for their inaugural matchup against Rim Valley next Friday. Coach Ben Hansen wasted no time getting his boys in shape, handing them grueling drills that included sparring with the school bus and running alongside the ore train, which first-string quarterback Felix "Red" O'Sullivan looks to have beaten.

Hansen then marched his men to the high school auditorium for a film presentation in Kodachrome, demonstrating in living color just what they will be up against if the team takes All-Northern and battles the South at the end of the season.

Hansen showed footage of Phoenix United scoring on an 80-yard run to beat Flag-staff last year. If the Muckers manage to win the Yavapai Cup against the Southern championship team, the remarkable feat, attempted only twice before—first in '24 led by Edward Mackenzie and Luther B. Sims Sr., and second in '41 led by Robert O'Sullivan—would cap off the final season in Mucker history.

WANTED—You to try Today's Special: Chicken Chop Suey with Noodle 65¢. LEE FONG'S CHINESE KITCHEN.

A N T I - T E T A N U S SHOTS—Dr. A. C. Brown to go door to door today along the Verde River. Inoculations voluntary. NO CAUSE FOR ALARM.

Chapter 3
VERY SATISFACTORY

TUESDAY, AUGUST 22
7:40 A.M.

MY LOCKER'S AT THE END of the hall in the basement of our main building. I'm locker number 7, the last one on the top row before the staff john, marked TEACHERS REST ROOM— PRIVATE. The trophy case is directly behind it, made of cherrywood, with glass shelves lit up around the handful of sports trophies we've won, and Bobby's closest to the top— right below the empty shelf where the Yavapai Cup is supposed to be.

Bobby's trophy used to be golden, throwing flashes of corn-colored light clear across the hall. Now it's coated in specks of oily blue, and the punter standing on top of the pillar kicking the football to high heaven is mostly orange with some dingy brown running through his jersey, the same as an old copper penny. I suppose nobody cares enough to bother unlocking the case every once in a while and polishing them up now that the school's closing.

"Looks like they'll be counting on you this year, won't

they?" Principal Mackenzie says. He just walked out of the john and is standing behind me, eyeing the trophies, too. I can see him in the glass. But I heard the sound of him limping before anything. "That's a whole lot of pressure, isn't it?" he says.

"I know." I don't tell him that I can handle it, like I would Coach Hansen, because you can't fool Mr. Mackenzie. He's found a way somehow of keeping everyone's secrets.

Ask anybody who they write to after they graduate and they'll tell you it's Mr. Mackenzie. Bobby wrote to him every week from the Pacific, and Cruz's brother Manny did, too. Mr. Mac's the one who gave me Bobby's locker right after Bobby died, though I wasn't even a freshman yet. I suppose he felt kinda sorry, watching me leaning up against the locker crying pretty badly the day after we'd gotten the news, and not being able to do anything about it except tell me that I could have it.

"The one on the bottom's from my year," Mr. Mac points out, tapping on the glass in front of the trophy marked ALL-NORTHERN CHAMPS 1924.

I ask him what'll happen to them once the school shuts down.

"We're not entirely certain yet, Felix," Mr. Mac says, then he pauses, closing his eyes, as if he's worn out or maybe feeling something that goes much deeper—like an aching sadness or a deepening regret. This school's as much Mr. Mackenzie's as it is ours—maybe more, since he's principal on top of being a former student *and* a Mucker. He must be having an awful time of it.

"As long as it isn't Cottonville, the kids will be able to stomach the new school," I tell him.

"It might be," Mr. Mackenzie says, and he adds how

consolidation's an option the board must consider. "You do realize, Felix, that Cottonville isn't the enemy, but merely an opponent on the playing field?" Which is what you're supposed to say if you're the principal standing in the middle of the hallway with a student.

But then Mr. Mackenzie looks at the trophies again and shakes his head, remembering how it feels to be a Mucker. Before he played at Flagstaff for Arizona State College, until the summer he worked in the mine and a runaway ore car tore up his knee.

"Just try to end the season in one piece, all right?" he tells me. "Oh, and I think you'll find the locker arrangements satisfactory this year. We've grouped all the grades together so this floor won't look quite so depleted." Then that smile comes back as he hobbles up the stairs, and I haven't a clue what Mr. Mackenzie's aiming at.

I look at some of Bobby's stuff that I keep in the locker. Mostly snapshots of him winning, some with his fellow marines at Iwo Jima, plus the Eagle Scout medal and the kimono they found in his duffel.

Cruz says all I need now is a candle and a picture of Mother Mary to make the shrine complete. That he could special-order me a heart-shaped *milagro* with all the thorns going through it from his uncle down in El Tiro.

I told him to screw off and be happy that his brother's still alive. But I'm thanking Mother Mary now and Mr. Mackenzie, too, because Angie's at her locker and that's catty-corner from mine this year, in the 200 section. *Very satisfactory.*

I caught glimpses of Angie all summer while she was at the pool on Mexican days lifeguarding. I'd be on my way to teach swimming at Scout camp, walking as slow as I could without seeming like a loafer and wondering if Angie was really looking at me. She'd have on these huge black sunglasses like the film stars wear, so I could never quite tell. But just last week on the final day of camp she said, "Don't look so sad, Red. Maybe you'll save somebody's life today."

So all I kept thinking on the way to camp wasn't how to rescue one of those cubs from drowning, but about saving Angie from marrying anyone but me, and how giving mouth-to-mouth to those red lips of hers would solve it.

Angie looks away from her locker, so I call out, "Miss Villanueva," which was stupid. I know the second it comes out, bouncing over the rusty tin of the khaki-colored lockers like a whiny morning announcement.

"Hey, Red," she says, throwing me a weak smile before going back to her locker business. "I haven't seen him."

"Seen who?"

"Aren't you looking for Cruz?" she says, squinting up at me.

"Yeah. I mean . . . no," I mumble, focusing on the copper floor before asking, "You at the pool this afternoon?"

"Uh-uh." Angie shakes her head and that curly mane of hers goes just about wild, bobbing and bouncing sideways over her shoulders like a rodeo pony's. "Not until tomorrow," she says.

"Well, I know the best place to swim around here, anyway."

"Oh yeah?" Angie finally stops messing with the books on the middle shelf and aims her eyes at me. "Where?"

"The Verde."

"Too far," she says, curling those red lips into a frown.

"I know a shortcut. I can bring you along."

"What are you gonna do, carry me with you like a sack lunch?" She laughs, holding up her lunch bag.

"No. No. Like a swim. Two people swimming. I could meet you at the tracks after school sometime. You pass right by them going to the Barrio."

"What do you know about the Barrio?"

"I know you live there."

Angie studies my face like she's about to bore a hole right through it with those powerful brown eyes. Then, just as sudden, they let go of me and she looks down at her watch. "Better get to my class, Mr. Sad Eyes," she says, even though she's got fifteen minutes. "Besides, don't you practice football all the time?"

"We're done by six," I yell over to her in my announcement-sounding voice.

Angie hesitates before going up the stairs, and I can't tell if she smiled at me or not—she's in shadow. But I'm pretty sure she waved.

"Yeah, okay. See ya around," I call over.

I'm trying to figure out if that went smoothly or not. I'm thinking *not*, if Angie thinks my eyes look sad when I'm happy to see her and that I'm just being nice to her because she's Cruz's sister. I pry stuff out of Cruz all the time and I don't think he ever suspects. If he did he'd probably never speak to me again, then find a way to kill me. Slit my throat in the middle of the night. Blame it on the enemy, saying a Cottonville Wolf did it.

I look over at Angie's locker. Number 207. Maybe I'll slip in a note in case she forgets. We can swim into October sometimes, if the wind coming over from Flagstaff doesn't take hold of the peaks and send the snow down to the Valley. *Two months.* Gives her plenty of time to change her mind. There's bound to be a perfect day. I'll be there, waiting by the tracks.

Chapter 4
EEJIT ICING

THE MORNING SUN HASN'T HIT the front steps of the school yet, so me and Cruz lean against the pillars, since I can hardly bend after fighting with the bus again at practice last night. Three freshmen quit already because of all that pushing. Now we're down to fourteen players.

Rabbit's sitting on the cold cement, gnawing at a pencil and facing the mansion of the man who made our school the finest in Arizona. Beats Phoenix United hands down. P.U.— the school that's won twenty-three championships and plays football on lawn Cruz swears looks too perfect to be real.

"Like they hired a bunch of crop planes to spray green dye over the field, then white right after, on the kids at their games," Cruz is saying. "And what do they mean *if* we manage to win against the South?" (He's talking about the newspaper.)

"Because it's never been done before," Rabbit says. "That's all they're saying . . . *as journalists.*"

"Then they should've never stuck 'manage' in there . . . *as idiots.*"

"Well, we *are* on the small side," I tell Cruz.

"Who is?" He shoots me a look. "The only one who comes close to Rabbit's height is Sneep, and he's a bench-warmer." Cruz nicks Rabbit's shoulder with the sole of his high-top. "Sit on the cement too long and you won't have children," he says.

"What do you mean?" Rabbit asks.

Cruz is messing with Rabbit already and it's not even first bell. And Phoenix may have a green field to go with their state titles, but they don't have copper underneath their school. We've got a hundred miles of it in tunnels snaking under every inch of our town. Hatley's mined about a billion dollars' worth of copper ore, and William D. Ruffner, the owner of Eureka Copper, lives across from our school on a mesa he blasted out of Bitter Creek Gulch. Ruffner plopped a lily-white adobe house on top of it as a wedding present for his bride. Takes up the whole plateau.

It's a real eyesore and something you wouldn't expect to find out here. Like John Wayne talking Spanish to an Indian warrior at the cowboy matinee, it's strictly meant for show.

Maw liked calling that house "the silliest, most peculiar topper an eejit could fi-end for a weddin' ceck."

"Go on now, Felix," she'd beckon, pointing at the house and tracing lines in the air with her finger. "Squeeze your eyes a wee bit and follow the mounds to the mansion." But I'd watch her instead, until she took my hand and we'd sift through the layers together. When we got to the top of the imaginary cake, she'd laugh, then we'd go to Peila's for some flour to make cookies we'd cover with "eejit" icing.

"Don't you know when a girl sits on cold cement, it stops

her from having kids?" Cruz points at his crotch and assumes the huddle position, getting down on his haunches to meet the screwball look Rabbit's giving him. "Freezes up her privates or something. Shrinks her pink taco."

"No fooling?" Rabbit asks. He's already slid *Geometry* under his bony butt and is looking at me for an answer.

I mouth the word "no"—Cruz is so full of baloney it's practically coming out of his ears—and I shake my head in disagreement, getting jabbed in the neck by one of those double-fisted plumes Ruffner had carved into the pillars.

Our school didn't start out as the finest, but by the time Ruffner was through with it, we'd gotten solid copper doors as tall as two men, five-foot-high windows with HHS etched in Italian stone above each and every one, and these Roman pillars I'm leaning on. Before that, it was just a plain old structure, the color of sunbaked skin. Ruffner said if he had to keep looking at three stories of flesh every morning, he didn't want it bringing up his bacon and eggs.

"What, you think I never been inside one before?" Cruz says, snatching Rabbit's pencil away. "That all the girls at Hatley High are virgins, especially the gringas?" Cruz slices through Rabbit's perfectly Brylled bangs with the eraser tip.

The truth is, I don't really know if Cruz has been with a girl. He shoots pool, giving lessons to the women at the Copper Star and moving his body so much that I have to look away, so he might have. But when he's anywhere near Beebe Vance and her blond curls, his hips don't act crazy like that.

And it's beyond me how Ruffner could've felt sick to his stomach about our building and not want to puke whenever he sees the dilapidated shanties in the Barrio on the other side of his dining room window because of those lowly wages he pays the Mexicans.

The ground trembles beneath us, heaving like an aftershock, and I hit the cement, crashing into Rabbit, not anticipating the morning explosion.

"That was only a charge of fifty thousand. No big deal, Ugly." Cruz grins, pointing to my books sliding onto the road. "You should know by now your pop only orders a tame one before nine so it won't scare the ankle biters walking to school. Wouldn't even get the jail to slide again."

"Just enough to wake up Father Pierre so he can say Mexican Mass, he's so deaf," Rabbit says, handing me *Advanced Typing*.

"Not when you owe him money for a pew." Cruz smirks. "He hears real good then. Even when they're blasting."

That's how Pop and his crew get the ore out of the mine these days—filling coyote holes with long brown sticks of dynamite and shaking up the whole town. The E.C. doesn't work the tunnels underneath us anymore since the shafts caught fire.

Francisco's charging down the hill on Paradiso, his burro. Paradiso's loaded with a sack of empty dynamite boxes to heat up Francisco's garage.

"You better hurry before Loco Francisco's ass shits all over your books." Cruz is doubled over now. "He can make that donkey do it, you know. If God tells him to."

"That would be a good omen, shittin' on your books!" Francisco scowls. His shirt's coated with dirt in the creases as if he still worked the mine, picking up steel as a tool nipper. "A job," Pop says, "left for those too daft to do anything but crawl on their hands and knees."

Paradiso chaws at my arm while Francisco takes out an orange. He offers the fruit to me, like he did when I was a kid, but I'm too embarrassed to take it. And I can't tell what

Francisco thinks—his face is hidden under that fedora and the silver beard, bristly as a pipe cleaner. Then he's gone.

"Gonna work for Loco again," Cruz jokes, "tearing up those dynamite boxes for kindling? Must be worth at least two oranges."

"Brace yourselves," Rabbit warns, pulling out a handkerchief as the rotten-egg smell from the explosion reaches us. I swing *Advanced Typing* against my face, and Cruz makes like he's sniffing the inside of his elbow.

I know the blasts don't happen as much as when we were kids, but they still get to me. The broken windows and shifting buildings. The reeking mix. But what I hate most are the sirens. Pop knows which rocks not to tamper with, and even when he's had too much to drink he can sniff out the ones that might kill you. I suppose only God knows for certain where every shaft lies. But when a siren goes off, you know a miner's gotten too close to one that was hidden and gone up with the dynamite hole he'd been filling.

"Hey, look at the Ruffner mansion," Cruz says. "I think it moved a foot. It's a wonder our field hasn't fallen right into the pit."

"His house has been doing that for years," Rabbit sniffs, "just like the rest of the town."

"Makes our school into a holy shrine but he doesn't give a shoveling shit about our team," Cruz says, heaving a wad of spit into some ivy. "How come he won't get us new cleats for the big games anymore?"

"Because they're shipping the Hatley kids to Cottonville next year," I tell him. "At least, that's what Mr. Mackenzie thinks might happen."

Cruz fishes in his pocket for a cigarette. "There's no way they'd go," he says. "They'll ditch school by then. And there's no Mucker I know who'd put a Wolf uniform over his head instead of setting it on fire."

"You can't smoke that on school property," Rabbit says, pawing at Cruz's cigarette.

"What are they gonna do, Rabbit, ship me to Cottonville?" Cruz sticks it in his mouth anyway. "Just let them try," he says, taking out his lighter. "I'd rather get sent to Korea."

"You wish," Rabbit says.

"What's that supposed to mean?" Cruz shoots Rabbit a look like he's popped a gasket, same as Pete Zolnich when a miner can't pay at his tavern.

Somebody comes out of the mansion. It's Jigger Datchi, Ruffner's Apache servant, carrying a bucket of suds. He splashes it over Ruffner's Packard and the soap drips off the swan ornament and onto the yellow hood, bubbling up like the macaroni and cheese Mrs. Slubetz serves in the cafeteria.

"A car like that's gotta cost more than new uniforms or that shift he cut out at the mine," Cruz says. "They should strike and make Ruffner pay."

"Ruffner wouldn't care." I look at the traces of grease caught under my fingernails from all the flats Ernie's had me fix on that yellow machine.

"Nick Managlia's dad got fired when he asked for a raise," Rabbit says. "He thinks it's because there isn't anything left in the mountain worth blasting."

"Don't believe it." Cruz scowls, glaring at a few anxious freshmen brushing past us to get inside. "I bet Ruffner's getting them to close our school to make it an open pit."

"Then why are all those houses for rent, huh, Cruz?" Rabbit asks. "Up on Company Ridge."

"How many times have they closed the mine and opened

it again?" Cruz says. "Besides, your opinion does
Rabbit. You flunked kindergarten." Cruz shoves his
my direction as if I might know something. "What
pop say?"

My face goes all sweaty when Cruz asks about Pop. Like
I've done something wrong, which I haven't. "He'd never
tell," I mumble. I don't think I've seen Pop this week. *Big
deal.* It's not like we keep track of each other. All I know
is that he took the Chevy early this morning—it's been on
blocks since they took his license away. Pop never lets me
drive it.

"You'll see, stupid," Cruz says, tossing Rabbit's pencil at
him. "The mother lode might be right here." Cruz jumps
over the front steps and scrapes up a clump of dirt, shaking
it around in his palm like dice. "Or down there, under Charlie's place." He lets the dirt escape through his fingers and
looks through the caretaker's window.

"Like who, Cruz? Who'd you go inside?" Rabbit asks,
and we're back on the subject of vaginas.

"Shut your mouth, Rabbit," Cruz whispers. "Think I'd
tell you that on school property?" He grabs hold of the collar
on Rabbit's flannel. I don't like it when Cruz gets this way—
picking on Rabbit when he's really sore about something else.
Rabbit barely reaches Cruz's shoulders and maybe my chin.

"And what does it really do to us guys, huh, Cruz?" I
want to make him work hard at a comeback. As hard as Rabbit does getting those Levis to look like they fit, rolling them
over his copper belt buckle so they won't drag across the entire Valley.

Cruz lets go of Rabbit and eyes me, disappointed, as if
I've let him down. And I hate that part, too. It happens when
I throw him a lousy pass because my fingers are way past

frozen, or if my arm's all shaky because I'm starving and Cruz doesn't say anything after, so I can't even be mad.

"It gives you a shriveled-up pecker like Sims, that's what it does to you, Ugly," Cruz says, throwing his smoke in the ivy.

"It just makes you go to the bathroom," I tell Rabbit. I'm not any good at lying.

"Dammit, now I have to take a piss, you idiot," Cruz moans, jiggling on one foot while me and Rabbit laugh our faces off. He'll have to hurry not to miss our class with Sims. Being late for him just isn't worth it.

* * *

Sims has on a striped necktie knotted tightly below his Adam's apple. He's got his arms folded like he's hiding something, and looks up at the three letters written in yellow chalk on the blackboard: *ISM*.

Sims is always putting on a show. Monday it was about *"mulligatawny-as-in-the-stew."* He had the girls so confused at the opening-assembly spelling bee, saying the word so fast that it tripped up most of them. Except Angie.

She looked calm—especially for a sophomore—her brown eyes staring into space like she was taking in more of the word. Not intimidated at all by Sims's sloppy delivery. She reached for the microphone and it made that loud, eardrum-breaking sound. But Angie just waited for the shrill to stop and spelled out the word.

"M-U-L-L-I-G-A-T-A-W-N-Y."

There was a long pause. Then Sims pulled in his microphone and announced, "That is correct, Miss Villanueva."

Cruz gave me a nudge and whispered, "Damn straight she's correct, Mr. Ass-in-the-Hole." Cruz sure was fired up. "You might be able to kick me around in English class, but you can't stump my sister." Smart-assy, too.

It's true that even if you try in Sims's class and screw up, he can make you feel small. That's when Cruz's ego erupts. He'll either sulk in his chair or march over to Mr. Mackenzie's office. Cruz says Mr. Mac's about the only Anglo teacher who thinks like a Mexican or maybe even Jesus. But I think that's too much to expect out of anyone. Even Mr. Mackenzie.

It's a funny thing about our town. Despite Sims having a pickle up his butt, everyone's got the spirit of good ol' Hatley High. They rally on the sidelines at our football games, but if you want to go for a swim or, say, get married, it better be "with" or "to" your own kind. We come together during the day, but we all head home to our places on the hill. And whichever way you go lets people know who you are. If you climb up from Main to Company Ridge—Gringo Ridge, Cruz likes to remind me—you're rich and help run the mine your house overlooks.

If you stay on Main and follow it to the city limits, just before it curves around toward Hatley High, you could be Rabbit's dad, Vince Palermo, heading to a clapboard in the middle of Little Italy. If you walk down the hill in either direction from the pool hall that fits your nationality, chances are you work *in* the mine.

If it's the Copper Star and your legs are draped over a burro laden with firewood, you're Mexican, maybe Santiago, Cruz's father, working your way down the switchbacks to the bottom of the Gulch and a little wooden shanty in the Barrio.

And if you just left Pete's Tavern, you're either a Slav or Irish and you live down the hill, too—in the Hogback section like we do—or maybe even in the Gulch, but high enough and far enough away from the Barrio. "Because we speak English," justifies Pop, knowing that's a definite advantage.

After all, he does shout orders to Santiago in the pit every shift—the way Sims does with us in English.

"What is an ism?" Sims asks, scanning the classroom for an answer. "Anybody?"

"An awful itch you can't get to?" Clem Pratty says. A few of us laugh, and Sims shoots an accusatory look in our direction, since Pratty's sitting behind us in the last row.

"It looks innocuous enough, doesn't it?" Sims says, tapping the letters with the tip of the wooden pointer. "Just three letters that sound odd and look even more peculiar." He tugs at the ring of the projector screen and the screen snaps and coils, rattling Penny Bruzzi in the front row. "But once you put another term in front, it's not so harmless, is it?"

It spells *COMMUNISM* now that the screen's up.

"What's the jerk going on about this time?" Cruz asks me.

I'm not entirely certain. I thought this class was supposed to be about sonnets, but Sims is always springing something on us.

"He means war," Rabbit whispers. "You know, fighting for what you think is right?"

"Why else would you be fighting?" Cruz says.

Any ism makes me think of Bobby. Only I'm not sure how different communism is from the Nazism or the fascism he was fighting. Maybe they all just mean hating and fighting and getting yourself killed.

Sims moves through the center aisle like he's searching for prey. He's acting a whole lot different than when he's talking about Shakespeare. "America has become the ism battleground of the world. If we could simply scratch it to make it go away," he says, squatting to go eye to eye with Pratty, "don't you think we would have done that a long time ago? The fact is, communists have been here since the First World War."

34

"There's Russians in this classroom?" Cruz says. "All I see is Red."

Penny giggles and Sims swerves to look at Cruz.

"Mr. Villanueva," he says, "how would you like to be told where to work? Or how much you shall make? And if you refused, they'd send you to the mines?"

Cruz shrugs. "We're already there."

That gets the whole class laughing, and Sims's chin breaks into blotchy little stains.

"I was referring to the salt mines, not Eureka Copper," Sims says. "As a slave for no wages." He tries to get the pointer behind his back, weaving it between his elbows like a pool cue—though I doubt he's ever played—and it falls to the floor.

"He wouldn't last a minute shooting pool at the Copper Star," Cruz whispers.

"Of course, they could also deny you the right to go to school," Sims says, picking up the pointer. He's by Lupe Diaz, our halfback. "Decide that you aren't intelligent enough."

"They're not."

It comes from somewhere in the middle of the class—but I can't tell for sure—stabbing the air with an invisible sting, just like those sulfur explosions. Nobody laughs, and Sims lets it hang there, all knotted and tense. Then he splays out his hand and says, "Five people from this very community voted for the Communist Party."

Some kids look surprised, and it's news to me, too, but I have my doubts. Rabbit nods, and that's not like him.

"We know these people. We may even have lunch with these communist spies," Sims says, watching the kids watching each other.

"Wake me up when it's time for practice," Cruz jokes, closing his eyes.

"This is more important than winning at Muckers football," Sims says, a bit more sharply.

"Didn't your father take All-Northern . . . with Mr. Mac?" Cruz asks. "He was the first Sims, no?"

Sims looks like the A-bomb just hit but quickly regains his composure and starts rattling on about how we should preserve our ideals by practicing good citizenship.

"He means white citizenship," Cruz whispers. And I wish Cruz would know when to stop.

"Did I hear someone willing to tell us about good citizenship? Did I?" Sims asks.

"I still don't know who we're fighting." Cruz is really asking for it. "Except for those Cottonville Wolves."

The guys laugh, but Sims shakes his head.

"Ah, you can be cheeky all you want," he says. "You've become complacent—that means smug, Mr. Villanueva— playing football and not worrying about Korea because you're not old enough to be called. But when we're complacent"— Sims dashes to the blackboard, changing the *ISM* to *IST,* the chalk crumbling into spray when he stabs an *S* onto the end, then the number *5* in front—"that's when the enemy strikes," he says. "It only takes a handful to start a revolution."

"They're always stirring things up."

Rudy Kovacs. That's who it is. He turned when he said it, tilting his shoulder and aiming it at Cruz.

Cruz's jaw tightens and flexes, but he doesn't say anything because it's Rudy. His father's a company man that the E.C. brought in from Bisbee last month to decide which mining men to keep and which ones to cut.

Everybody eyes Cruz and Rudy, but I can't tell which one they think might be the enemy.

Sims turns to face the blackboard, but I caught the smile. He underlines *5 COMMUNISTS,* then taps a prop on his desk with the pointer. Not the bust of Shakespeare, but the metal box in front. It looks like a tackle box, except there's a slit cut into the lid, and he gives it a shake.

"Part of good citizenship means identifying those who don't share our democratic ideals," he says. "Let's put their names in this box."

There's rumbling and a few anxious whispers. Even a hiss.

"Bet there won't be one Anglo name in there," Cruz mumbles.

"Anyone can be a commie," Rabbit says.

"Like who, Rabbit? Name me one." Cruz punches Rabbit in the arm with a knuckle.

Sims has really lost his brain, thinking your neighbor could be a spy. As if Lee Fong's plotting to overthrow the government while he's fixing you a dish at the Chinese Kitchen.

And I'm surprised at Rudy—he's on our team. He should know by now Hatley's made up of everything. But Rudy's just a scrub, practicing drills with Wallinger. He won't play much.

"You mean students, or teachers, too?" Margaret Menary asks.

"None of us is immune," Sims adds. "Teachers. Men of high office. We'll hand the box over to the school superintendent before the November election."

He gets us to stand and say the Pledge of Allegiance, in case we forgot about those freedoms.

Cruz jabs me in the ribs. "We'll never pass senior English," he says. "Goodbye, graduation."

"Sims never failed anyone yet," I say. "He just likes scaring people."

"It's gonna be nice picturing Sims's mug on that tackling dummy at practice," Cruz says.

Still, I press my hand against my heart, thinking, *He's done it.* Sims has let the kind of hatred you read about down in Phoenix slip into our classroom. The kind where Mexicans go to the Indian schools and Negroes go to Carver. Charlie may be our only Negro, but I saw what segregation does when the bus rolled in from Carver High last year.

Those boys stared out the window, heading up to our field with eyes as empty as the open pit. Until they saw the Mexican players on our team. They must have figured we'd be civil, and I thought so, too. Then Wallinger hollered, "You gonna let those niggers beat us?" loud enough for everyone to hear, including Charlie. Coach Hansen and Wallinger went at it, yelling and arguing about it so much that the officials asked if we wanted to forfeit the game.

"I know what an ism is," Cruz whispers to me. "It's Sims's name, all twisted around and screwy, but it's there."

THE VERDE MINER

Twice-Weekly News of the Mountain

HATLEY, ARIZONA   WEDNESDAY, AUGUST 23, 1950   FIVE CENTS A COPY

MID-WEEK EDITION

Hatley Muckers Gridiron Bound

The Hatley Muckers head to the gridiron Friday for their opening game against Rim Valley and their final attempt at a state championship as the school prepares to shut down.

Attendance records are unlikely to be broken, with the mine cutting back shifts, but are certain to exceed last year's turnout, when the Valley's polio outbreak shortened the season.

The final Muckers team is definitely on the bantam side, averaging 135 pounds. They will have to depend on speed, deception, and passing for of-

38

fensive punch from the 14 players Coach Hansen has on his team. When told his squad could be the lightest in all of Arizona, Hansen shook his head. "Footballs don't know how much you weigh," he said. "They only go where they're thrown."

WANT ADS

(Minimum charge, 25 cents.)

PIANO INSTRUCTION— Harmony included. Your home or mine. See or write Mrs. Featherhoff, Upper Main.

Chapter 5
GAME NIGHT

FRIDAY, AUGUST 25
4:15 P.M.

"JUST DO LIKE I TOLD ya, Red, and you'll be fine."

"Remember, get the ball to Managlia," another helmeted miner says, "and he'll light it up."

They've come off shift—the four o'clock bell rang about fifteen minutes ago—and the miners who just worked the morning are headed along the catwalk across from the high school when I make the turn for home.

They're the mining men with seniority: the foremen and steam-shovel operators carrying empty lunch pails and grime-faced grins, heading home to get washed up and guzzle down dinner their wives have made them. Then they'll hike up to the field at least an hour before kickoff.

I'm getting hungry, too, only I know what usually happens to me if I eat before a game. Especially meat. Not that there's much to chow on at our house. So I forget about raiding the kitchen and go right for the banister, dashing up and down the stairs and missing every other one for a pregame sprint. I usually do a couple hundred push-ups in between the beds right after, but I need to save my shoulder for tonight and it looks like I need a shave.

There's a crack in the bowl on the washstand between Bobby's bed and mine, but it can still hold water. It rinsed the blood off my father's razor and maybe a few fathers before him, too. And the mirror above it from the old country has seen generations of O'Sullivans scrape themselves clean. Including Bobby.

I shared this room with him. Wait, that's not right. Bobby shared it with *me*. He was six foot two with broad shoulders and a lean waist, forming that all-important V that makes you a great athlete and the kind of fellow girls fawn over, though Bobby only cared about one girl—Faye Miller. Me, I'm five foot seven . . . with wingtips on. I form the letter *i*, in lowercase only.

I was the kid brother in fourth grade and nowhere near puberty in '42 when Bobby went to war. Now he'll miss another birthday. Tomorrow.

I'm still waiting for Bobby to walk through that door, hand me the football, and slap me on the back, chanting, "Red-ee." But all I have left are the things I'd taken for granted. Like how he threw rockets on the field and just smiled, watching the touchdown, not making a fuss or anything. Then he'd talk about it with his gang after—holding on to Faye on the cushioned seats in the front window at the diner.

Me and Rabbit and Cruz would be walking by, so I'd look back like something had distracted me, giving Bobby just enough time to see me—or at least recognize his old Hatley High sweater I'd practically slept in. He'd knock on the glass with a knuckle for us to come in, then put up three fingers for Benny behind the counter, signaling chocolate malts for us.

I look at the photos from the Mucker annuals I tacked above my bed. They're of Mr. Mac's team and Bobby's. You can't miss Bobby smiling and sitting cross-legged in the middle of the front row after handing young Teddy, their mascot, the football to hold.

That's how it was with Bobby, never wanting it to be about him, but making others feel puffed up and proud. I remember the day that snapshot was taken and going to the field with Bobby right after, tossing the football he'd thrown against Tucson. He showed me the best way to grip the pigskin before you release it: not too tight, but as if you were holding something you'd never want to let go of—like a baby—while still giving it room to breathe. And when I first managed to do it, I felt all puffed up and proud.

Even Pop wasn't so angry when we came home after and Bobby told him how well I'd thrown. Then he asked to see Pop's rock collection. Pop told us about every one of those rocks and where he'd found them, before there was an open pit. He held those rocks like they were babies, too, cradling them in his palm like downy chicks so fragile you forgot that they were stone.

I don't look like much in the mirror. My eyes are bloodshot, and Angie was right: they do look sad. But then they get mad, seeing the letter that's been clinging to the mirror. I keep it there because it still gets me P.O.'d, and somehow being sore about it helps keep Bobby's memory alive. I kicked in the bedroom wall the first night I read it, and almost let the notice go up in flames in a bonfire down in the Gulch. But Cruz was there and held out his arm, grabbing my wrist just in time.

It's not even on official stationery or anything, those cheap army bastards. It looks just like the stuff Mrs. Normand hands out for us to fool around with in typing class. Anybody could have typed it from here. That's why it's still so hard to believe:

HEADQUARTERS, 2nd BATTALION, 28th MARINES,
5th MARINE DIVISION, FLEET MARINE FORCE,
c/o FLEET POST OFFICE, SAN FRANCISCO, CALIFORNIA

May 2, 1945

Dear Mr. and Mrs. O'Sullivan:

It was my sad duty to notify the Commandant of the Marine Corps regarding the death of your son, Robert.

Your son, Robert, met his death on Iwo Jima, in the following manner: He began the operation as a rifleman, but because of his capabilities Robert was made a radioman, a position which requires a man of courage and clear thinking while under fire. Your son had these qualities and accepted this position, which he knew to be dangerous.

It was while he was carrying out his duties in a most commendable manner that he was struck by enemy small-arms fire. Robert died instantly and suffered no pain. You may be assured your son gave his life as a true marine, gloriously, fearlessly, and proudly.

As his commanding officer, I wish you to know that Robert was a man of whom we were all proud and with whom we were all honored to serve.

The Marine Corps and the nation can ill afford
to lose the valuable services of such a person as
your son.

Please accept my sincerest sympathies on your
recent bereavement. I remain,

Sincerely yours,

J. D. Hutterfield
Lieutenant Colonel, U.S. Marine Corps,
Commanding Second Battalion, 28th Marines,
5th Marine Division

* * *

5:54 P.M.

The screen door whams shut and then there's a thump, like
a big juicy cantaloupe's rolled off the counter and onto the
floor. But I'm always thinking about food when it's supposed to be suppertime. With Maw not here anymore, Pop
eats wherever he feels like it: Duvall's Service Station one
night, the diner, even the Copper Star—whatever can get
delivered to the doghouse during meal break over at the
mine.

He has Maggie Juniper, the widowed squaw living in an
old gypsy caravan down in the Gulch, come in once a week
to clean the place up a bit, and sometimes she'll make us
food. That's on Mondays. Now that it's Friday there's nothing left to speak of in the way of nourishment.

That's how come I know it's Cruz in the kitchen instead
of anything to eat, like a ripe-heavy cantaloupe that's gone
rolling. He must've dropped his helmet on the floor. Cruz is
always stuffing way too much in his gym bag.

"Hey, Ugly. Aren't you ready yet?" he hollers up the stairs.

44

Cruz sure is fired up if he's at my house this early. The game's not until eight.

"What'd you do, eat up all the food on the shelves and then chomp on the ice, too?" he says. I can hear him in front of the Frigidaire, scratching up Maw's linoleum floor with his cleats.

"I'm not hungry," I tell him. Cruz is getting on my nerves already, walking around the kitchen as if he owns it.

"Whaddya mean, you're not hungry? You eat already? Better not be meat. *¡Ave María Purísima!* You know what happens if you eat meat."

"I said I'm not hungry. *Comprendes?*" I sprint down the stairs and shove Cruz and his yapper out of the way, swinging the refrigerator door shut. It's nobody's business how much food is in there.

He plugs his nose and shifts a pile of my dirty laundry onto the step stool.

"Good thing you're not hungry." Cruz starts pulling out a red bandanna from his bag but he doesn't even have to untie it. I caught a whiff. I know it's a burrito. Smells all fresh and full of those Mexican spices Mrs. V grinds up with her mortar and pestle.

"*Frijoles.* That's what you need . . . beans," he says, poking the bandanna at me.

"I said . . . I ain't hungry." I try not to lick my lips or swallow or anything. But the scent's all over the kitchen and my mouth sure is watering.

"I thought you said your pop leaves leftovers every night, no?" Cruz tugs on a cupboard handle. "That your fridge is so full you can't even close it."

"Threw all that stuff away on account it was turning sour," I tell him. Which is true: the one rotted-out tomato covered in fuzz that I scraped off the butter dish.

Once in a while Pop'll remember to bring me something home, but I can fend for myself. Ernie still keeps me on the payroll two days a week, though there's not much to do at the garage, and if Mrs. Slubetz has anything left in the cafeteria, she lets anyone take it, so I'll bring stuff home and mix it up with some hot sauce.

Cruz takes out a plate, wiping off the dust with his elbow. It's the orange china dish with the little grooved lines around the edges that was Maw's favorite.

Pop acts like Maw will walk right down from the miners' hospital and start making us an Ulster fry like nothing ever happened. Like everything's all right.

"If you don't eat something fresh, Ugly, you'll pass out, and I don't want us losing the game on account of you." Cruz is acting cocky, as if he's got the upper hand. Like he's better off because his mother's still at home making enchiladas and taking care of ten kids, three of them snot-nosed and barely potty-trained. They run around the Barrio with mud-covered feet, their painted-pony-colored hair flapping in the wind.

"You still have a rusty ol' icebox, Cruz. What do you know about keeping food fresh?" I tell him.

He cuts the burrito in two with a bottle opener he found in the sink, but it's not an even half. He slides the plate in my direction, leaving me the bigger piece, before wiping his forehead with the bandanna because of the heat.

"We may not have a big fancy white Frigidaire, but we don't go hungry, Ugly," Cruz says. "You tell that shift boss—"

"Just worry about your own performance, amigo. And I don't need your food," I say, giving that half burrito a fierce stare like it's a vulture-pecked rat. The same way Mrs. Hollingworth and those ladies on Company Ridge looked at Maw when she turned.

I remember when they first took Maw up the hill, the Hatley women would leave all sorts of things in our kitchen: buttermilk biscuits, spaghetti-and-meatball casseroles, chocolate cream pies with notes pinned to them. Like we couldn't take care of ourselves. Like we were a bunch of lowlifes or eejits or something. That's what Pop used to say. The gifts lasted two, maybe three months.

I pretend like I'm just casually opening the fridge to see if there's any eggs I might've missed. The ones from Mrs. Palermo's chickens that I scramble up with the half-rotten cabbage heads I find behind Peila's—if the burros haven't gotten them first.

There isn't an egg in sight, just a few pickles in a jar.

I know it's stupid turning away food when I'm starving, but I don't want anyone knowing how it is behind these walls and getting all righteous like Sims or judging what they don't even know.

"You tell that shift boss to stuff this fridge before he does anything else tonight, you hear me, Ugly? I know he eats plenty. I've seen him at the Copper Star with—" Cruz shuts his mouth in midsentence when he sees me glaring at him. Not that he's about to tell me something I don't already know.

"Hear those Rim Valley players ain't been anywhere near five thousand feet since last season," Cruz says. "Hello, nosebleeds."

I don't like it when Cruz changes the subject, especially after smarting off at me. And there won't be any Copper Star for my father tonight. He'd rather work a double shift than watch me play.

"I can't wait to shred their knees and elbows into Hell's Corner."

"Too dry for Hell's Corner," I snap back. "And they beat us last year, remember?"

"That's because the chalk line was wrong."

"You mean *you* slipped on your ass and never got the ball over in time, so you said the chalk line was wrong."

Cruz's mouth is full, but by the look he's giving, I'm thinking he'll spit out what's in it and tear a verbal strip into me. Then he grins. A few pieces of rice and beans fall out, so we both start laughing and he nearly chokes on the rest of the burrito. "Whoever made that call must've been born in Phoenix, no?" Cruz mumbles.

"No," I tell him. *"Cottonville."*

Cruz swallows before laughing this time. "They promised to go heavy on the markings for tonight, so they can't make us lose."

It's just like Cruz not to see that we might get beat tonight fair and square or how small we are. And it's no use telling him any different. Cruz has never given a horse's ass about the other teams or what people think. But he's not the one throwing the ball. I am. And I've got to be pretty much perfect this year.

Cruz doesn't know much about Hell's Corner anyway. Not the way Bobby did. He'd take me to the field on Sunday afternoons and teach me all about that northeasterly patch of ground. How it's hiding the rocky elbows of a boulder embedded in the sand and that you need to set your spikes around the edges and dig so you won't slip. It's bad enough on dry days, but after a monsoon, Hell's Corner can suck you deep into the mountain, twisting knees and ending seasons, not caring which team you're on.

"Rally sons of Hatley High. Sing her glory, sound her fame. Raise her Orange and Black!" Rabbit walks in singing our fight song, which Notre Dame stole off us, and wearing the token sweater Coach Hansen gave him for being such

a good sport, writing those articles about us in the *Pick & Shovel.*

"How's traffic out there?" Cruz jokes.

"I'd say you could shoot a cannon from here to the post office and you wouldn't hit anybody," Rabbit says.

"They're all at the field already?" I can't believe it.

"Last I heard was nearly five hundred," Rabbit says. "My dad ran out of French loaf already. And Beebe's not even in her cheerleader outfit yet. She had to ask Angie to help collect the two bits for admission just to keep up."

"Rah! Rah! For Hatley High!" Cruz wiggles his hips and whistles, following the curves of some imaginary gal with his hands, but I know it's Beebe. "We're not even there yet, Ugly. And already they're dying to see us."

Rabbit hands us each a copy of the *Pick & Shovel.*

"You wrote about the game already?" Cruz asks.

"I wrote an *essay* about the game," Rabbit says.

"Good." Cruz nods. "Keep writing essays and acting smart so you won't get drafted when you turn nineteen come December. And don't grow. They're not looking for soldiers the size of eighth graders."

Rabbit ignores Cruz and gets out his notebook, drawing a line with his pencil to split up the page. "You nervous, Red?" he says. "'Cause it's okay to be nervous. Gosh, if I was you I'd probably screw up the first play."

"You write about that and your fingers'll be taped up for a year," Cruz warns him.

As if I didn't know that I can't screw up this year.

I take the half burrito, kick the trash can open with my cleats, and shove it in, plate and all. I'm no charity case. And I don't need anyone acting ornery—not Cruz, not Rabbit, not my pop. Or feeling sorry for me either. I'm the first-string quarterback for Hatley High. The second O'Sullivan to be one. Coach says I've even got the same arm as Bobby. That my skills are similar, only I'm shorter. And maybe even a little bit quicker. Not as strong, though, but just as accurate.

We'll find out by the end of the night.

* * *

7:00 P.M.

It's impossible to cut through the line of cars, the chrome grilles are bunched so close together they're nearly touching. Not even Francisco can squeeze through on Paradiso. And the spots behind the goalposts are already taken, so I don't know where the Rim Valley cars are going to park.

Our bleachers are full, too, though kickoff's an hour away. Even the drag-ons that can seat a couple hundred extra: pretty much old ladies and little kids spreading out blankets to save seats before climbing down to get ice cream. But mostly Mucker people standing with their arms folded, waiting for us to score.

Rabbit's sitting by the water jugs stuffing his face with a hunk of French loaf so I guess Mr. Palermo found some more bread. What I wouldn't do for a piece of that right now. I haven't eaten anything and Cruz was right, that was stupid. My head's pounding inside like a tom-tom and my hands go all clammy, but my face is burning up and the sun isn't helping.

It's barely starting to dip behind the mountain. Shafts of light are streaking onto the field and I have to cup my hands to see it from here, the outline of the miners' hospital. Its clay-colored roof is shaded brown, but the rest is blurred together so I can't make out stories or balconies or where Maw's window is.

Maw used to be the first one at these games, tying markers on the bleachers with her handkerchiefs—some black, some orange—and me hauling a hamper full of soda-bread sandwiches.

People used to joke how Maw was a walking example of good ol' Hatley High—a living mascot with her copper-colored hair and shiny black blouses covered in orange polka dots she'd special-ordered from Penney's.

I could pretty much starve to death and it wouldn't make a lick of difference to Maw now.

"He got his job back," Nick Managlia says to me, all happy and pointing to his father leaning against the side of the bleachers.

"That's good," I tell Nick, eyeing his dad. He's lighting a cigarette and putting on a show, grinning and laughing like he could actually be proud of Nick. Only I know what he's become. Him and Pop. But at least Nick's father shows up for the games.

A shadow darts by—it's Cruz and he's jerking his knees up high, sprinting from goalpost to midfield, giving the folks a performance. But I've got to save my strength. Besides, if I put a helmet on now, my head might bust right through.

"Shake the thunder from the sky. Old Hatley High will win!" Beebe calls out, going over a yell in her shiny black skirt.

Cruz doesn't look up. He curls his lip instead, then trots backward, diving higher than he needs to in order to catch an easy pass. He must know I'm feeling skittish. He's been taking handoffs from Marty Quesada, who's second-string quarterback this year and will move over from halfback, I guess, if I really do screw up.

I glance to Rim Valley's side. Their quarterback's beaten us before. And they lost a player to polio last year who'd be in the lineup right now, so I'm certain they'll want to get even. They still blame the outbreak on our mountain air.

I jog over to Ricky Sanchez and get into position to take a snap, swinging my arm for an aerial to Pete Torres.

"How you feelin'?" It comes from behind and stops me cold—Pop's voice. You're not supposed to be talking to anyone except the team once you're on the field, so I keep throwing.

"Your arm, I mean," Pop says.

It's heavy as a jackhammer and throbbing. I weave it around the socket a few times and it begins to loosen by the fourth throw. *He's finally here,* I'm thinking, *to see what his other son can do.* And I can't help but smile when I turn to face Pop. He's eyeing me like he would a pony at the races or one of those illegal cockfights he bets on behind the theater in the Cribs.

"Tink you can win?" he says, tugging on his cap. Those brows are still thick with black from the mine and brooding over me as he crosses the sideline with his hands on his hips, making his belly flare out even more.

My gut starts cramping up and I have to run. I race for our goalpost as fast as I can and make it just in time, heaving what little that's left in my stomach into the open pit below.

Coach Hansen's yelling at us to hustle over and I don't think anybody saw. My throat's so dry I guzzle down all the water Tommy hands me in the huddle before Coach blows the whistle for us to come closer, fanning the air with the newspaper.

"I'm sure you've all read what's in here, about us being the lightest team in Arizona," Coach says, "and maybe the history of the state." Coach looks at some of the guys and they hunch over, feeling embarrassed, and start shrinking into themselves. Except for Cruz and Tony. "Well, the last time I checked, a newspaper's never won a game."

"Damn right!" Cruz shouts, jumping on the spot.

Coach crumples the paper into a ball. "Remember, this isn't a weight contest, boys, it's a football game. The pigskin can't read. It only goes where *you* tell it, not some reporter." Coach kicks the crumpled ball off the field and I didn't think paper could go that far.

Tony grins.

"So you're small," Coach says. "That means you're fast. Too fast for your opponent. And what you've got is all muscle or brawn. That'll take the football as far as you want it to go."

The rest of the guys nod and start loosening up, but I'm too nervous to even try.

Coach clears his throat and focuses on the slag. "You've got something else, too," he says. "Take a good look around you, boys." Coach tilts his head toward the bleachers, where Mr. Villanueva's kneeling at the fifty-yard line, adjusting his tie and beaming like the Cheshire cat. Mr. Casillas, Tony's father, is there, too, with his hair all shiny, and he's wearing a starched shirt as if he's going to church or a funeral instead of the sawmill.

"You're all they've got," Coach says, eyeballing us one by one. "Torres, didn't your father have to book off ten months ago just to watch you play tonight?"

Pete digs the tip of his cleat into the gravel and nods.

"See, they want to remember this game," Coach says. "To savor it and take it home with them until the next one, because you know what they have in between?" Coach jerks his thumb at the open pit behind us. "Another week down there in a black hole, breaking their backs and coughing up ore dust."

Alonzo Cushman, the fat freshman who lost to the school bus, starts fidgeting, shifting his weight from one foot to the other.

"And you know what they've got next year?" Coach jabs Cushman's shoulder, then circles the 0 in his number 60 with a fist. "Nothing."

I stare at the slag underneath my feet. It's dry and hard and ripe for cutting.

"*This* can make the difference." Coach jerks at my throwing arm and hoists it in the air. "The O'Sullivan magic!"

"Yeah!" Cruz springs up and down. The other guys slap me on the back.

"*Muckers! Muckers!*" The bleachers are chanting for us.

"Let's give them what they paid for!" Coach yells.

Torres starts clapping and we all do. Slowly at first, then faster and faster.

"You think they came here to see Rim Valley shellac us?" Coach barks. He slaps our shoulders as we jog onto the field. "You're Muckers," he says. "What do Muckers do?"

"Muckers fight!" we holler.

"What do Muckers do?" Coach screams.

"Muckers dig!" we roar back.

I take my place near the end zone for the opening kickoff, trying not to let my nerves take over the heat of the chant. In my head I go through the plays Coach told me earlier, but I'm drawing a blank. I think I could throw up again, too, I'm so shaky.

The pigskin comes flying at us. It's spinning toward Lupe Diaz. He scoops it up and cuts toward the sideline, dodging an Elk tackler and heading upfield.

The kicker's racing for Lupe but doesn't see me coming. The one thing I can always do is run. I focus on his number, then throw myself at his legs and knock him flat. He's gasping and bucking and spitting out chunks of black slag. I let him go and hop up to see that Lupe nearly made it to midfield. The guy I just blocked gets to his knees and wipes some blood off his arm. I don't notice that I cut up my elbow, too, until the blood trickles onto my knees, and I'm glad. I feel good again. *Familiar.* Now that I've had the nervousness ripped out of me.

"Nice block, Ugly." Cruz slaps the side of my helmet.

We huddle up and I remember to keep it simple, that my first call's an easy handoff to Cruz, but he's so primed he barrels forward for seven yards. We get six more on second down, and within three minutes Cruz is diving over the goal line and hitting pay dirt.

Coach smacks a fist into his palm after the touchdown. I look out at the bleachers but the faces go fuzzy with all that clapping and hollering and me feeling so weak. Then I see Angie leaning by a lamppost and smiling at me like it's Christmas Eve and I must be Santa Claus who just flew in from the North Pole. The shift horn blasts, scaring the living daylights out of the Rim Valley players, and we both smile, knowing the night watchman's caught wind of the touchdown and is telling the entire valley about it.

A little kid tugs on Angie's skirt and shows her the money in his fist. She puts it in the cashbox and his mother points to the field. The kid starts jumping up and down all excited and looks at me like I've done something special. Faye Miller— that's who the boy's mother is. Cheering like she did when she was Bobby's girl. Before she moved to Grasshopper Flats a couple months after Bobby shipped out.

"Turn on the lights . . . ites . . . ites!" The boom from the referee's voice echoes from the megaphone as the tiger moths

gather, hovering above the lampposts. I suck back some water, watching the stars come out, covering the sky with shiny specks of white. And it doesn't seem like we need the lights at all. That we could play in the dark underneath the stars and be just fine. Except I'm way past hungry.

Second quarter and Rim Valley toughens up on defense. They manage to score, so we're tied 7–7 at halftime.

Late in the third quarter we're driving toward another score. I call for a handoff then glance over at Cruz. By the look on his face I know he's here—that Pop's back. Probably to make sure he wins his bet now that we're tied. I wonder who he's rooting for. He always played Bobby to win. With me, I'm not so sure.

What did I just call? Sanchez snaps the ball and I pivot to the right, expecting Lupe to take the handoff. But Managlia's there instead. The ball hits him in the thigh and rolls to the ground. I dive for it, but a Rim Valley guard shoves me back and pounces on the ball.

"What was that?" Lupe shouts. "You called twenty-four!"

I know he's right. I shake my head then punch my thigh, knowing that I really did screw up.

The game's still tied in the fourth quarter and we're running out of time. I've only thrown four passes the entire game, but we've got no choice now.

"Just hurry up and win this thing so they can shut off the lights!" Coach is acting kind of screwy on the sideline and squinting pretty badly.

I take the snap and drop back, scanning the field, reminding myself to settle down. That we just can't lose on opening night. Torres is clear near the Rim Valley sideline, right where the ground stays firm so he can get enough traction. The blood pumps back into my arm and I throw a bullet in his direction. He grabs it on the run and, with an open field ahead, sprints toward the goal line. A defensive back finally knocks him out-of-bounds, but he's five yards from pay dirt.

I know I'm racing down the field and I can hear the crowd calling out for me, but the game's gone into slow motion, I'm feeling so weak.

We huddle up and I go by body recognition, faking a handoff to Lupe and pitching the ball to who I think is Managlia. He cracks through the line and breaks a tackle, rolling across the white stripe for the score. We're in the lead and I'm happy, but nothing comes out of my mouth. I can't get off my knees. Somebody hoists me up by the shoulders and drags me off the field.

"Just hold on, Ugly." It's Cruz, splashing water in my face. Telling me Quesada's conversion kick is good. That we won.

"Muckers! Muckers!" The shift horn blasts again and you can hear the miners cheering from the open pit. I'm still down on the ground, but the guys start lifting me onto their shoulders, shouting, "Red-ee! Red-ee!"

The Rim Valley cars flick on their headlights and start backing up, driving onto the field, trying to make it out of here without any problems. But I know the Mucker crowd will let them go without much trouble. Winning makes them awful generous.

Coach is throwing up on the far end of the field so no one will see him. And I don't know why—we won it. I guess he was as nervous for this game as I was.

The boys finally let go of me and I collapse on the ground, I'm so spent.

Rabbit leans over me with his camera and snaps a picture.

"You're not running that." I try pulling the camera off his neck, but I can't even do that. "Got any bread left?" I ask.

Rabbit shakes his head.

"What happened to it?"

"I ate it all."

"You didn't even play, Rabbit."

"I was hungry."

"You idiot, Rabbit!" Cruz says. "Ugly's about ready to pass out." Then Cruz lets out a wolf whistle. "Señor Francisco," he beckons. "*¡Ven!*"

I hear rattling. It's Paradiso. Trotting over to me.

"*Come esto*," Francisco says, tossing a bag of pecans at my number. I tear the paper open and shovel them into my mouth.

"God gave you strength to finish," Francisco says. "He gave you the strength of Goliath. He always gives us what we need."

"'Cept a brain," Cruz says, punching my arm. "Not only are you ugly, you're stupid, too. So do me a favor?" he says, hauling me up. "Don't ever not eat before a game again."

* * *

10:08 P.M.

I'm walking fast up the thirty-degree incline since there's still a maze of cars working their way through Hatley after the game. I'm too close to the top of Hill Street not to go see Maw.

I know it's past visiting time, but we won. And Mrs. Mackenzie usually makes an exception for me—she's just as nice as her husband, Mr. Mac.

Ricky Sanchez's mother is polishing the floor in front of the elevator and stops scrubbing for a minute. "Congratulations, Felix," she says, smiling at me. "*Muy bien.*"

I mumble "*Gracias*," making my way up the stairs. I wouldn't take the elevator anyhow.

They keep it clean and the floors are always polished, but the Eureka Copper Miners' Hospital still smells like disease. I never much cared for the place even before Maw came here. It's shadowy and dank. And no matter how warm it gets outside, the heat can't burn off the stickiness holding in all the soiled smells. I've seen them wash down the walls first thing in the morning, but how do you get rid of something that's rotting from the inside?

I pass the second floor—the only one where you still see flowers in the rooms and other signs of life: young miners with broken bones that'll mend in a few weeks or wailing babies too small to go home yet, but they will. Things go downhill pretty quickly as you climb. And the higher you go, the stronger it gets. The scent of sickness. Overtaking any hint of talcum powder or ammonia from a newly bound cast, so that by the time you reach the fourth floor—which is the top floor—you know the stories must be true. And I don't want Maw being part of them.

One time on the way home from first grade I looked up at the hospital after hearing a terrible cry. They were rolling a miner out on a gurney, his light still strapped to his head. He'd let out a bloodcurdling scream from a pain I can't imagine, his two arms—if you can call them that—aimed at the sky. Only they weren't long enough to be arms; they were more like a pair of stumps, wrapped like meat from the butcher. I sprinted the rest of the way home.

Those two severed limbs shooting skyward—and that scream—stayed with me all summer. Only I couldn't tell Pop. He'd just accuse me of going soft. "Whatcha expect, you tink mining's pretty?" he'd say with a deep-throated laugh. "'T'ain't fer whisses." But I'd heard him cussing and going over things with Maw that night, about how they'd sent another to the fourth floor and that even if he did get to go home, he'd be forbidden from walking the streets in daylight—for the sake of the women and children. How daft the rule was. "'T'ain't no secret," he'd howled, "what the mines'll do to ya."

I feel a sudden urge to turn back and sprint home all over again because I'm never the same after these visits. The sadness sticks with me and I go over how it went with Maw, no different from a combination I haven't got right on the field. Both needle my brain until only a hard tackle or a win can change how I feel.

I don't turn back, and it sounds like Opal Hubbard's winning again. I can hear those checkers skipping to victory in the fourth-floor lounge. *Rah, rah, sons of Hatley High!* Opal sings when he sees me, marching on the spot. Then he smashes the board with a fist and the pieces scatter like popcorn. "You cheated!" he shouts at his imaginary opponent. "I saw you."

Phyllis Crawley shuffles over and buries her face in my shoulder. "I can let down my hair," she says, showing me her long silver braid. "Then you can go home if you'll do the same for me."

"It's another one with short hair, Phyllis," Tuffy Briggs tells her. "You're not going home." Tuffy's reading in a wheelchair by the window, his pajama bottoms billowing empty where they amputated below the knee.

"It's 10:18, Red. You're late. Two minutes and forty-five seconds late," he says, holding up his stopwatch.

"It's all those Rim Valley cars," I say. "Wanting to hurry home after a loss."

Tuffy likes holding my helmet, so I rest it gently on his lap and he fingers the indentations where the stitches grip into the leather. "Should've never lost in twenty-four," he says. Tuffy drove the school bus back then. "Saw it with my own eyes, what the Phoenix officials did."

I lean closer and he takes my throwing hand, turning it over to examine it. "It's your year, Red," he says.

"I hope so."

"You'll make things right and let those Southern boys have it."

Mrs. Mackenzie waves me over. "Your mother's still awake," she says, so I follow her down the hallway.

"Did she get out on the balcony at all?" I ask.

Mrs. Mackenzie pauses. "I was making the rounds in the maternity ward, so she very well might have."

I know she's just being kind.

"Mrs. O'Sullivan, look who's here," she tells Maw before I go in. Then Mrs. Mackenzie turns to me and says, "Just for a little while, okay, Red?"

I don't find Maw at first—the light's too dim. But when I do, I'm caught off guard—blindsided—every time I catch Maw this way, like being brought down to my knees the way it takes a while to recover from a sack. I keep imagining Maw as she was before, not who she is now—a shell of herself in the corner of the room in a wheelchair, slumped over, chin to chest.

I come closer and kneel beside her but she doesn't move. The choppy layers of hair covering her face lift a little, sort of to a rhythm, so I know Maw's breathing—that she hasn't given up completely.

"Maw?" I whisper, turning up her chin so she can get a look at me if she wants to. "It's me . . . Red."

Maw rolls her head back and blinks at the ceiling. Her neck's all shiny, which means she's been drooling. I wipe some off her chin and gnaw at my lip.

Pop used to joke how even though Maw's eyes were as

green as the Glens, she was destined for Hatley since they'd been sprinkled with flecks of copper. I angle her face so I can see those eyes, but they're empty. Cloudy as ice cubes, hazy and dull.

"Would you like me to comb your hair?" I take the sable brush Pop got Maw five Christmases ago, just before she came here, and start at the temples.

Cruz asked me flat out one morning if Maw was like Loco Francisco, which she's not. I know they call it "the ward for the insane" or "the nuthouse" but those are just names, really. Maw isn't crazy, and I don't believe Francisco is either. They call him *loco* because he aimed higher than most and started going on about God's plan, telling them about his visions. Things like starting his own church to preach at and building it with his own two hands. It made the rest of the town so uneasy they kept giving Francisco hell for it, so he up and quit the mine. Now he keeps to his Bible and won't share a word about what God tells him, living off the land instead.

Maw doesn't say much at all anymore, but that doesn't mean she's crazy, or even gone for good. You can give up for a while and then snap out of it like you can with a coma, which is a lot worse than what Maw's going through. You read about stuff like that all the time in the paper—little miracles, really. People waking up from the worst after years, asking for a cherry Coke, then remembering all the people who love them sitting around and staring. Never giving up.

I was helping Rabbit collect eggs from his mother's hens last week. When one of them wouldn't let go of the egg she'd been nesting, Rabbit wanted to know when Maw first let go of me. He said I was like an orphan.

It was when we first got the death notice. Maw stayed in bed for a week and only got up for Bobby's funeral. She never cried either. "Strong as the white rocks in Antrim," Pop kept saying. Then Maw stopped baking soda bread on Saturday mornings.

When school started up again, I came home and there was Maw, sitting in the parlor with her nightgown still on, counting the roses lining the wallpaper. When I asked why she hadn't washed up, she just shrugged and said, "What for?"

By Christmas, Maw'd cut up her hair pretty good, and she thought the living room carpet was a wicked, screaming beast. "Open the windee and we'll shoo the bleemin' hallion away!" she'd cried, beating the border with her crimping iron. And I knew I had to tell Mr. Mackenzie.

That's when Pop started taking on more shifts—night shifts especially—and I saw him even less, so by the time Sundays came, I'd eat up most of the bread meant for Holy Communion, and Father Pierre didn't want that kind of altar boy around.

"Ten more minutes, okay, Red?" Mrs. Mackenzie says, poking her head in the doorway.

"Did he come visit?" I ask.

"Not today."

I don't know the last time Pop did.

I keep brushing Maw's hair, which used to be like mine, but it's pale and brittle now, as if the pigments have given up, too. When I reach the nape of Maw's neck, she simply lets go and an envelope falls from her lap to the floor.

I know it's a letter from Bobby. There's a pile of them on Maw's dresser in the old Victory cigar box next to her pearls.

It's the one where he's at sea writing to Mr. Mackenzie, who gave it to me the day we found out Bobby died. It's the last one Bobby ever sent. The thing about Bobby was that you could never catch him hurting.

Februrary 3, 1945

At Sea

Dear Mr. Mackenzie:

Here's hoping you and your family are in the best of health. Everything is just joto as they say over here. That means okay. But it looks as though I'll have to stay out here for a few more months.

I saw the damege caused by the Jap suicide planes and it's nothing to scoff about. I can see where I am going to need lots of luck in order to stay alive if one should ever hit the ship I am on. Almost all hit near the con-tower, where the captain is. I guess they figure that if they get rid of him the war is won. The captain says if he makes it home he's gonna lie in a hamock for a month and have his wife pour beer down his throat. That he won't even bother to swallow.

All these waters are mine-infasted. At night you have to pray that you don't hit one. It's hard to see them in the dark and it really gets dark up this way. (Please excuse the mistakes but the typewriter isn't any good and I can't type real good when the kid below keeps shaking the bed. I know those are excuses but I don't want you thinking all the time you spent on me was wasted if I can't spell.)

(Over)

Had two good liberties. Bought a nice silk kimono for my future bride. It cost me fifty yen or in american currency it runs to three dollars.

Any way lets give the teams a good going over next season, especially Cottonville. I'd give anything to be there that day but I don't think I could make it.

Well Mr. Mac, keep the home fires burning until I reach home and tell everyone hello. Don't forget we are still out here trying our best that freedom shall not perish from the earth.

> Very sincerely yours,
> *Bobby O'Sullivan*
> Robert O'Sullivan

P.S. I will try and write as soon as I reach my destination. That's a promise!

Don't do it, I tell myself. *Get all weepy and sentimental. It won't bring Bobby back, will it?*

Maw starts getting restless and reaches for the doors that lead to the balcony. She's never done that before. "You want to go out?" I ask. She keeps reaching, so I take her outside. It's a beautiful night. Not dark and murky at all, like it was in the Pacific. You could pluck any star you want from the sky. And Maw wants to see it.

"We won the game, Maw." I lean over and whisper it in her ear. "I threw a pass that was nearly as far as Bobby's."

I rest my cheek against hers and look out at the sky. You can see everything from up here. We're at the highest point before the mountain goes vertical. The hillside below is covered with light and it's blinking. And I can't tell which houses are Mexican or Irish or Slav—they're all blended together, forming a single glow.

On nights like these I feel like I can fight the sadness by throwing farther and running harder. That I can actually beat the odds. We've already got one game down—why can't we take the rest of them?

I know this place is the opposite of Rapunzel's castle. That no one's clamoring to get up here and that the chances of leaving are slim. But if an awful event brought Maw here, then why couldn't a happy one bring her back home? Something so important it would make her decide that it's worth it to come back. To take that chance.

Maw reaches out again the way she did before and I give her my hand, but that's not what she wants. She wants the letter.

I miss him, too.

Soon the glow over Hatley begins to fade as the town goes to sleep, like candles getting blown out on a birthday cake.

And in a few hours it'll be Bobby's birthday. He would have been twenty-six.

I hand Maw his letter. It's all I can give her. Someday it might be something more. They say the Yavapai Cup weighs twenty pounds and that it bestows great things on anyone who wins it. If we do, they'll be cheering so loud in this part of the state Maw won't have a choice but to come around and see what all the fuss is about. Then I can finally bring her home.

THE VERDE MINER

Twice-Weekly News of the Mountain

HATLEY, ARIZONA   SATURDAY, AUGUST 26, 1950   FIVE CENTS A COPY

WEEKEND EDITION

MUCKERS WIN PIGSKIN OPENER, 14–7. RECAP, P.2

Miners Request Raise

Hoping to secure the raise they've been trying to put through since April 1945, the Brotherhood of Hatley-Cottonville Miners & Smelter Workers has petitioned for a pay increase of 40 cents a day for all workers at the Eureka Copper mine and smelter.

When asked about the threat of a strike if the request was not met, Dell Bruzzi, spokesman for the Brotherhood, said that as of yet there is no plan to do so. He said the facts show the inflation of prices in this locality after every past raise was greater than the increase in wages. If the trend continues, Bruzzi said, the Brotherhood may find no other alternative than to take constructive action.

SOCIAL NEWS & ARRESTS

—**Mrs. Faye Cosgrove** (nee Miller) and her little son are houseguests of Faye's parents, Mr. and Mrs. Virgil Miller. Faye is back from Grasshopper Flats to manage her father's furniture store since he took ill last month.

—**Mrs. Reginald Hollingworth** entertained the Women's Garden Club with a bridge party at her Magnolia Street home on Company Ridge. Bouquets of white asters decorated the tables, and glace cupcakes were enjoyed by all. High was won by Eulene Vance, second high by Hilda Booth, and low, Wanda Menary.

—Featured guest speaker at the Elks fund-raiser will be Hatley High English teacher **Luther B. Sims Jr.**, who has prepared a speech entitled "Creeping Communism in Your Community."

Draft Registration for All 18-Year-Olds Monday at Cottonville High. Draft Call Still Set at 19.

Chapter 6
EVERY MAN FOR HIMSELF

POP'S SURPRISED WHEN I WALK into the kitchen this early in the morning the day after a game. He's got on his red unions—he always has them under the white shirt every shift boss wears—and should be using a fork instead of those fingers when he starts fishing for a pickle out of the jar. But I'm glad he's aiming for something to eat. Pop never does when he's drunk, so I know I'm in the clear.

"Dammit!" he hollers. I can see his fingers dangling inside the jar. "I'm stuck," he says, his face burning red.

I get out the lard Maggie Juniper keeps in the cupboard and bring it over to the sink, trying not to smile or laugh or anything. I can see his wrist is bleeding since he keeps trying to yank it out when it just won't go.

"Stop thrashing it around," I say. "It'll only make it worse."

Pop sighs and watches me spread the lard around the rim, then onto his swollen wrist.

"If you say I'm in a pickle you'll be sorry," he mumbles. But I can't stop myself from smiling.

When the wrist wriggles free, he dumps the pickles into the sink and grabs the first one that slides out, looking at me in between chewing.

"So you're the king of happiness, eh?" he says.

I don't say anything. I never know what to say to Pop anyhow. I wonder if he'll let me take a pickle, though. There's only three. I lean into the sink to get one, but Pop latches on to my arm. He's quick for fifty-four, at least before he gets to coughing, but his hearing's definitely shot from all that blasting down in the mine.

"The game last night," he says. "Remember, it's every man for himself out there. Same as in the mines." Then he lets go of my arm and I stuff the pickle in my mouth.

"Wipe that smile off your face," Pop says when he catches me grinning.

It wasn't even a real smile. How could it be? Not today.

Pop doesn't bother to shave much anymore. He's due at the mine before it gets light out. I know they like their shift bosses clean-shaven, but they ease up the rule for Pop.

Except for his big hands and gut, Pop's pretty thin, especially in the face. He never took on any muscle, even after all those years of mining, and his nose hasn't looked like a nose in a while. There are little round things sprouting out from the sides like on those saguaros that grow down in Phoenix we saw in that Kodachrome film.

Pop's nose turned purplish-red once they started blasting open the pit. Every time a miner got killed on his shift, you couldn't find Pop for days. Then he'd come home and throw one of his rocks at the mountain. When Bobby died, there weren't any rocks left to throw, so Pop hurled a chair at me instead.

He puts the empty pickle jar in the Frigidaire without the lid and gets the newspaper I left on the back porch.

"It'll never happen," Pop sniffs, wiping his mouth with his hand and pointing to the part about the miners wanting a raise. "The E.C. don't need us like they used to," he says, sitting back down at the table, "or we'd have 'em again by the balls."

"Ever think it'll shift back," I ask, "or isn't there enough ore down there to keep the mine going?"

"There's ore, and enough of it. Gold, too," Pop says. "But I don't make those kinds of decisions." He scratches his belly and looks up like he's seeing me for the first time. Then he goes to the sink and gets the last pickle. "It's still good," he says, handing it to me. "There may be no future for you here, Red. And the mine—it's no life for you. Once football's over, you best be tinking about what comes next 'cause there might not be anything left for you in Hatley."

Chapter 7
FOUR O'CLOCK WIND

COACH LET US OFF PRACTICE early after grinding hard all week. He says he wants us to be fresh for our second game tomorrow night in Prescott so we should head home.

People are always calling four walls a home. But ours doesn't feel like one. To me, this field is home, so I showered and came back.

The train's almost loaded at the depot when I see Angie heading down the hill for the Barrio.

"Hey, Angie!" I call out. "How'd you like to go for that swim?"

She turns and puts her hands on her hips. "We're not anywhere near the Verde," she says, coming over.

"We can be." I point to the train getting loaded up in front of the tunnel.

"Red, you're crazy."

"No I'm not. You jump on before the train gets going." I jog over to the tracks and hop onto the last freight car, then reach for Angie's hand. Her eyes go wide and she starts biting her lip, so I know she's doubting it already. "Come on, Angie. I'll catch you if you fall."

"From up there?"

I dangle a foot in the air, out toward the Barrio, and jump off. "Here. I'll even make you a doorstep." I get on all fours and wait until I feel her foot push against my tailbone.

"And why would I hitch a train ride with you?" Angie says, looking down at me from the doorway, her red lips smirking and both arms splayed across the opening of the car.

"'Cause you want to."

"How would you know?"

"You're up there, aren't you?"

The train lurches forward, shaking Angie's stance, and she's startled.

"Red, get up here. Don't leave me!" she cries, gripping the rattling steel.

"Not until you tell me you don't hate me."

"I'm not going on this thing by myself."

I know I've got about thirty seconds before Dell makes the switch. So I grab my letterman's jacket and break into an easy jog. "Well, then . . . ," I say to her.

"I don't hate you. You're a nice gringo, okay?"

"And you want to hitch a train ride with me."

Angie hesitates, so I stop running and let the car get ahead of me.

"And I want to hitch a train ride with you!" she shouts.

I can hear two low-pitched barks and they're bounding closer. I know they're Father Pierre's angry dogs, but I focus on the opening in the car and lunge forward, hurtling through it and onto the train floor, sliding a few feet on my stomach.

"You scared me," Angie says, pummeling my back with her fists. They don't hurt. No more than a flood of piñon nuts falling off the pines by the Verde, shaken loose by the four o'clock wind.

"Didn't mean to." I roll over and smile. "Guess you never caught a train like this before."

"What if somebody saw us?" Angie says.

"Like who? Dell Bruzzi's the only one driving this train. He'd never tell. And Father Pierre's dogs can't speak human."

"Don't be so sure. Father tells them everything in French. And they always chime in at the best parts."

"That's right . . . you're good at languages, aren't you?"

"I just know three," Angie says. "So far. It's how I got the job at the telephone company." She won't let our eyes meet and peers through the gap in the freight car instead. "Would you care?" she asks, looking into the rushing scenery.

"You mean, if somebody saw us?"

She nods. "Would you?"

"Why would I?"

"I don't know. You're a gringo and I'm—"

"Hey, doesn't *gringo* mean 'green' in Spanish? I'm Red, you know. In case you hadn't noticed."

"*Verde* means 'green,' silly." Angie messes up the top of my hair and laughs. "It's really beautiful," she says.

"And I didn't even get a haircut yet."

"I meant, *the view.*"

"See. Aren't you glad you jumped on? Though you don't look like a girl who gets into nature much."

"What do you mean?"

"I don't know. The skinny skirt. That pearl necklace."

"These? They're not real. They're fake. I got them at Penney's. We could never afford real pearls like the ones at Robinson's. And I was hiking down the hill when you caught me, remember?"

"But you'd like real ones."

"Oh no." Angie blushes. "They cost nearly forty-nine dollars! You know how much real ones could buy? There's ten of us. New shoes would be nice." Angie looks down at her black-and-white ones. "I can't keep polishing these saddle shoes forever. It just makes the cracks deeper."

I come closer and touch one of those pearls. "Bet they'd match your teeth," I say. "*Real* pearls."

Angie looks down at my fingernails. "You work a lot at Ernie's, don't you?"

"Enough, I guess," I mumble, pulling away. Doesn't matter how much I wash them, the thumbnails still keep in the grease.

I wish Angie hadn't seen them. Not this way. When I'm throwing out on the field, all you notice is how smooth they hug the ball, buried deep in the pigskin. Not how filthy they are, but how well they listen. Then the precision of the quick release, so all you can do is follow the direction of the toss.

"I don't mind," Angie says. "Papá's grimy like that all over when he gets home. You know, from down in the mine. He makes Mamá take a banana yucca and scrape the black off, even if it cuts into the skin." Angie takes a loose nugget of churned-up ore that's found its way into the car. Then she starts laughing.

"What's so funny?"

"I was just thinking about the stone the train's carrying," she says. "And how half of it's probably from my father. Or my brother Manny."

"Yeah. And I bet my pop made them shovel it in there."

Angie's expression turns cold, so I know I said something wrong.

"I mean . . . I didn't mean it like that," I tell her. That was stupid. Talking to Angie like she was Rabbit or Cruz.

"I know. It's true," she murmurs.

The train rounds a sharp corner before heading into the tunnel and she leans into me when the darkness covers us. Her body's firm and warm. She steadies herself when we get back into the daylight, then inches backward until she's against the closed side of the car. "Papá would kill me if he saw us right now."

"Us? Or *me*?"

"Anyone who's not my brother. I'm only fifteen!"

"Yeah, well, he'd have to take a number because Cruz would slit my throat before your father even got to me."

"You think so? But you're Cruz's best friend."

"Exactly."

The train grazes past a shaggy juniper as it picks up speed, and I know that it's time. "Get ready to jump," I say.

"Are you joking?" she says. "Can't we wait until the train slows down?"

"It'll be in Cottonville by then. Nothing but sidewalks with people gawking at us. And the sheriff's office. We'd be found out for sure."

"But it's going so fast."

I take Angie's hand without waiting for an answer and pull her up quickly. "There's a sandy pocket ahead," I tell her. "When I yell 'gringo,' we jump, okay? One. Two. Three. *Grin-go!*"

Angie screams before we leap into the sky but she doesn't let go. Then we land, tumbling down the valley together all entangled and heading for the river until a cottonwood breaks our fall. And she's laughing. Just lying there with me, laughing.

"You all right?" I ask.

Angie looks down at her skirt, then feels around the back of it. "My seam split," she whispers.

"Uh-oh. Is that bad?"

"Nothing that can't be fixed," she says. "Close your eyes, okay? And I'll see just how far it ripped."

I do what I'm told and after a while she says, "It's not too torn. I'll be able to fix it."

So I open my eyes and Angie's standing there at the edge of the river, the ends of her skirt flipped up above her knees. "How cold's the water?" she asks, kicking off her shoes and stuffing her ankle socks inside their toes.

"Not too cold." I roll up my jeans and untie my sneakers. "It's had most of the summer to get warm, and the shade hasn't hit yet," I say. "Come on. There might even be some trout in there."

Angie stands at the bank, one foot in the water, the other swirling around at the surface. "It's warmer than the pool water," she says, circling her foot wider and wider. "At least— *our* water. Is your water cold, too?"

"Pretty cold." I turn away and make like I'm eyeing a fish. It's such a stupid rule. "From what I hear. I don't go in much. I'd rather swim here in the Verde."

"It takes me three hours just to bleach it."

"How's that?"

"When we're done with our days and it's about to be your—*their* turn." Angie stops circling and splashes her foot in the river. "We have to bleach it after it gets drained. I wear gloves but it's just so strong. The solution they give us."

She examines her hands and that's when I notice they're

different. They're covered with patchy stains that don't match the rest of her skin.

"I'm becoming whiter. See? Isn't that a laugh?" Angie says, holding up her hands. "I bleach the pool because I'm not a gringa, and then the bleach ends up making me one." She's smiling, but it looks pasted on. Her voice has gone all shaky, too, and her lip starts quivering. "I wonder if they bleach it after they're through and it's our turn. I mean, who checks?"

"Angie—"

"I never see the sheriff by the gate when they close, like he is when we do."

"Angie, stop." I wade over and cup her hands in mine. "It's a stupid rule, okay?"

But she's crying. "Maybe they just leave it dirty after white days. Dirty for the Mexicans. Filthy white water."

I take her shoulders and she lets me bring her close, only I don't know what else to do. Holding her doesn't seem like enough. It can't be enough. *Would a kiss be all right? No, a kiss wouldn't be right.*

"*¡Ay, Dios santo!*" Angie screams. "A fish just swam right by me. I could *feel* it!" She lifts her face from my chest.

Some rainbow trout swarm by us, treating our legs like they're bulrushes. "See that big speckled one?" I point out.

"Yeah." Angie nods and follows my finger.

"I'm gonna catch it."

"Oh sure. And I suppose you'll do that with your bare hands."

"You know it." I've caught one before. I'm pretty quick. I can anticipate where they'll go. I take off my jacket and aim it at the banks. It lands right where I wanted it to—on a ruddy manzanita branch.

Then I go find the fish. It stalls for a split second, barely an inch from the surface, and I pounce. But all I end up with is a face full of water.

"Nice going!" Angie says, and it's good to hear her laughing. I don't move, and scan the surface for bubbles. Then I see the fish in between the rocks to the left of me. Wedged between the banks. I know it's only got one way to go and that if I dive for him, he'll wriggle out from behind. So I reach for him with my toe and aim my body just behind his tail.

"Got it!" I shout, hoisting him up for Angie to see. "Here, catch!"

"Red, you wouldn't. Please don't throw it!"

"What, you don't like fish?" It's nearly a two-pounder and slices into my fingers struggling to get free, but I've got a good grip on it.

"I do," Angie says. "But not when they're moving!"

It would make a good supper and I'd keep it if I were alone. Stuff it in my shirt once it stopped breathing. But not with Angie. She doesn't know how hungry I get.

I catch a glimpse of the tail shimmering pink and green and blue before I give him back to the Verde and it scares her. His heavy splash into freedom catches her by surprise. Angie slips on a rock before I can get to her but hops back up faster than that trout.

"Hey, you're quick. Those pearls didn't even get wet." I look down at Angie's skirt and it's the only part that's soaked. Still, she's shivering, and I can see her legs through the wet material as she walks to the bank. She's wearing pink underwear. They've got flowers on them. Angie turns around and I notice that her shirt has splashes on it, in places I'm longing to see once we've grown closer.

"My jacket's dry." I walk up to shore and give Angie my letterman's jacket, and we sit on the bank.

"Thanks. It's really warm," she says. "Hey, would you look at that cactus? It's blooming right in the air."

There's an agave behind us and it's loaded with yellow flowers on a spike going ten feet up.

"See. It's coming back," Angie says. "The mountain."

I smile because she noticed, too, and watch as she lies down and gazes at it, the same way I do.

"Maybe it's because the smelter only belches out half of what it used to," I say.

"No." Angie shakes her head. She leans on an elbow and fingers a clump of fuzzy white sage. "I think it's because Nefertiti's fighting it. She's a tough mountain. And she's still got plenty to give."

I'm not sure about that. "You know they die right after they bloom, don't you? Those agave plants. It takes so much out of them just to make it up that far."

Angie jerks forward and stares at me, disappointed. But a part of me believes that the mountain gave all she had a long time ago, and even though things are blooming, it's too late. For the mountain, anyway.

"My parents won't sell the house, you know. Papá doesn't think the mine will close."

"Neither does Cruz," I say.

"What, so you think they will? That they'll ship every last piece of the smelter to Ajo or Bisbee? Is that what the white folks think?"

"You mean, like me? You really believe I think differently than you?" I look down at my hand where the gill caught my finger and squeeze out some blood. "See this?" I say, showing her the cut. Then I break off a piece of agave. "Now give me your hand. This won't hurt much—I promise. You can close your eyes if you want to."

"No. I don't need to," she says.

I prick the fleshy part of her middle finger until there's a tiny drop of blood. "See?" I put my cut-up finger beside hers. "They're both the same color, aren't they?"

Angie sucks her finger and looks up at me with those eyes. "I'm glad you kidnapped me." She smiles.

"I didn't kidnap you. And you sure don't look like a kid to me. You're already a sophomore."

"It'll be strange," Angie says, "going to Cottonville next year."

"Yeah, well, don't plan on talking to any of those Wolves, all right?"

"Who's gonna stop me?" she teases. "You won't be here, will you? Not if the mine really does close."

"There's no way I'd ever work in the mine."

Angie looks at me, surprised. "So, what will you do then?"

"Play football."

"No, I mean after," she says.

"I don't think about after. That's getting too far ahead. 'After' makes you forget about what happened before and forces you to lose sight of now. And right now I've got to win something."

"Don't worry," Angie says, resting her hand on my arm. "You'll beat those Wolves this year. That'll make you happy."

"No." I shake my head and turn to face her. "I mean something really big, like going undefeated and taking the Northern Crown. Then the state championship."

"Is that all you think about?" Angie sighs. "It's the same with Cruz. And Manny before that."

"That's because we have to."

"And what if you don't, Red? What if you don't take Northern and go to the state? You'll still graduate. Things'll be the same."

"Same as what? Nothing's been the same for a while, Angie. Not like before. I've finally got a chance where I can get some of it back and I'm not gonna let that be taken away."

Our eyes unlock and she leans back into the sand. "I'm getting out of the Barrio," she says. "It's practically all I think about—the future. What's in store. I know I'll teach. And Mexicans can buy houses right on the main streets in Cottonville."

"What's wrong with now?" I ask. But Angie won't look at me.

"I don't want to think about now," she says. "Now means separate swimming days. The Barrio. These hands. You can get the grease off yours if you really scrub, but I can't wash out the stains. They're permanent."

"I don't care." I take her speckled hands, pulling her toward me, and she starts crying again.

After a while Angie looks up at me. "You really do have red hair everywhere, don't you?" she says. Then her face goes pink. "I mean on your arms . . . your legs." She runs a finger over my arm. "It looks just like a copper ingot in the sun."

"Yeah, we all do—" I catch myself. "Did."

"He played football, too, didn't he? Your brother."

I tighten up for a moment, then pick up my shoes.

"I'm sorry I brought it up," Angie says. "You're happier when you forget."

"Forget? About Bobby? Not a chance," I say. "Come on, we better head back to catch the next train. It's getting late."

We walk past the mesquite brush along the tracks for a

couple hundred yards, waiting for the train to slow down as it reaches the tunnel. Then we scramble on.

Angie's more comfortable on the way back, maybe because it's familiar now, and she lets herself be rocked by the motion of the train.

"It was his birthday on Saturday," I say, looking out at the scenery.

"Bobby's?" Angie asks. She looks sad when I nod. "I'll light a candle for him right away when I get home," she says softly.

"What'll that do?"

"It will let his soul know that I care."

I don't know how to answer that. All of a sudden there's so much more going on in my head, but the rest of me feels warm, not wound up tight like a coiled spring you'd find under a Chevrolet. Angie leans over, wanting me to look at her, but I can't. Not yet.

"They're the same age, Manny and your brother," Angie says, breaking the silence. "We're lucky Manny came back, that's for sure. Even though he's missing a few fingers. And he still talks about Bobby."

"What about?"

"Football. That big season they had right before they left to go overseas. He also said—" She waits for me to look at her. "He told me about your brother's fiancée, Faye Miller. She was at the game last Friday. She has a son."

"I know. I saw them, too. She said hello."

"So, how come you don't visit the Barrio anymore?" Angie asks.

"I haven't been invited. Not since I was a little kid, anyway. And now Cruz won't let me. Not if he knew you were with me. I'd be getting shot at every step of the way down."

"Papá's gun is so old he'd miss every time." Angie smiles.

"I like your lips when they're not so red," I tell her. The sun and the water wiped away the makeup, uncovering a pale glow, and she's glistening. There's really pink underneath where the red was. And both the top and the bottom are all fleshy and shiny, just like the back of that trout.

Angie blushes. "I must have dropped my compact somewhere. Down by the river." She reaches inside her skirt pockets but comes up empty.

"I'll have to kidnap you again. To go see a picture show. One that Cruz won't want to see. Maybe I'll ask Bigsby for a private screening. I could fix his flats for nothing."

Angie laughs and says something more about Cruz, but I'm not listening. I'm focused on those pink lips. How they must feel. Then I lean over and kiss her. Just flat out kiss her. "In case I never get the chance again," I say, not waiting for a reaction.

"Planning on leaving anytime soon?" Angie asks, stroking the spot where my lips touched hers.

"Nope."

She wraps my jacket tighter around her and I think it looks better on her than me. And I get this feeling inside, like I could rest in this moment a whole lot longer. But I know what happens next, because it always does. Time never gives me more when I need it. It just keeps getting away, snuffing itself out like a dying candle. Like it's some sort of game, handing me way too much when I could care less— like when I'm alone and wanting to be with someone I can't, but not giving me enough when I am.

The train slows down and this time I don't let go of her hand when we jump off. Angie pauses and looks up at me but we don't speak. I can't speak.

She hurries down the hill, then rushes back. "I almost forgot. Your jacket!" She hands it to me and leaves much too quickly. I wanted to catch those eyes one more time, but she's already sidestepping the prickly pears and the bear grass to get down to the Barrio.

I'm alone again. And way past hungry. I'm hungry for a lot of things. Hungry for Angie, hungry to have Bobby here with me, and hungry for a win against Prescott tomorrow night. But I need to eat something first. Too bad I didn't keep that trout. I'm so hungry I could start up a fire and cook the whole thing right here.

Chapter 8
A SQUEAKER

SATURDAY, SEPTEMBER 2
6:40 A.M.

WE BARELY WON AGAINST THE Badgers last night. It seemed all of Prescott was gunning for us, crowded on the bits of grassy field at the fairgrounds. We were the show, and I wanted to win so badly that it cost us the touchdown that would've let us relax in those final seconds until the gun sounded. All I kept thinking was how once we win and notch two victories, I might have less of a reason to get so nervous, since winning two games in a row doesn't mean you just met some kind of lucky—it means you deserved to win. Then a Badger got me.

Tony kept him still as long as he could, but I just stood there frozen like one of those people buried alive in Pompeii, eating away too much time figuring on a pass, so the Badger wriggled a hand loose and got me. Reached out for my ankle and down I went. The ball did, too. Cruz pounced on it and made a nice recovery, but not before swearing in Spanish and bucking like the rodeo ponies waiting on the sidelines for the game to finish.

The guys were all joking on the bus ride home, with Coach calling the win a "squeaker" like some muddy pig had just made it through the gate in the nick of time. And when he thought all the others had fallen asleep, Coach asked how things were going with me. I didn't know what to say, so I just looked out the window. But then I wanted to ask Coach the very same thing whenever we got to a stop and he squinted like it was painful to watch the light changing from red to green.

That was six hours ago—we didn't get back home until past midnight. Now it's not even seven o'clock on a Saturday morning, but me, Cruz, and Rabbit are meeting in the back of Ernie's garage so no one will see what we're up to. Looks like it took another crack from a blast. I lean against the shed and wait for them to get here with the supplies we'll stash inside.

Ernie will be here in half an hour so I'm starting to get nervous, plus the garage sits below the Sacred Heart of Mary, where Father Pierre gives the Mexican Mass at seven. But it's stupid that I'm starting to feel found out before we've even done anything. I mean, all Cruz wants us to do is hike up to the H and write HELLO on the hill. It should get a good rise out of the kids, and they ought to have one, after knowing they might end up at Cottonville next year. And it's not like it'll last for more than a few months or anything. It's only whitewash. We paint the H every year.

"Hey, Ugly, I need some help," Cruz says. He's coming up the hill with the burros and snapping his gum. "There's two cans of paint on this one, and brushes on Kissy," he says, untying the flour sacks from the saddles.

"You seen Rabbit?" I ask, not wanting to leave room for any talk of the game. I open the shed and clear a spot on a rickety shelf for the paint. There isn't much space for anything else in here, with Ernie's motorcycle and the stacks of magazines he doesn't want customers seeing.

"Still at the bakery filling his face," Cruz jokes. "One day he'll be a blimp, I swear."

I hold up a magazine—the one featuring a naked girl on the cover with a Valentine box over her privates. "Guess you'll just have to give him one of your girls, then," I say, showing Cruz the cover. He tells me he's seen better than February '49.

"What about you?" he asks, pointing to my hair. "If you don't dye those carrots, you'll stay a virgin, too, no?"

"What's wrong with red hair?"

"Orange hair."

"Kiss my ass."

"So they're here!" Rabbit pokes his head inside. "Your dad say anything about the burros?"

Cruz shrugs and hands Rabbit a can of paint.

"How old are these?" Rabbit asks, swirling the can around. "They're so lumpy you can't even shake 'em."

"What do you know about paint, Rabbit? It's not a ball of dough."

"I don't roll the dough—I get the *ingredients* for the dough," Rabbit says, shaking his head. "So, did you get any sleep after what happened in the game last night, Red?"

"Oh, here we go," Cruz says. "Rabbit being an expert on a game he never played."

"I see things," Rabbit says. "You're in it, so you can't."

"And you better not write about Ugly freezing up either."

"I didn't freeze up. I was reading the field."

"Oh yeah? What do you call *this*?" Cruz jokes, pretending like he's the Tin Man who just ran out of oil midstride. "Don't matter. It takes a lot more than that to make them win against us, no? You can throw anything in your sleep, Ugly—better than all those quarterbacks we play. Nobody can stop us."

"Everybody can be stopped," Rabbit says. "You just have to keep pushing until they notice you."

"Not this year. They'll be talking about the Muckers in Phoenix and Tucson soon," Cruz says.

I don't want to think that far ahead yet—it's already ten to seven—so we take the burros and make the trek past the Ruffner mansion and down to the cemetery at the bottom of the Gulch, where they'll graze in the Barrio by the graves all day before we pick them up. Which will be in about fifteen hours.

"Oh shit," Cruz shouts.

He just stepped in some. Carl Purdyman's cows must've wandered down here overnight. There's cow patties everywhere.

"Ever notice that the dung's mostly around the tombstones?" Rabbit says, careful not to step on any of the drying brown clumps.

"Ever notice that this town is full of shit?" Cruz fires back. "In the streets it's the burros and in the graves it's the damn cows! And since when do you go calling shit 'dung,' Rabbit?"

I know they'll be arguing all morning about what to call the crap spread over the cemetery, so I say, "Meet you guys back here tonight." I start work at eight and practice is at twelve-thirty.

By the time I climb up the hill and reach the Copper Star, my letterman's jacket's soaked right through. The blinds in the restaurant are drawn this early in the day, but Cruz'll be there later working the pool tables—maybe even giving a lesson, though the only ones who can afford them these days are the prostitutes who still work the Cribs behind the theater. Cruz says the older ones are the biggest tippers, so he doesn't mind when they get too close.

The sun's bearing down on me so hard along Main that I strip to my undershirt, but it isn't helping. Any minute now the sun will flatten me into the ground like a heel pounding in a tin can. Then I'll melt into a gooey cow patty. And Cruz will step on me, just before he runs out of oil.

I decide the only way to stop my frightening imagination is to get a copy of the *Verde Miner* from Benny at the diner.

THE VERDE MINER

Twice-Weekly News of the Mountain

HATLEY, ARIZONA   SATURDAY, SEPTEMBER 2, 1950   FIVE CENTS A COPY

WEEKEND EDITION

Muckers Nip Prescott

Hatley squeaked out a 19–14 win over Prescott last night at the fairgrounds, overcoming a sluggish start that saw the Muckers trailing 14–6 at halftime. Cruz Villanueva, the swivel-hipped wingback, saved the game with a spectacular 53-yard touchdown run in the fourth quarter.

Hatley quarterback Red O'Sullivan kept his accurate throwing arm under wraps most of the game, often underthrowing his receivers. The result was a pair of interceptions that killed potential scoring drives.

Halfback Lupe Diaz scored the Muckers' first TD on a 6-yard run in the second quarter. He had set up the score with a 42-yard gallop on the previous play. In the third quarter, Nick Managlia reeled off an 18-yard run into pay dirt that sliced the Prescott lead to 14–13.

"Our defense and our run-

Elks Warned of Creeping Communism, p.2

ning game were very good tonight," said Coach Ben Hansen, whose boys are now 2–0. "We're fortunate for that, because our passing game was not at its best."

SOCIAL NEWS & ARRESTS

—After the defendant requested a change of venue to Cottonville, the jury there found **Peter Zolnich,** owner of Pete's Tavern, guilty of simple assault in the sawed-off-pipe attack involving Ronaldo Managlia. Zolnich was sentenced to 60 days in jail. He'll serve his time in the temporary jail in the basement of the Sacred Heart of Mary.

—**Horatio "Peach" Kellerman,** melon farmer, was taken to the miners' hospital after experiencing digestive trauma. His condition is unknown at this time.

—**The Sacred Heart of Mary** will hold a fund-raiser on Mexican Independence Day to collect money to repair the roof leak. **Father Pierre** expects all children to attend and try their luck at cracking open the candy-filled piñata with his cane.

* * *

NOON

I'd rather be spending the end of my shift thinking about Angie and that swim, but Ernie's got me on a call. I turn onto Gomez Street and see Father Pierre's Buick straightaway. It's definitely upside down this time, with two of the tires spinning on silver spokes like pinwheels caught by the afternoon wind. Looks like it was parked at La Paz Grocer, then it cut loose and rolled, crashing through the iron railing but stopping short of Miller's storefront window. The grille's butted up against the window ledge with the roof blocking the alleyway below like a saggy tarpaulin, though you can still get down the stairs to the basement of the furniture store.

"Holy shit," Cruz says, walking past on his way to practice. "Would you look at the *santos*! They're still lined up in a row."

He points to Mother Mary clinging headfirst to the dash, then makes the sign of the cross. "You'd think they'd go running when they could," he says. "And how'd Father Pierre get the money for a new Buick, anyway, when he took that vow of poverty?"

"You swore!" Frankie Tucker gasps, pointing at Cruz. "In front of the Madonna and Saint Christopher." Frankie's an altar boy in training.

The kids have formed a semicircle around me, Cruz, and the empty Buick, the bigger ones holding up the smaller ones so they can get a better look inside. Faye Miller's kid, Samuel, is standing back from the rest, looking timid and rubbing at his freckles.

"Yeah, well, don't be getting any ideas," Cruz tells Frankie. "And don't be late for practice, Ugly." He punches me in the shoulder, timing his jab as I bob up from an eyeball inspection of the car. Nothing's leaking. I'm guessing the radiator's okay even though I can't get to the cap—no steam's coming off the hood. Father Pierre's rosary is tangled up around the steering wheel, but that's about it.

"You know how many Hail Marys you gotta say so you won't burn in hell?" Frankie says, but Cruz is already climbing the hill. "And even if you don't get hell, it's near as hot up in Purgatory."

Cruz turns and grins. "Can't be any hotter than it is in Hatley," he shouts, thrusting his helmet into the burning sun. "I'll tell Coach it was an emergency, Ugly."

"Sure he's not in there?" Frankie asks me.

"Nah." I shrug. "The car's empty."

"So we still gotta go to Mass on Sunday?"

"Looks like it."

Some of the kids boo. A handful of their haltered burros, sweaty from the heat, crane their necks to get a lick at the garbage the wheels picked up from La Paz's.

Faye Miller comes out of the furniture store and shakes her head. "Did Father Pierre's car hit anyone on the way down this time?" she asks.

Frankie points to Leon Brewer, huddled up and crying in the corner of Miller's stairwell. His striped T-shirt's streaked with blood and I can see that his forehead's been cut.

"You okay?" I ask him, ducking onto the stairs.

Leon tightens the grip on his knees and nods.

"Joey went to get his ma," Frankie says.

"Samuel, get me a washcloth from the store," Faye tells her son. The cut's clotting up on Leon's forehead, but Faye brushes back his bangs anyhow.

Leon smiles, tracing the number on my jersey. "Seven," he says. "That's *my* age."

"Then it's got to be lucky, doesn't it?" I tell him. "We'll win the next game for sure."

Leon stretches out his legs and smiles.

"Anything broken?" I ask.

He points to his burro, hopping around in a circle on the sidewalk above us, favoring the right foreleg.

"We were coming back from a swim in the river," Leon says, "and Bear got hit."

"Leon!" Mrs. Brewer cries out. "My baby!"

"He's okay," Faye tells her.

Clipping down the stairs, Mrs. Brewer examines Leon's cut, then eyes the overturned Buick. "Oh, thank goodness it was Father Pierre's car, or Leon could've been killed!"

I don't share the town's view of the Father, and Cruz doesn't, either. Cruz says if you're a Mexican you're not supposed to doubt God, though. That a parish priest is His anointed ambassador, or the go-between—like a shift boss—working in the middle of the Lord and the rest of us. That's why Father Pierre can get away with anything. Ernie isn't Mexican but feels the same way—he'll say this call's on the house. Something about it being like giving God a bill.

"My burro!" Leon wails. His lower lip quivers as Faye leads the Brewers into the furniture store.

"I'll bring him by," I say. The Brewers' house is on the way to the field. But I'm not sure what to tell Ernie about the Buick. It could be a straight tow, or we could lose more than a fender if it takes a nosedive as we haul it out. Either way, I've got to get to practice.

"He's coming!" Frankie shrieks, his breath blowing shallower. The younger kids aren't sure what to do—Father Pierre's all nice when you're little, but just wait till you become an altar boy (or choose football over Mass) and get conked on the head with his cane.

The yelping from Father Pierre's dogs comes lightning quick, riding the wind in angry bursts, first one and then the other a split second later. They keep echoing each other, picking up speed and tumbling loose as red rock down Nefertitty Hill.

I reach for Bear, but the barking startles him and he skitters away like the rest of the kids, who leave their burros to fend for themselves, ears cocked, cowering on the sidewalk.

The black sash holding Father Pierre's cassock in place swishes like a cranky snake every time Father stabs the umbrella he's holding into the cobblestone. Father's eyes—a bullet-gray—catch mine even a hundred yards away. Seeing me makes his lips tighten, and his wire-rimmed glasses slide down his nose, so the lower half of his face seems all beard, clotted yellowy-white.

It's nearly ninety degrees out, but Father's wearing his woolen shoulder cape and the hat—a beaver *cappello* he had shipped over from Rome. Said it was blessed by the Vatican. I forget by which pope. And I know what's underneath the silky lining—a liturgical comb at least as old as the conquistadors who discovered our valley. Father Pierre bought it from an ivory trader in the Belgian Congo. With what, I don't know. And I'm sure priests less ornery combed their hair with it before Mass four hundred years ago. But Father had me douse its teeth with Barbicide every Sunday before Mass so he could comb those African lion hounds with it. Relieve them of any mites or fleas. I didn't want to burn in hell so I did what I was told. Now I know that's just a crock. And I'm not his altar boy anymore.

The dogs have sniffed out Bear shivering at the corner of Hull Avenue. They're lunging and snapping at the burro, the Roman crosses Father had branded on their ribs rising and falling with every bark.

They should have been destroyed a while back when they bit the fleshy part off Baldo Gallegos's thumb. People like Leon's mom and Ernie think that's just a rumor, but seeing the dogs like this, you know it could be true. I heard Baldo aimed at shooting them in the middle of the night, but Father Pierre got wind of it and that's the reason he took the nameplate off Baldo's pew.

I grab Bear's halter, ready to take a kick at those snarling dogs if I need to.

"Benedictus! Fidelis! Come!" Father says to them. The

two dogs stop barking and sit statue-still on either side of the Father while I lead Bear toward Miller's and tie him to the railing.

"You weren't in church last Sunday," Father says.

Which is true.

"No, I wasn't," I tell him. I'm almost always at church, by the way, but last Sunday was different. Not that I go to church because I think it'll help or because of Father Pierre. He's so certain there's a direct pipeline to God reserved just for him. I go because of Maw. I made her a vow. "You'll get to church now, won't you, Felix?" she'd pleaded before they took her away. "And sit in Bobby's pew."

I reach for the keys still dangling in the ignition, and the rosary comes with them. Cruz was an altar boy once, too, until he swung at the Easter piñata before Father Pierre said we could and got pummeled across the neck with this rosary. Walked right out of the churchyard and never assisted at Mexican Mass again. And I suppose Cruz still goes to church every Sunday because of his mother, too.

"Hours for the Sacrament of Penance are still the same at the Sacred Heart of Mary," Father says, prodding my throwing arm with the tip of his umbrella.

What do I have to confess? I didn't do anything wrong. So I say, "There doesn't appear to be any damage to the interior," pointing to the whipcord seats. But my voice is tight, giving away how I feel, and I can see Father bristling already. I won't let him poke my shoulder with that umbrella one more time, so I try another line. "Looks like that chrome fender must've cushioned the blow, but you'll still need a tow so Ernie can take a better look at the damage."

And it's only happened twice in five years that I skipped. Once this past Sunday, after the Purdyman baby got the whooping cough—his family's seats are next to ours—and once when Maggie Juniper needed to get paid. I had to go find Pop and I did, hauling him out of Pete's Tavern and taking his billfold while he slept curled up on the sidewalk, too tired to be in a mood. Not that any of that is Father Pierre's business.

"I'm driving to Prescott tomorrow, so it must be ready by noon," Father says, like it's a commandment or something, when all he had to do was use the emergency brake. That's what I should tell him, but I don't want to be run out of town. I know how news travels. They'd be saying how I smarted off at Father Pierre and what happened to the O'Sullivans? What a sorry lot they've become.

"I'll work on it after practice," I say. "And show you how to use the emergency brake, too."

Father's eyes narrow and his throat starts swelling up. "Who are you to tell me how to act in an emergency?" he bellows. The dogs heel closer on either side of him. *Father's personal patron saints.* "You think you can be the savior of this town," Father says, picking up my helmet with the hook of his umbrella like it's got stuff on it from Purdyman's cows, "but Hatley doesn't need football, it needs an exorcism."

"Your Buick hit Leon Brewer," I tell him. "He'll be all right, but he might not be able to help you on Sunday." I toss Father the keys with the rosary and take back my helmet.

"Leonard is obedient," Father says. "He will attend." Then he tells Fidelis and Benedictus to follow him.

"I expect to see you in church tomorrow," Father says. "Didn't you promise her? You wouldn't want your poor mother to be in worse shape than she already is, knowing that you lied."

* * *

The paint cans are rattling as we head out of the cemetery into the darkness up the hill, and it sounds like thunder. We've got the cans of whitewash strapped to our three burros, Kiss, My, and Ass. Cruz named them. Guess who's being led by the Ass and feeling pretty low because I played so badly again in practice.

I took a nap after practice with a wet blanket over my head, trying to stay cool. I dreamt that when I went to shave, Bobby's death notice wasn't on the mirror anymore. Then when I got to school, Bobby's locker had disappeared and nobody knew who he was. And Maw and Pop kept staring at me with strange expressions on their faces when I mentioned his name. I tried shaking them out of it, but Pop ran away and Maw kept staring at me like she was a zombie.

"Jesus, Rabbit, would you watch where you're going?" Cruz says. "Your burro's ass just stopped dead in my face."

"Can I help it if I got the slow one? Why don't you and Kissy go up ahead?"

"Or maybe I can get in front of Cruz," I offer, snickering. "So he can kiss my Ass."

I think that's really funny and Rabbit does, too, but Cruz looks back and gives me this dirty look. "We gotta be quiet, man," he whispers.

"For who? All the dead people?" Rabbit jokes.

Rabbit's wearing his father's straw hat, even though it's dark out. We've barely made it through the cemetery but he's already stripped down to his undershirt since those scrawny pits have worked up such a sweat.

"Just get up that hill without opening your mouth, you two," Cruz says. "You know how sound carries up here. You wanna get found out?"

We're coming at the H from the side so we won't be obvious, climbing the mountain through the cemetery and past the open pit—which is where the town ends or begins, depending on how you look at it.

It's hard to see, so I bring my burro alongside Rabbit—he's in charge of the flashlights. The night is heavy and the clouds are hanging low, covering the stars and cutting off any light from the moon. "Hand me one of those," I whisper, reaching for a flashlight. They're hooked on a tool belt that's hanging off Rabbit's bony hips and slapping his thighs with every stride.

"Too soon, Ugly," Cruz warns. "They'll see us for sure."

Rabbit hands me one anyway.

"We ought to see where we're going, or we might get bit by something poisonous," I tell Cruz, aiming the beam at a thornbush. Two eyes glow. A ringtail. But it could have been something that stings.

"Jesus, Ugly, do you have to be so dramatic?" Cruz says. "You're scaring the hell out of Rabbit."

The hill probably is full of rattlers with no intention of hibernating yet, and it's definitely loaded with vermin this time of night. Bottom-feeders like that ringtail and raccoons displaced by the mine. I don't care much about any of those, but if you hit a prickly pear or a yucca they can pierce through anything and jab right into your flesh. Try not screaming then.

"I'm not scared," Rabbit says. "Doc Brown says you've got two hours to get an anecdote for snakebite before you die, and we're a ten-minute climb down to the hospital from here."

"What the hell's an anecdote?" Cruz says. "Isn't that from Sims's class?"

"You mean an antidote," I tell Rabbit. "The serum that

counters the poison. An anecdote will just give you a few minutes of conversation."

We stop to catch our breath since it's getting steeper, and they finally quit bickering. A few people are walking Main Street, not many, looking no bigger than a pinky finger from up here. Down in the Gulch there's a faint glow from a fire. Somebody burning trash, I suppose. Then it swells up and grows large enough to be a bonfire. And I'd sure like to be down there enjoying it with Angie, rather than up here with her brother.

"Hey, isn't that Sims down there?" Rabbit points to our toy town and a man wearing a shiny suit crossing Main near the Sacred Heart of Mary.

"Turn them off!" Cruz says, cupping his hand over the lens of my flashlight.

"He can't see us," I whisper. At least, I'm pretty sure. We're behind the spindly gables above Company Ridge, eye level with the mile-high markers, painted white across the clapboard houses.

"He's got a little kid with him," Cruz murmurs. "Didn't think he could make one."

"That's not Sims," I say. "He doesn't have kids."

"He's in charge of the crippled-children's fund this year," Rabbit whispers. "Maybe that's one of the kids."

My burro brays, no longer interested in hiding, and we persuade them to go another fifty feet, then leave them there. It's mostly crushed stone anyway, fiery red from lime and slippery, with only a few hairy patches of coldenia, scrubby and green, to break up the sandstone.

Cruz gets the brushes out from Kissy and says he'll paint the first L. We start crawling, following him with the paint cans. I've been up here twice before but still can't believe how huge the H is. Must be nearly two stories high.

"You think Sims has really lost it this time, don't you?" Rabbit says to Cruz.

"You'd have to be some kind of saint," Cruz says, handing us the brushes, "or kill off the Red Army to get an A in Sims's class. And even then he'd accuse you of being a commie, no?"

"What if you put his name in the box?" Rabbit asks.

"He's the one reading it, stupid."

"Yeah, and weeding out which names to keep and which ones to tear up," I whisper.

"You want a big E or a little e?" Rabbit asks me, dipping his brush in the paint. "Little e's faster."

"Little e then."

"Hey, the lights in the church are still on," Cruz says, pointing to the bell tower with his brush. "What's Father Pierre doing up so late? Counting all the sinners he can charge?"

"Or their offertory money," I say. "You'd think there'd be enough to fix the leaky roof by now."

"Sims can't flunk everybody," Rabbit says, eyeing those big pale boulders of basalt left in chunky piles. "Then what'll they do next year?"

"Send us to Korea."

I keep going over my L, not wanting to think about what Cruz just said. Or next year.

A coyote howls, startling Rabbit, and he balks, losing his footing. Cruz catches Rabbit's arm, pulling him back up. A spray of pebbles loosened by Rabbit's stumble trickles down the hill like pennies shaken from a jar.

"Stupid war," Cruz says. Then he looks at me. "Even if you win, you lose too much."

I suck in some air but it shakes going down. "Bobby would've been twenty-six, you know—last week. He would've married Faye Miller. She was at the game last week, smiling and laughing. She has a kid already." The back of my throat's all moist and my voice breaks. "Should've been Bobby's."

"He fought for what he believed in," Rabbit whispers.

"No he didn't, you idiot," Cruz says. "He fought 'cause they made him."

"So, we shouldn't fight?" Rabbit looks at Cruz, then at me, his brush suspended over the e.

"And get yourself killed?" Cruz says, stabbing at the L.

"I'll do the O," Rabbit says, reaching for my brush.

"No." I push him away. "We're stopping here." I throw my brush down the mountain as hard as I can. It breaks a hunk off a banana yucca.

"What if we get found out?" Rabbit whispers.

"Shut up," Cruz says. "You're gonna work at your mom and pop's bakery for the rest of your life. What do you care?"

Something springs out from the darkness below then skitters away. An antelope or maybe an elk.

"Antelope season's starting up," Cruz says, sitting down beside me. "First one we've had in years. I don't like the taste of that meat, but I could kill a Cottonville Wolf." He slices an imaginary slit across his throat with a finger, then aims it at the Cottonville smelter.

"You don't mean that," I say. "You're such an idiot."

He smiles and I go to punch his arm, but he leans back and I miss.

"Let's get going," Cruz says, gathering up the paint.

It's starting to rain. Just a light drizzle. Misty and warm by the time it reaches us and I don't think it'll cool off the Valley, but it's a start. We haven't had rain in months. Cruz nickers at the burros to wake them up, tying the flour sacks onto the saddles. We head down the hill in silence, lulled by the rhythmic swaying of the sleepy-eyed burros as they navigate the inclines imprinted on their hooves. We get near the iron fencing around the cemetery and my flashlight finds the first monument, a tiny one sticking two feet up with a lamb on top of it. Below, it reads OUR BABY IS RESTING.

"I joined," Rabbit says.

"Joined what?" Cruz reins in his burro.

"The army."

"You can't join the army." Cruz laughs. "You're too small."

"I already did. I got a number."

"You got a number." Cruz waves his flashlight across a row of monuments. "Congratulations, Rabbit. Pick out your plot, 'cause this is where you'll be. Six feet under with a pile of shit on top of you. What should we put on your stone, Rabbit? THE IDIOT IS RESTING?"

"Not everybody who goes to war gets killed," Rabbit says.

"You really want to take that chance?" I've caught Rabbit by surprise, and he cranes his neck to get a look at me.

"Somebody has to fight the commies in Korea," Rabbit says. "It's the right thing to do."

"Says who?" Cruz lets his beam linger on the monuments. "How come you've gone changing all of a sudden, Rabbit? You're acting like a stranger."

"Nothing's how it was anymore," Rabbit says. "In case you haven't noticed. And maybe you never knew me in the first place."

"I know what won't suit you," Cruz says. "Like shooting things. You think having a gun in your hands makes you some kind of hero?"

"You think catching a football makes you one?"

"It's not my fault you're too small to play," Cruz says.

"Is that what you think? That I'm sore about not playing?

I don't care about football, and I don't hate everyone who's not from Hatley, Cruz."

"Stop it!" I say. "Listen to the two of you fighting like you were enemies."

"I just want to matter," Rabbit says. "To count."

The ground has flattened out, giving up most of its incline, and my burro dips his neck to graze. Cruz gets off Kissy and unleashes a flour sack.

"Gotta get rid of these brushes and cans," he says, walking over to Rabbit.

"I'm going into the service, Cruz. You can't stop me. I'm gonna be a private. Private Salvatore Palermo."

Cruz drapes the sacks over his shoulders and slaps Kissy on the rump. The burro bucks out a little, then wanders off. "Just get to the bakery, Rabbit," Cruz says, but he won't look up. "And make like you've been baking while I'm gone. And you both better get that paint out of your fingernails and wherever else it's on."

"Where you going?" Rabbit calls after Cruz. He takes off his straw hat. Even in the dark you can tell Rabbit's hair's been shaved down to the nub.

"I'm gonna drive down to Cottonville and leave these in their schoolyard," Cruz says. "Who else would want Hatley to go to hell?"

Chapter 9
STRAIGHT TO HELL

SUNDAY, SEPTEMBER 3

8:39 A.M.

THE SUN ROSE PALE AND quick above Nefertitty Hill, un-
sullied by sulfur smoke—they're not allowed to blast on
Sundays with Ruffner being a Roman Catholic. Now the
sun's hanging right above *HeLL*—there's no mistaking that
word—and both are bearing down on me as I walk to church
thinking, *How could anyone know it was me who painted that
word?*

The church is nearly empty and the oak's waxy and cool
when I slide into our pew. It's third from the back on the
right-hand side, across from where Jesus is being stripped
of his garments in station number ten. The *ofrendas* left
over from Mexican Mass flicker in cherry-colored glass by
the front window—the one that Ruffner took the stained
glass out of so he'd have a clear view of the pit while he's
praying.

I know that's what I should be doing. That I ought to
be halfway through my first Hail Mary instead of thinking

about what people might be saying when they look up and catch sight of the hill.

I open the kneeler and it groans, coming to rest on the floor with a thump that reaches up to the sanctuary, where Jesus and the archangels are still in shadow, and I'm grateful that I don't have to face them yet. Or the letters forming that word. My back's to the hill, so it shouldn't matter, but the fact is I'm caught between the Savior and the worst possible outcome, spelled out behind me in whitewash. And I don't like being cornered. I'm better off when I can run. But our field's thirty yards from here, outside that first window.

Somebody coughs a little baby cough up front, then a veiled head rises to meet the *ofrendas* and I see that it's Rabbit's mom. She gathers the lace ends of the scarf to her throat and hunches over, lighting the highest candle. Maybe for her brother; he died a year ago, I think.

"Hey, Ugly," Cruz says, then takes hold of my shoulder since I just about jump out of my skin. "Relax," he says, stroking his hair. It's still wet from Bryl.

"What are you doing here?" I whisper. "Weren't you at the Mexican Mass?"

"I slept in. Shove over."

"You can't sit here."

"How come? You got room." He punches me in the knee until I move. "Besides, you should be flattered. I usually take old man Ruffner's pew for our Mass if it's empty."

"You shouldn't be here."

"What are they gonna do, throw me out? It's a church," Cruz says. "And I'm sitting next to our quarterback. Hey, there's Mrs. Palermo. Hi, Mrs. P," he calls, waving to her sitting next to the Buffo family. "How'd the Palermos get the third row? Just because they donate their stale bread for Communion?"

"What'd you do?" I ask him. "Drink before you got here?"

"Huh?"

"'Cause you sure smell like it."

"That's not booze, stupid. It's cologne."

The church is filling up fast. Mrs. Murdock waddles into the pew behind us with her kid, Reuben, poking her elbows into my shoulders every time she looks around for someone to gossip with.

Reuben gets excited when he sees us and taps our shoulders, saying, "Go, Muckers!"

Beebe Vance walks by. I guess you'd call it more like gliding, the way the ice skaters do and those girls on the floats at the rodeo with the pageant crowns on their heads.

Cruz sticks his elbow into the aisle. It nicks Beebe's handbag, so she stops and looks at Cruz like she's seeing a ghost. Mrs. Vance shoos her away and Beebe blushes brighter than that pink lipstick of hers, taking the piece of mesh stuck to her hat and pulling it over her eyes with a little white glove.

Cruz rests his chin against that elbow and eyes Beebe all the way to her pew ten rows up by the Walshes. I don't think I've seen Cruz this happy since he won the Ford Deluxe in that pool match that lasted three days. And I know I'd be doing the same thing if that'd been Angie and I was in Mexican Mass.

Mrs. Featherhoff starts playing up in the balcony. I turn and see her face in the mirror above the pipe organ—a funhouse-type mirror that makes her cheeks go all squatty like a cabbage. It takes a few violent pumps before the air sputters out and I recognize the deep, brooding hymn "Save

Our Souls." Then Father Pierre walks up the aisle in layers of purple, wearing a biretta puffed up and crowned with a pom-pom bigger than the buttons on a clown suit. Leon Brewer's tagging alongside him, with the Father using the top of Leon's head as a cane.

Father's gaze is too quick and he catches my eye, then he smiles, probably thinking I'm here because of him, which I'm not. Leon hobbles along the red carpet to keep up. He opens the gate to the sanctuary, where he and Father Pierre will stay, barricaded from us, until Mass is over. Father raises his hands to the ceiling, making the ends of his chasuble tremble. And we all make the sign of the cross before saying "Amen."

"Who do you think did it?" Mrs. Murdock whispers to Mrs. Dearing. "I just can't imagine who would've done a thing like that."

"Idle hands, that's who," Mrs. Dearing says. "There's not enough shifts to go around at the mine anymore."

Cruz pokes out his chin to claim more room, as if he belongs at English Mass and just might come again if he feels like it. Me? I'm sweating. My good shirt's stuck to my chest and I'm sitting too long when I should be standing or kneeling, swatting the back of my neck so Mrs. Murdock won't bore a hole into it like those carpenter bees do on our porch.

"Whoever did it, that's straight where they're going," Mrs. Murdock says. "H-E-L-L. What's the town coming to?"

"Mommy, why's hell so high up?" Reuben says. "Ain't it down there, below China?" he asks, stomping his feet on the floor.

I focus on the statue of Jesus perched in his niche across from the altar, arms outstretched, with his heart ten times the size of any of ours. He looks sad, maybe even a little disappointed at what's happened to this town and how my part in it's only adding to the pain.

"There's the idiot," Cruz whispers, looking over to the third row where Rabbit is. "Bet he won't look back."

"He doesn't even know you're here."

"Aren't you the cheerleader?" Cruz sniffs, adjusting the knot in his tie.

I ignore the jab and look at Rabbit's big ears. We've got a clear view of them since the Heydorn kids are down by the kneelers in the pew behind Rabbit, unlacing people's shoes.

Rabbit's staring at the altar. It has a lamb painted on it, shorn pink and waiting to be slaughtered. The lamb looks calm, considering, with its eyes half shut and its legs folded like it's about to go to sleep. They painted golden shafts of light around it and sat it on a fleshy pink carpet, as if that's supposed to make a difference.

Rabbit's even skinnier with that army buzz cut. He looks like he did when he was twelve. *Helpless.* Just like that lamb. He dozes off and sways to the left, his head landing on Mrs. Palermo's shoulder. She smiles and lets him stay.

Maybe she didn't light that candle for her brother. Maybe Mrs. Palermo lit it for Rabbit. I've read that those things are supposed to work either way: as a prayer for the dead or a wish for the living.

Father Pierre walks past the lamb to deliver his sermon. He leans into the railing as if he's about to tumble over it, but then clenches his hand into a fist and punches it into the wood.

"The idiot's up now," Cruz says, nodding at Rabbit.

"Stop calling him that."

Cruz gives me a dirty look. "Whose side are you on, anyway?" he says.

"Nobody's."

Father Pierre keeps scanning the congregation. "Only *He* knows who desecrated our hill," he begins. "And when a sinner mocks the work of God, even the Lord gets angry." He's facing our direction now, glaring at me. *He knows.* I'm sure of it. My foot kicks the top of the kneeler, folding it back up and making a crashing sound like pieces of wood splitting in two.

"It's those teenagers," Mrs. Murdock whispers. "They don't know the meaning of hard work."

"They just want liquor," Mrs. Dearing says. "Did you see the *Verde Miner*? It's called alcoholism. I'm marking prohibition on my November ballot."

"Look!" Reuben calls out. I turn around. He's pointing at me and Cruz. The itch starts coming out of the wool in my suit collar, but there's no way I'd move a finger.

"They know it's us," I whisper to Cruz.

"The kid's pointing at the window. Stop being so jumpy," he says.

A wasp's flying around in the blue part where the window comes to a point, next to Jesus falling for the third time in station number nine.

Father's going on about the unraveling of family values. How if you're not a family, that somehow it makes you do bad things. But I can't see his angry eyes anymore because of Mr. Weetman's onion-shaped head.

The chandelier above us flickers and the rain begins. First a few fat taps like a BB gun firing, then stronger, gushing heavy against the glass.

And what does Father Pierre know about family anyway? Even if you have one, that doesn't mean your world won't get torn apart. Mary and Joseph are a perfect example of that, standing in the altarpiece in their flowing robes. They're acting all happy, gazing down at Jesus. And I wonder if Mary knew her son was going to die and how she took it after. They don't tell you that in the Bible. She's smiling down on him as if she couldn't know.

A drip falls onto Cruz's shoulder as the rain finds its way through the roof, and the ushers get out the buckets.

"Hey!" Reuben shouts. He's been at the window taunting the wasp. "Hell's gone."

Mrs. Murdock rushes over and takes Reuben's hand. "Would you look at that," she says, peering outside. "The rain washed those letters away. All that's left is the H."

"Told you the paint was old," Cruz whispers.

All eyes focus on Father Pierre.

"It appears we have the Lord to thank for cleansing our hill," he proclaims.

Some of the men laugh.

"Yet—the sinner is marked." Father's eyes dance around the church like little rubber balls. "You know who you are."

That gets the whole congregation muttering.

"What gall," Mrs. Murdock says, putting up her umbrella. "To be here at Mass after doing a thing like that."

I close my eyes and try to think of something cool, like icicles or polar bears, since I'm not getting dripped on and my body's burning up.

The ushers start coming around with the offertory baskets, and I tell Cruz I'm not going to take Communion.

"Are you crazy?" he says. "You gotta go. If you don't they'll know for sure."

The basket reaches across our row and Cruz fumbles with his pockets, jingling some coins until the usher's about to leave. Then he grabs the rim of the basket and puts in a five-dollar bill. "For the candles," he says, dropping the money into the basket like a slow molasses pour.

"Where'd he get that kind of money?" Mrs. Murdock whispers.

"Probably stole it," Mrs. Dearing says. "Don't they live in a shack?"

"Are all the Anglos this distracted during Mass?" Cruz whispers, loud enough for them to hear. "*Our* women recite the rosary the whole time. I think they must know God better."

"Well, I never," Mrs. Murdock sniffs.

"Knock it off," I tell him, "or you're gonna get kicked out."

"Not before you do. You're doing everything wrong."

"So you're going?" I ask. "To Holy Communion?"

"Why shouldn't I?"

The wooden kneelers for Communion are lined up on either side of the sanctuary against white spindle railings three feet high. Me and Cruz take the two places near the window, where Jesus is being condemned to death in the first station of the cross.

We wait for the Father, who's on the other end spooning out morsels of soggy bread into a chorus of open mouths. Then a hint of liniment hits my nose, and the golden threads running stiff through his vestments brush against my hand as Leon lifts the white towel toward my chin like a bib.

"Corpus Christi," Father says, gazing over the top of my head. He doesn't want anything to do with me either.

Father spoons the mixture into my mouth and I swallow. Then I realize he's given me an empty spoon. It catches me by surprise and I should have gotten up already, made the sign of the cross, and moved on. But the Father's not budging either, and he should be at Cruz by now, only he isn't.

There's a break in the singing. I guess they must've run out of verses. Father turns to Leon and says, "Get me the longer spoon."

Even Mrs. Featherhoff in the balcony must have heard it.

Cruz is staring at the statue of Guadalupe, his lips tracing the words of a prayer I can't understand. My knees are numb, but I won't leave him. I gaze up at Mary and Joseph and Jesus all together and think how Cruz is just about as close to being family as I've got right now.

Leon comes back with the spoon, but Father Pierre starts in on another row. And what he's doing to Cruz, it would've been better if he'd punched him instead of this: kneeling here in front of the town waiting for scraps like a mangy dog.

Father finally takes the spoon. It's a long silver one— the kind Benny mixes chocolate malts with. Father Pierre grips the end, leaving a good four inches between him and Cruz. His eyes narrow, and it's clear to me now who the enemy is. He's hiding under saintly robes and feeling mighty powerful.

"Corpus Christi," Father murmurs.

Cruz grabs the chalice instead and takes a good long drink from the wine.

There's gasping and Leon drops the towel, making the bell under his cassock fall and let out an unexpected *ping*. But I'll never forget the look on the Father, his face turning the color of that pom-pom: a mixture of pink and red, like a maraschino cherry.

Cruz hands the chalice back and gets up from the kneeler. I make the sign of the cross and follow him, just like those hundred other sets of eyes. All you can hear is the *drip drip* of the rain against the metal sides of those buckets. I expect

Cruz to curve back into our pew and kneel to pray, but he keeps walking down the aisle and out the front door.

I stay in church a long time after, thinking about Cruz. I run my hand across the gold lettering on the nameplate nailed to the end of our pew: *In loving memory of Robert A. O'Sullivan. Beloved son, cherished brother. Laid to rest 1945.* All of that's true. Except the last part. I can't imagine him resting after what he went through.

"I prayed for snow," Father Pierre calls out to me from the back of the church, "but He gave me rain." Father takes a few steps, then thumps his cane on the carpet until he reaches my row. "I can take your confession now, Felix." He points to the curtain lining the confessional in the vestibule.

"I've got nothing to be sorry for."

Father squints to get a better look at me. "Is that the attitude you learn on the football field? You think you're better than the rest of us, don't you? You and your little brown friends. I saw you jump on the train with that Mexican girl."

"Why do you hate football so much?"

"The town draws its strength from this church, not a football field."

My throat tightens. "You're wrong," I tell him. "We'll win."

Father looks at Bobby's nameplate and taps it with his cane. "This will be removed by the end of October unless it is paid in full."

"How's that?"

"It's a privilege to have your own pew, Felix. Even God needs assurance of our daily love. It's fifty dollars for the year, and I'm afraid I've already given your father three months' grace."

"You'll get your money," I tell him, and head for the door.

I'll find a way, somehow. I catch sight of myself in the organist's mirror before leaving. My eyes look twisted and my face so contorted that I barely recognize who I am. I might know who the enemy is, but I don't like the sight of me either. It's the look of being afraid.

Chapter 10
WHERE THE HELL'S KOREA?

THERE'S NO SCHOOL BECAUSE OF Labor Day and no work for my pop either. He's sitting in the kitchen staring at the Frigidaire, and I don't remember him looking this sad in a while. He's getting ready for another funeral. That's why he's clean-shaven. The mine took another one of his men, and his fingers are no good with a tie.

"I'll do it," I tell him, reaching for the red knot he's trying to make. "I can do a Windsor knot, you know."

"Not bloody well," he says. "And don't be siding with the Queen."

But I try again anyway.

"Not too tight," he tells me as I draw the knot close to his neck and fold down the collar.

"Poor bastard didn't deserve it," Pop murmurs. "He never said a harsh word. At least there's no family left behind to be missing him."

He brushes my hand aside, but I'm almost finished with the knot. I catch him looking up at me the way he

116

does when he's gone too far—like I must be thinking that he's the one who deserved it. Then he sighs in the same way he did at Bobby's funeral, looking broken—like an old toy you keep trying to fix but knowing it won't ever work the same.

"Rabbit's going to Korea," I tell him.

Pop takes his jacket off the step stool and walks toward the door. Then he pauses. "Poor bastard doesn't deserve that either," he says before leaving.

I head up to Main Street to meet Cruz and Rabbit, who's sitting on his duffel bag.

"Where the hell's Korea?" Cruz asks.

"In the Sea of Japan," Rabbit says. He rubs his shiny scalp, which is the color of chalk except where the shaved hairs are starting to poke through.

The Greyhound bus is already here, idling on the slope and caught in shadow across the street in front of the cigar store.

"It's a peninsula," I tell Cruz.

"Oh, that explains it," he says, scowling at me. "We're fighting a peninsula. Sounds like another new screwball disease, no?"

"I might not even get to Korea." There's a tinge of disappointment in Rabbit's voice. "I could end up in Japan. That's where Pete Torres's brother's been stationed. Going over drills and building foxholes at the base in Sendai."

Rabbit stuffs a sack of Mrs. Palermo's food into his duffel. Cruz says she was bawling something awful in front of the ovens and too shook up to come.

"At least you won't be fighting the Reds," Cruz says. "Get anywhere near an A-bomb and you'll be screaming bloody murder."

"You can live through one," Rabbit says, tugging the

drawstring secure before eyeballing Cruz. "Don't you ever read the paper? They write about it all the time."

"I don't need no paper telling me to be a few countries back when that atom bomb hits. And all the *Verde Miner* writes about is those stupid pineapple parties up on Gringo Ridge."

"Pinochle, not pineapple," I tell him. "And the Russians are the ones behind Korea."

"Pee-knuckle." Cruz repeats it like he's some bratty kid. "Bet they play that on the peninsula, too. Huh, Ugly?"

"Half Korea's communist, Cruz," Rabbit says.

"Think I don't know that? And you ain't been further than Kingman, so don't be showing off." Cruz takes a kick at the duffel bag before Rabbit hauls it over his shoulder. "If you don't come back, I don't wanna hear about it, idiot. No griping."

Rabbit waves a hand in the air and keeps walking.

"You know we play Cottonville in three weeks," Cruz hollers, throwing a silver lighter at the duffel bag.

"What's this for?" Rabbit bends down for it and gets whacked in the head by the bag.

"For when you smoke," Cruz says. Then he starts laughing. "But don't be trying it when you're carrying something. *Like a gun.*"

"I don't smoke." Rabbit tightens his fist around the lighter and whips it at Cruz, but the lighter caroms off the sidewalk and dribbles toward us, settling next to my foot.

"You will." Cruz grins. "Keep it." He tosses the lighter back, gently this time, so Rabbit can make a one-handed catch. "It was my grandfather's," Cruz says.

Rabbit takes it and heads up Main, waiting for a cranky old Studebaker to pass. We keep watching him from the other side and it's strange, him walking away from us. Then Rabbit hops on the bus like he's headed for Smelter City to visit a cousin or something—no different—and we lose sight of him.

Things get quiet—there's not even a wind—and the sun is leaving an amber trail of ninety-degree heat, like yesterday's rain never happened. A bead of sweat from Cruz's brow drips onto his nose. He lets it slide all the way down his chin.

"What are you looking at?" he growls, but the air's already gone flat between us. Cruz reaches for something else to say, but now there's only me.

"He'll be home by Christmas," he finally grumbles.

They said that about Bobby, too.

"Think he'd miss a free meal at the Square on Christmas Eve?" Cruz jabs me in the ribs with his pack of Luckies. "Maybe he'll be home sooner. He's only got enough smoked-meat sandwiches to get him through the first hour. By the time they get to Prescott, his stomach'll be rumbling."

The first time I ever saw Rabbit was at Christmas, lined up to see Santa. I think he must have been six. I already knew Santa didn't exist. I'd found out the year before, when they'd asked Pop to play him at the Square. Only he couldn't go through with it. He'd managed to get the beard on and the shiny, fat belt before passing out on the chesterfield, stone drunk. The furry red-and-white costume was lying on the dining room table still wrapped in cellophane. So Santa was a no-show at the Square and we had to go to Cottonville instead.

Maw took me to the Square the following year, maybe thinking I hadn't remembered. And I still wanted to believe, to be like Rabbit. But you can't undo a thing like that.

That year Rabbit wouldn't get on Santa's knee unless he got the candy cane first. Cruz was in line right behind him and wondering why Mr. Mackenzie had taken Santa's place. He walked right up, pulled down that flimsy white beard, and said, "Hey, Mr. Mac."

Rabbit screamed and Cruz knocked him over. "What's the matter?" Cruz said. "You think the *real* Santa's got time to be here when he's busy making a million toys?" So Rabbit stopped crying, took the candy cane from Mr. Mackenzie, and told him what he wanted for Christmas. But I couldn't believe Cruz. I knew that if Santa was real, he would have never asked Pop to stand in for him.

All the passengers are on the bus now, and Rabbit's grabbed a window seat on our side, about halfway down. He leans into the glass and I'm waiting for him to glance back at us, but he doesn't. And he's got to know we're still here. No one else is around.

I guess it's no big deal going off to Korea. The only other person I know who's there is Buddy Ritz, and he's been in the service since 1938. Not like when Bobby left for the Second World War; that felt like a party. There were nearly two dozen boys who'd signed up, calling it "the pursuit of happiness" or "fighting for the noble cause." And I swear the whole town filled up Main Street, swarming the bus and yelling, "Kill a Jap for me!" They even had a police escort, with Faye Miller leading it, stringing a necklace of candy hearts around Bobby's neck before he walked onto that bus so he wouldn't forget they were engaged. Was *he* red.

"I don't even know which way their eyes go over there,"

Cruz says. "Do they slant up or down?" Cruz is acting like an idiot, the way he always does when things get bent out of shape.

"They must be waiting for the driver," Cruz figures, spreading his legs out and leaning against the fire hydrant. "Can't you see him sucking back coffee at the lunch counter?"

I think I do, so I nod, but I can tell Cruz is itching to argue. He grips the head of the fire hydrant and his legs start fidgeting. It's going to be tough on him not having Rabbit here to argue with. I'm more of a listener.

"It's not even a war," Cruz says. "They'll push those commies back to their line. What is it? Thirty-eight yards? That's all they need to do. How long can that take? Nobody beats MacArthur."

"If it's not a war, then why's MacArthur even there?"

Cruz just about falls off his perch when I say it. But MacArthur's the one who got Bobby killed, sending him over to the Pacific when he was due to come home. Now the general's taking ninety-eight-pound teenagers with him to Korea, who've flunked P.E.

The driver hops on and the bus pulls out. That's when Rabbit turns around and looks at us. He's got the biggest grin on his face and I've never seen him smile that way before. Like he's got something over Cruz and me. It gets even bigger as the bus heaves, coughing a black wad of smoke at us before rounding the switchback to Prescott.

"Hey, next time we see him, he'll be in a green uniform. Can you beat it?" Cruz says.

"Maybe even a Purple Heart," I joke.

"Or a yellow one." Cruz smirks. "He's still afraid of the dark."

It's true. At Scout camp the first time, Rabbit slept in

his bunk with a flashlight aimed at the ceiling the whole night, until Mr. and Mrs. Palermo came to get him the next morning. It's the only time he's ever been away from home overnight. And none of us has ever been outside of Arizona. The closest me and Cruz have come was the White Mountains, when we gave St. John's a good going-over on their football field last year, a few miles before New Mexico.

Rabbit will be halfway around the world, six thousand miles from here.

"That'll get him laid," Cruz laughs, looking at the sky like he can imagine it. "A Purple Heart's gotta be at least as big as an Eagle Scout medal."

By the time it's Christmas, we'll have taken the Yavapai Cup. That's what I'll focus on. *Rabbit getting back. Us winning the Cup.* I don't want to think about either of those things not happening. Rabbit could get lucky and so could we. Not everyone who goes to war gets killed. Only he doesn't have Cruz beside him anymore, and I don't know how much good a gun'll do.

"He'll miss the game of the year," Cruz says, tapping the butt of his cigarette pack to coax out a smoke. "Maybe the century. You'll have to write him about it."

So that's how it's going to be. Me still in between Rabbit and Cruz, interpreting them for each other long-distance.

"I'm gonna beat the living crap out of those Wolves," Cruz mumbles, the cigarette hanging from his mouth. "Shit!" he yells, fumbling around in his pockets. "I gave my lighter away, didn't I?"

THE VERDE MINER

Twice-Weekly Voice of the Mountain

HATLEY, ARIZONA   WEDNESDAY, SEPTEMBER 6, 1950   FIVE CENTS A COPY

MID-WEEK EDITION

Last Rites for Hatley Miner

Funeral services were held graveside for Milosh Maxim Diklovich, age 48. Mr. Diklovich, a long-time boarder of Mrs. Lillian Slubetz, and shaftman for Eureka Copper, died Sunday at the miners' hospital. After his shift boss, Alastar O'Sullivan, drove him to Phoenix last month, Mr. Diklovich underwent a lung operation and was thought to have been improving. Born in the village of Jošan in Lika, Croatia, he was known around town for his accordion playing. There are no known survivors. Mrs. Slubetz played Mr. Diklovich's accordion during the interment.

WANT ADS

IMMUNIZE AGAINST WHOOPING COUGH—Dr. A. C. Brown says all young children should be immunized since the Purdyman baby took ill. The disease has taken the lives of three Indian children working at the Navajo cotton pickers' camp at Black Mountain Indian Reservation.

Chapter 11
BENCHED

FRIDAY, SEPTEMBER 8
6:07 P.M.

PRACTICE FINALLY ENDED TEN MINUTES ago, but my face still feels like it's flaming hot. Not because I did much, but because I'm flat-out mad. And now Coach Hansen's asked me to stay. What's he want with me anyhow? I wasn't even late. And he's the last person I feel like talking to since he's the one I'm P.O.'d at. He didn't even know I existed the past two hours, giving Quesada all the quarterback time, with me relegated near the pit and punting most of practice, looking like a jackass instead of first-string.

Cruz kept coming over and asking if me and Coach were just fooling, like maybe this was a practice before practice, and aren't I the quarterback? I sure thought I was. Kicked the ball clear through the posts and into the pit, I got so heated. There's already two W's in our column, and there's no way I'm going back to being second-string.

"You know you're slipping," Coach says to me.

"How's that?"

124

"Usually you beat me to the field. Now it's the second time you're only slightly early." He takes the football from under his arm and tosses it, catching me off guard. It clips my elbow but I snatch it, and he smiles.

"You've always liked the heat, haven't you?" he says, taking out a handkerchief to wipe his brow.

"It's what we got," I tell him. "I don't mind it most days. *Especially when I'm playing.*"

Coach shakes his head and I'm not sure what he's disagreeing with: what I just said or the heat.

"Me, I'm from Missouri. I can't wait for the sun to go down and cool things off." He looks up to face it and closes his eyes for a second. "Not this year. I want it to take her time because we might never see it again, at least not this way, when we have a season and the chance to take it all."

Coach rubs his forehead, then adjusts his cap. He wears it all the time now, even when the sun's dipped below the mountain. And I'm pissed that I'm not so pissed at him anymore, watching him rub on that scar.

"Look, I know I caught you by surprise today, but I wanted to shake things up," he says. "Get your mind back on football. *And winning.*"

"No one wants to win more than me."

"But you're afraid to. And it's slowing you down."

"Who's afraid?" I throw the ball hard, past Coach's shoulder. I think it might have nicked his ear but he won't duck. He just stumbles a bit, letting the ball wobble around in the slag.

"You know, they tell me I shouldn't do this anymore. That another blow to the head and it could be my last." Coach taps the side of his forehead. "Something about not having enough skin between that steel plate and me."

"Sorry . . . I didn't know."

"I didn't expect you to." Coach picks up the ball and tosses it to me. "Now throw it back," he commands. "*Harder.* Come on. Don't hesitate," he says, squinting at me. "That's right. Good. Now aim for the shoulder again."

I wing it even harder this time and Coach catches it about an inch above his shoulder, the force making him lose his cap.

"See? You were afraid to hurt me but you threw it hard anyhow." He raises the football in the air. "You didn't hold back. If you were scared, you would have."

Coach motions for me to come over, and we start walking toward the school bus parked under the goalpost.

"I remember when I got this scar," he says. "The moment it happened. June twenty-sixth, 1944, thirteen hundred hours. The date's etched in my brain and not even a tank of gasoline could blow it out of me." He pauses for a moment, and I try not to stare at that scar. "People were talking all around me right after the explosion, but it felt like I wasn't really there. Just watching it all."

"You snapped out of it, though," I say. "You survived."

"Things felt different in the hospital." He nods. "When they told me I couldn't work out with the kids, to stop coaching, all of a sudden I came to. It's like I shook loose. And I knew I couldn't be cautious. How do you hold back on living? Not doing things because you remember the pain from what happened before."

Coach looks up at the goalpost, and I finally take a look at that scar. It's fleshy and red, like somebody ran the fruit of a prickly pear across it, staining the whole thing raspberry. It cuts a deep gully along the side of the temple, dividing his forehead the way the Gulch does to our town.

He must have lost a lot inside, the scar's so deep. And I wonder if some of the pain's still there but he fights it. Like at the game, when the lights were burning down on us. It must have set that scar ablazing. Only maybe when that happens Coach taunts it—the way he does with us at practice—until the pain finally goes away.

"Climb up," he says.

"What?"

"Go 'head. Climb up on the hood like this," Coach says, catching the rim of the tire with his sneaker, then pulling himself up on the bus. "You haven't forgotten how to climb, have you?"

"Course not."

"Then follow me and you'll get the second-best view in the Valley." Coach grips the side of the goalpost and I don't know if I should stop him or let him keep going. Then he's up there sitting on the crossbar. "There's enough room for you, too," he says, sliding over.

The last time I was up there was on Cruz's shoulders—we couldn't have been more than thirteen. He was standing on Kissy, which was stupid. Cruz had made some stirrups out of binder twine, but it got botched up when the burro walked away and we just hung there. Me clinging to the crossbar, and Cruz holding on to my ankles until our hands slipped away and we fell, rolling onto the slag, laughing but feeling like idiots and hoping nobody saw.

"The best view is up there on the hill," Coach says when I reach him. "Where the H is."

"I like this better."

"It's not bad, is it?" He points to the mountain range across from the H. The one we wake up to every morning, a hundred miles away.

"Flagstaff doesn't seem so far away from up here," Coach says.

The Peaks are tinged with pink and orange and blue like

girls' dresses. And even then, it's still too pretty to be real. Mr. Mackenzie says that if you don't have the money to get to the Grand Canyon not to bother, we've got the same view right here.

"Somehow, it seems almost attainable," Coach says. "Like you can reach out and snatch those peaks." He lets out a sigh. "If only it were that easy."

"We've got five weeks to get tough," I tell him.

"That was the first game I ever coached," he says. "The lowly Muckers against the mighty Flagstaff Warriors, the most decorated team in the North. Bobby was the quarterback and folks thought the T formation I brought in was just about as bad as sin itself. But Bobby, he just took to it, without question. You knew he was fast, even as a freshman. But now he could really show them." Coach looks sideways at me. "You can be even better, Red."

"That's not true."

Coach keeps looking at me and I don't want him to. I want to keep thinking about Bobby without having to think about me.

"You've got a feel for this field like no player I've coached. You'd think you're made of slag and mud, knowing where the good patches are and how that can change. But for the first time you looked scared out there."

"We won both games," I say. "Isn't that what matters?" But I focus on the skyline instead, where puffer clouds have stalled halfway down the peaks, making them all blotchy.

"You're afraid right now. And that's a whole lot different than being nervous," Coach says. "It's okay to be nervous. But being afraid only leads to regret. You're second-guessing, which spoils the gut instincts you have and everything you've learned. You never make the right moves then. I know you'll get over it, Red, but I'm taking you out of the quarterback spot against Coldbrook, until you settle down."

I can't believe what Coach is saying.

"You'll still play defense, of course," he says. "Your drawbacks are those wobbly legs and your fear."

"You're making a mistake."

"Am I?"

I don't answer and slide over to reach for the post. Then I hop onto the hood of the bus, thinking, *I'm up two-nothing, Coach has to be wrong.* But I'm not entirely certain that he is.

"If you need to be living somewhere else, just let me know," he says. "I can't have my quarterback going hungry."

"I already have a home." I spill out the words, not bothering to turn around and look at him or anything. "And I don't need help."

"Then find the kitchen," Coach says firmly. "And get yourself something to eat."

My ears feel singed, like I'm way too close to a campfire. I start jogging, but the air's moist and stale and there's no wind to move it.

The door of the school bus slams shut and I know he'll overtake me in a second. "Then come back and throw that football like you own it," Coach hollers. He maneuvers the bus past me, and I can't see the Peaks anymore. Just two red taillights blinking back at me.

Chapter 12
ANGRY EVER SINCE

I'M ON MY OWN BEHIND the school, throwing the football through a tire hung from the old cottonwood by the baseball diamond. It's first thing in the morning and I'm waiting for Mr. Mackenzie to walk by. Rabbit's been gone for a week and that's hard to believe, though I'm reminded of it every time I look at his empty desk.

The benching hasn't sunk in yet either, even though it's been three days since Coach told me I wouldn't be playing quarterback against Coldbrook.

I keep throwing until I hear Mr. Mackenzie saying good morning to someone before rounding the corner. I exhale and start breathing normal again. Mr. Mackenzie will look at me like it doesn't matter how I play, or if I play at all. He'll look at me like I matter just because I'm Red.

"Getting a little practice in early, are we, Felix?" he says, leaning his leather satchel against some ivy and resting his cane on top of it.

"This is the only practice I'll get when it comes to throwing today, Mr. Mac. I'm benched."

He goes over to the tire and stretches it out to a forty-five-degree angle and stands clear so I can volley the football through it.

"Nothing wrong with some good old-fashioned solitaire to build acuity and acumen," he says. "It'll serve you well on the gridiron."

"It'll be almost two weeks till I get to play quarterback. If I do at all."

"Everyone gets benched at least once in his football career," Mr. Mackenzie says, tossing the football back to me. "Thank goodness it isn't a life sentence. And there are as many different reasons for being told to sit out a game as there are teams in this state." He smiles. "Remember when Bobby got benched?"

I didn't know Bobby got benched. "When was that?" I ask him.

"October of 1941—you must have been eight years old then. We'd had a freak October snowstorm, remember?"

I cradle the football under my chin and nod.

"Bobby went sledding down Nefertiti Hill with Faye Miller. He thought it would please the kids at the matinee, seeing him start his shift at the theater arriving by sled like Santa Claus. Faye wanted to come along and be the elf. But the mountain had other ideas and sent those two kids and the sled veering left, down into the slag field. The bleachers prevented them from ending up in Cottonville and they escaped with only a few minor bumps and bruises, but the sled took out the first row. That's why Coach Hansen benched your brother."

"So Bobby got benched for ramming into a bench?" I

can't help but smile, and start tossing the football up in the air a few times, just for fun.

"That's about the size of it." Mr. Mackenzie laughs. "And they still made it all the way to the state. Now, my benching was different."

I stop throwing because I find it hard to believe Mr. Mac could do anything that would get him benched.

"It happened two games before the state championship." He nods, seeing how surprised I am. "We were playing Prescott and a referee made what I considered to be a poor call. He'd done it twice so I thought it best to tell him about it, but I was ejected from the game. Then Coach Kerr benched me."

"Even though the call was unfair and you were right?"

"It wasn't for me to decide or to let the referee know what I thought. I was very troubled about the whole thing after and spent the rest of the weekend holed up in my room." Mr. Mackenzie lowers the tire, gesturing for me to come over.

"I knew we had more than a good shot at making it to the state and I wanted to be there," he continues. "Then I realized I could, but that it was up to me. And that the only way to do it was by not worrying about calls and playing better than I ever had."

"And then the officials went and did it again when you got to Phoenix."

"Yes, they did," he says. "But the Coyotes were a great team—give them credit—and to be truthful, the game could have gone either way. It would have been better if it had been a draw, though it doesn't work that way in football, does it now, Felix?"

"I guess that wouldn't seem fair either," I figure.

"But we knew we played our best," Mr. Mac says. "The home-field advantage went their way that year. Pete Zolnich and the rest of us knew who really won. I'm not sure Peter ever got over what happened, though—he's been angry ever since—but I did."

I think about Pete and his sawed-off pipe. How he's sitting in the temporary jail at the Sacred Heart of Mary—likely stewing.

"I know you think you're not as good as you need to be, Felix, but you're wrong." Mr. Mac stops the tire from rocking and looks straight at me. "You've got a lot to carry on your shoulders to begin with. Don't add anything that shouldn't be there by judging yourself too harshly. There's already enough of that going on around here, don't you think?"

"You mean the commie box?"

"Is that what they're calling it? Good Lord. I suppose you'd know all about that box Luther Sims has been keeping, since he unveiled it in your class." Mr. Mac shakes his head. "If Luther senior were still here, he'd have a long talk with his son—I can tell you that," he says, reaching for his cane. But I get it for him and dust off his satchel, too.

"I'm putting a stop to all this nonsense," he says. "I have a meeting with Mr. Menary this week to plead that sanity prevail and that differing points of view or nationalities won't be lumped into the convenient label of communism." He takes his satchel and we start walking toward the school. "But the superintendent and I have always approached things differently. And we're all foreigners for that matter. Except the Indians. But if I say that too loudly, I just might be deemed a communist spy, so keep that close to your vest, all right?"

"You could never be a communist spy."

"And you could never disappoint Bobby."

I repeat in my head what Mr. Mackenzie just told me—
I could never disappoint Bobby. And I hope that it's true.

"He'd be the last person wanting you to be feeling this way," Mr. Mackenzie whispers.

We reach the front steps and he gets out the keys—it's too early for Charlie to have unlocked the school yet.

"Thanks," I tell Mr. Mac.

"For what?" he says, keeping the door open with his cane.

"For remembering. And letting me know."

"Which reminds me," he says.

"Oh no," I say, teasing, but wondering if I've opened the door for a lecture on homework.

"Remember how I said Phoenix had home-team advantage back in twenty-four? Well, this year the pendulum's moving our way. The championship game gets played on the field of the team that wins the Northern Crown. And even though I believe we won that day in Phoenix no matter what the scoreboard showed, what I forgot to mention is that I'm not entirely opposed to a little revenge when it's warranted. And getting even in our final year seems like the right time to do it, don't you think?"

I go back and throw awhile longer and it feels different this time—solid. I work up a sweat and then head to my locker for a towel. There's a note sticking out of the vent.

Dear Mr. Sad Eyes
    So what if you don't play quarterback on Friday? I know you'll still get a win for us. You'll wriggle your way through their line somehow just like that trout.
            Angie

* * *

We've gone from pushing to pulling since Coach saw those old snapshots of the fire boys hauling hoses attached to a carriage. Coach had a bulldozer dump boulders near the field and now we're pulling them with fire hoses, too. Across a line Coach drew in the slag. You'd think Tony would've been over the line first or Cushman, the big freshman, but I was right there with them, with Cruz behind me yelling, "Don't hurt that shoulder. You need it for Cottonville," and Quesada saying he didn't need to be quarterback against Coldbrook on Friday with the way I'm looking. But I know you can't take a thing like that back. Coach already made up his mind.

Still, I'm ready. Even if it takes hauling these rocks all the way up to the top of the mountain.

THE VERDE MINER

Twice-Weekly Voice of the Mountain

HATLEY, ARIZONA WEDNESDAY, SEPTEMBER 13, 1950 FIVE CENTS A COPY

MID-WEEK EDITION

Muckers Host Coldbrook with New QB

The unbeaten Hatley Muckers will take to the field Friday night with a new look on offense. Despite their 2–0 record, Coach Ben Hansen has decided to play Marty Quesada at quarterback this week, opting to give starter Red O'Sullivan a breather. Hansen said O'Sullivan will play a key role as defensive back, but "time away from the pressure of quarterback will do him some good."

Eureka Copper Miners Win Raise

In an unexpected turn of events for Eureka Copper miners, the company has agreed to the Brotherhood of Hatley-Cottonville Miners & Smelter Workers' demands for a wage increase. The increase of 40 cents a day will affect approximately 500 employees at the local mine and smelter and goes into effect in 30 days. While the office won't comment on whether or not this means the mine won't close, diamond drilling has commenced on the old Buttercup claim, though company geologists fear all veins have been pinched out.

WANT ADS

136

Chapter 13

BOWLING UNDER THE STARS

THE COPPER STAR IS BUSIER tonight than I've ever seen it because of the news about the raises. Zefferino Avilar's singing on top of the bar and who's gonna stop him? He owns the place. Zeffy's long apron is tucked below his vest and pretty near grazing the counter as he swoops down to raise a glass of tequila at me with his lanky frame, those brown eyes glinting like it was the old days again. *"¡Arriba los Muckers!"* he says when I go by looking for Cruz.

I spot him leaning over the pool table. Pretty near lying on it, actually, with a woman hooked around his neck who's not paying any attention to the shot Cruz is demonstrating.

I have to suck in my breath and walk sideways to get near him. Past a group of tool nippers still with bandannas covering their necks to keep out the dust. They're throwing marbles onto the roulette wheels, trying to get them to spin, but those games haven't been played since the Second World War.

Cruz sees me and drains the shot, and the woman lets go. She starts clapping; the gold cross hanging around her neck gets tangled up in all that cleavage when she plants a red kiss on Cruz's cheek.

"You wanna stay?" I ask him, knowing a night like this must be worth a dozen Saturdays. Cruz shakes his head. "Not with her husband around," he says, grabbing the money on the table and shoving it in his gym bag. "Besides, you need to throw."

"Not for this game," I remind him as we head out of the bar toward the field.

"Yeah, I know. But the way you're playing in practice, you'll be back throwing against Cottonville," he says, handing me a carbide lamp.

"What's this for?"

"So you won't have any excuses in the dark," he says. Cruz is so full of himself he's about ready to pop. "Told you they needed us," he keeps saying. "There's no way they'll close the mine."

"It's only a raise, remember?"

"Same difference. You think Ruffner would give us more money if they were shutting things down? How stupid would that be?"

It's just like Cruz, believing. Once he's got his mind bent around something like winning, or the mine going on forever, he'll keep riding you about it until you finally believe it, too. But if I throw one more time I'll end up in a sling, so after ten minutes of handoffs I tell Cruz to give it a rest.

I can barely see him anyway without the moon up; it's just the light from the carbide lamps and the heaps of ore burning on the ledges in the open pit behind us, flaring red like cherry Coke. His dad and my pop are somewhere beneath

138

it, wearing carbide lamps, too, one telling the other to shovel more steaming chunks of ore into the pyre.

We pass Husband's Alley, where the higher-ups in the mine—men more important than Pop—sneak out of the bordellos known as the Cribs. This early, though, it's just the Heydorn boys running up and down the alley, throwing oranges at Leroy Piggett, who's lying in the middle of Main Street stone drunk with the sheriff just watching, not wanting to arrest anybody when the town's feeling this happy.

"Look out for the piano," the oldest Heydorn kid says, pointing at the sky.

"Would you look at that?" I say. Mrs. Featherhoff's piano is coming out of the second-floor window, wrapped in a sling and with so many straps around it you can hardly see its black body except for the legs. Mrs. Featherhoff leans out the window, her hands clamped together like she's praying, and crushing that brooch of silk flowers she wears whenever she's teaching.

"Guess she won't be giving lessons anymore," Cruz says. And I'm hoping he's wrong. We pass the Hatley Telephone Exchange, where Angie's gotta be working. But there's no way I'd look up with Cruz right there.

We get to the sliding jail and Cruz kneels down, scanning the inside. The roof caved in when the whole thing went sliding last month and now you can pretty much see everything that remains. There's a toilet on its side in the middle of a cell and a few bottles scattered around it.

"We should be bowling," Cruz says. Which is what we'd be doing right now if this was a year ago. But they closed the alley since it cost more to keep it going than to shut it down.

"I mean it." Cruz turns on his carbide lamp, then hops along the brick wall and shinnies down a cell door until it swings open and he can jump into jail. "We'll bowl with these," he says, picking up two chunky rocks. "And think of all the people whose guts we hate. Same as before."

The rocks still have some malachite in them, so they'll be weighty enough, and their edges haven't been hacked off too badly either, so they should roll. I count four bottles that Cruz is lining up: you need two more to play six-pin.

"Toss me the gym bag," Cruz says. He unzips it and pulls two beer bottles from inside his helmet, then looks up at me on the sidewalk like he's waiting for me—no, *expecting* me—to climb into jail along with him.

"We gotta drink up if we're gonna play," he says, "and I ain't wasting these Acmes." Cruz holds a bottle in my direction then pauses—he knows I don't like to drink—still, he keeps the bottle outstretched in his hand and smiles when I take it.

It's not like I never drink; it's just that I can't look at one without seeing Pop, which is why I normally refuse. But I like to bowl and I can't imagine Cruz beating me, even if it *is* rocks we're using.

Then I remember about my throwing arm and dangle it in the air. "What about the arm?" I ask.

"We'll bowl left to keep things even," he says, taking a swig of the Acme.

Cruz picks up the first rock to start. It goes sliding across the lumpy cement, connecting hard with the first pin—a liniment bottle. "And Sims goes smashing to the floor!" Cruz says when it topples over. The rest of the bottles follow and Cruz yells, "Strike one!"

I get the other rock while Cruz lines up the pins, then I aim the greenest part of the malachite at the whiskey bottle to the right of the liniment bottle, taking out Father Pierre. "There goes the priest!" I say.

140

Cruz starts clapping. "What's he got? A silver spoon and a cane for a whip?" he says. "There's nothing he can use that's gonna break us."

One tequila bottle's still wobbling—the new kid, Rudy Kovacs—and he holds on, the jerk. But I get him the second time, sweeping him clear off the ground.

"We should have outdoor bowling," Cruz says. He leans against the gym bag and looks out at the stars. "There's plenty of empty lots around here. I could run it."

"Maybe you're right," I tell him, looking up at the stars, too. They're blinking and round as peaches, scattered all over as if they just fell off the moon. The more I look at them, the more they seem within reach.

"Damn straight I'm right," Cruz says. "And don't think I haven't thought about it before." Then he looks over at me. "What about you?" he says.

"What about me?" Cruz catches me by surprise.

"After you get that football scholarship," he says. "You could coach."

"Nah. Not me."

"I'm serious. You see all the positions."

"The school's closing, remember?"

"It ain't closed yet," Cruz says. "And I don't mean here. You'll get out."

"And what if I don't want to?"

He pauses, looking serious for a second. "Then I'll just have to make you," he says, looking me in the eye. "Now let's line these things up."

Cruz takes what's left of his battered rock as I straighten the bottles. He hurls it into the air and hits the toilet. "Now, that's something Rabbit would do." He laughs.

"If Rabbit was here, there's no way he'd be doing this," I tell him. "He'd be too scared of getting caught."

Cruz is quiet for a while. Then he says he'd have Rabbit take care of the food in his bowling alley. "Nothing fancy. Full-o-Flavor sandwiches on French loaf. Stuff like that. When he gets back from playing soldier and finally finishes school."

My bottle's still got an inch of beer, so I down it. "You know that piano Mrs. Featherhoff got lowered from her house? I'd learn to play it."

I'm waiting for Cruz to tell me how crazy that is. How old ladies who'll always be virgins are the only ones who play the stupid piano. But he looks at the horizon like he can imagine me playing.

"I always figured when Mrs. Featherhoff got too old and they'd wheel out the piano in the Square on Christmas Eve, asking who can play, I'd go up and start into 'Silent Night' like there was nothing to it. Not making a fuss or anything, no matter how hard they'd clap after."

Cruz takes a swig from the tequila bottle and starts humming "Silent Night" real low.

"I should have a piano in my bowling alley. And you could come and play it sometime." He finds another rock. "Let's go, double or nothing," he says, and we lift our rocks and roll them down the jail at the same time. This time we aim for those Cottonville Wolves.

All the bottles shatter, making a shotgun sound. Cruz looks up at the street to see if anyone noticed. "Can't do nothing to us. We're already in jail. Can you see Rabbit right about now if he was here? He'd be cleaning up the broken glass, feeling like a sinner. And you'd be helping him," he says, watching me scrape the pieces into a corner with the edge of my sneaker.

"You think I only brought two?" Cruz takes out a couple more beers from the gym bag.

"Got any food in there?" I ask.

He nods and hands me a burrito, or maybe it's a taco. I keep thinking they're the same thing. All I know is that it's good. *Very good.* "How many of these things can your mother make?"

"As many as you want."

"But no meat. Not before a game anyway," I tell him.

"*Arroz* and pintos," Cruz says, "à la Villanueva." He hands me a new bottle.

"To Rabbit," I say, lifting it. Then we get all quiet again.

"They'll be sending him home any minute," Cruz says, "when they see how he can't run."

"Looks like they've got the communists licked anyhow," I say, hoping maybe it's true and that this war will be a short one—that Rabbit won't even get to see it. Maybe the mine will stay open, too. Because tonight I'd rather believe Cruz and all he's saying. I'd rather be in this jail with a perfect record and the whole town all happy, even if happy means drunk.

"Just wait," Cruz says. "You'll get that scholarship and I'll start my bowling alley."

"We gotta win the next four games first," I tell him.

"That's the easy part," he says. "You, me, Tony, Coach. We beat Ruffner, didn't we? If we can do that, we can take the state."

Chapter 14
GOODNIGHT, IRENE

THURSDAY, SEPTEMBER 14
7:33 A.M.

YOU SHOULD HAVE SEEN MR. Mackenzie sweat yesterday, taking that stupid oath along with Superintendent Menary, having to prove to everybody that he isn't a Communist (they're putting a capital *C* on it now in the papers), and Sims right there holding the Bible up for good measure, though he couldn't look Mr. Mac in the eye.

This tree I'm under is as crazy as Sims is, growing up through the fire escape on the side of the school and reaching right up to the roof. Like it was natural as rain to be sprouting out of a flight of metal steps. I've been looking at its weepy leaves since the sun rose, and all I've come up with is that the tree's just plain crazy going through all the trouble, twisting its way around the grate I'm lying on. But then there's patches of craziness scattered all over our town.

Father Pierre is mean crazy, and I think that's the worst kind of crazy you can be. And I suppose Pop's copper crazy

144

and drunk crazy, too, though I never know which one will show.

But Sims is crazy in a cowardly way, hiding behind that Commie box. Mr. Mackenzie says Sims hasn't been the same since his father got killed in the mine years ago. Still, he gives that box such a violent shake, you'd think it would explode and blow somebody else's life to bits right along with it.

When it quiets down, he'll show us pictures of Communists, lining them along the blackboard railing. Yesterday he put up a poster of the Weavers and my jaw just about fell on the floor. You can't go near a radio without hearing them sing, and I really like the way they sound. But there they were, Pete, Lee, Ronnie, and Fred, smiling at me the entire class, so polite and neighborly, with Penny Bruzzi whimpering in the front row all shook up about it and me wondering if they really were Communists and maybe "Irene" was a code name they used to let other spies know what they were thinking.

I grab hold of the gnarly branch—the one wrapped around the railing—and give it a good shake. Sims is like that knot, too, right in the middle of things, twisting them around until it seems normal to be hating people you've known all your life, just because they're different.

The moon's gone and the satiny white moonflowers at the foot of the fire escape fold under the strengthening light of the day. But they've been blooming in front of Sims's classroom window all night, and that's crazy, too.

I get out my jackknife and carve SIMS IS CRAZY right in the middle of that knot, cutting it deep and in capital letters. I feel better while I'm writing it. But as soon as I'm done I just get mad all over again. Carving those words in that branch won't change Sims.

And the morning's starting off all wrong. I suppose the evening will, too. They play "Goodnight, Irene" on the radio at ten, but I don't know if I'll be able to listen without reading into those lines or seeing Penny whimpering, she's got such a crush on Pete Seeger and she wears her hair like Ronnie Gilbert's, too.

There's only one way I can get this day off to a better start, so I carve a few other words in the tree. This time the satisfaction lingers as I mouth what I wrote over and over again—MUCKERS WIN.

* * *

6:15 P.M.

There's a gentle knock at the bottom of the screen door—somebody tapping out the rhythm to "shave and a haircut . . . two bits." I haven't heard that since I was little, but I know who it is. There's only one person who made that knock every time she came to visit, and that's Faye Miller. She's standing on the porch. We look at each other through the screen until Faye says softly, "I brought you this," holding up a glass container that smells like our house used to smell.

"It's a casserole," Faye says, fussing with the tinfoil on the edges, making them tighter with her thumbs. "It's still warm," she says, telling me it's got beef and peas in it, but no carrots, since she remembered how I didn't eat them because, well, I didn't want people saying that's how come my hair's that way. And that she makes casseroles every week and it's no trouble at all to throw another one in the oven.

"Thanks." I smile, taking the dish.

"I saw you being kind to that little boy, Leon, in front of the furniture store after Father Pierre's Buick went haywire," Faye says, "and how the Father wasn't very nice to you after,

146

even though you were helping him out. I guess some things don't change, do they, Red?"

"Not when it comes to some people."

"You sure must miss him, huh?" Faye whispers.

"All the time." I bite at my lip. "Do you miss him, too?"

"Every day." Faye starts to say something else, but smiles instead and then tells me, "Good luck at the game Friday night."

"Thanks, but I won't be playing quarterback."

"Well, I'm sure you will soon," she says, stepping off the porch and onto the cobblestone road. "The recipe's from your mother, by the way. She's the best cook I know."

THE VERDE MINER

Twice-Weekly Voice of the Mountain

HATLEY, ARIZONA   SATURDAY, SEPTEMBER 16, 1950   FIVE CENTS A COPY

WEEKEND EDITION

Mighty Mites Win Third Straight

The undefeated Hatley Muckers, now nicknamed the Mighty Mites, are racking up points downing teams twice their size. But last night, minus the watchful eye of quarterback Felix O'Sullivan, their winning ways looked in doubt.

Cruz Villanueva, speedy wingback, pulled the game out of the fire for Hatley by running a late punt back 83 yards for a touchdown as the Muckers defeated the Coldbrook Roadrunners, 12–7.

Two unlucky breaks in the game kept the pesky Mucker 11 from chalking up a more impressive score. Early in the first quarter, Lupe Diaz, touchdown bound, fumbled the ball away just short of the end zone.

The second was a Hatley touchdown called back when Villanueva illegally pushed away his interference. Later, Martin Quesada, subbing in for O'Sullivan at the quarterback position, plunged over from the three to hit pay dirt as Tony Casillas held the line. Muckers Coach Ben Hansen says O'Sullivan will be back to lead his team against Cottonville in a week's time.

SOCIAL NEWS & ARRESTS

—**Leroy Piggett** was charged with obstructing Hatley traffic on Upper Main Wednesday evening. According to the citation, Piggett obstructed the road by sleeping on it. Fine notice of 25 dollars was pinned to Piggett's flannel shirt.

—Back to complete the visit interrupted by a call to Korea in July, S.Sgt. **Buddy Ritz** promptly asked Bernadette Cushman to marry him. They were wed the next day, before Staff Sergeant Ritz returned to duty.

—**Lee Fong** was called in for questioning by Sheriff Doddy on two counts. The first was for complaints that food served in his restaurant had been scavenged from the back of Peila's Grocer, which Fong hotly denied. The second was about registering as a member of the Communist party under the anti-subversive bill. Fong says he is not a Communist, nor has he contacted relatives in China since that country turned Communist last year.

Allies Land Behind Red Lines at Inchon. Take Offensive for First Time, p.3.

Chapter 15
INDEPENDENCE DAY

I DON'T KNOW WHAT TO do without Rabbit. He's always been here beside me at the fiesta for the Mexican Independence Day parade. It's our only chance to laugh at Cruz and get away with it, watching him march by us in the band, since he doesn't know how to play. And all Cruz can do about the ribbing is blast out more sour notes to the Mexican anthem, on the horn every Villanueva's blown into since the first Mexican Independence Day 140 years ago. So I sit on the cement wall across from Penney's to wait out the half hour until the parade starts, watching Tony singing on the Mexican Legion float.

Tony's standing next to his father, who's commander of the post—which means Mr. Casillas gets to dress up as Father Hidalgo himself. (He's the Mexican priest who planned the whole revolt against the Spaniards in the first place.) He'll shout *"¡Viva Mexico!"* in the Square a little while from now and ring a bell that'll start up the mariachis, which used to be my favorite part until this year, with Angie being in the pageant and all.

Tony's putting on a sombrero the color of holy wine. That thing's the size of a Chevy tire and nearly grazes the banner stretching from Penney's to Lee Fong's Chinese Kitchen. You'd think Tony would be feeling foolish wearing a thing like that. He's got to know there's about a thousand sequins sewn onto it, glinting green and red in the sun. But he taps on the brim whenever a woman walks by, not feeling like a horse's ass one bit.

I'm the one who's feeling foolish sitting here, nodding at the folks congratulating me on winning the game last night when I didn't do much. And I'm sure glad Marty held on to keep us undefeated. But how am I gonna laugh at Cruz on my own when he goes by? That would just feel hollow. And I wonder what Cruz'll do come Saint Patrick's Day if Rabbit still isn't back and it's just him watching me out there marching in that parade.

I spot a maroon letterman's jacket with SOUTHWEST MISSOURI STATE on the back, so I know Coach Hansen's here. And I guess I'm not surprised. Wallinger, yes, if he showed up. Which he won't.

"I was looking for you," Coach says, walking over. Little Homer, his boy, is hoisted on his shoulders and keeps looking down at me with a great big tamale-sauce grin. I'm thinking maybe I'm not in for the next game after all, despite what Coach said in the paper, if he's out looking for me in the middle of Mexican Independence Day.

"If you help me with this, you'd be doing me a big favor." Coach smiles, pointing to the tamale stuffed in the paper cone he's holding. "Eleanor's got a roast in the oven, and if I don't eat half of it she'll think there's something wrong."

I unwrap the tamale and try not to shovel it in my mouth all at once.

"Ever toss a beanbag?" Coach asks.

"Not since third grade when the circus came to town and I guessed the number of marbles in a jar. I'm pretty good with numbers. Pop said I was his lucky charm."

Coach grins and takes Homer off his shoulders. "This'll be the little guy's first try." He hands Homer a squishy green bag filled with rice and starts showing him how to aim it so it'll go in the monkey's mouth painted red on the board. Homer misses, but Coach keeps saying "Great try," even when the second bag lands on Coach's foot.

Homer throws his last bag. It lands in the dirt but he claps, he's so happy, and runs into my legs, looking up at me so I can tell him his throw was good, too.

"Nice try, buddy," I tell Homer, rubbing the top of his curly head. Then I remember how Quesada did last night—good enough to hang on to a win. I'm not sure where that leaves me.

"Quesada did real well last night," I tell Coach.

"Yes, he did," Coach says. "But Quesada's even stronger at halfback. That's where he ought to be and he knows it. Look, I know benching was a tough thing to have to endure, but you had a great week of practice, and you're our starter. From here on in we'll be challenged and we need you to lead this team. So let's quit talking about football and get to the shooting gallery. Homer could use a prize."

I keep grinning all the way to the gallery, where Baldo Gallegos is manning the counter. He hands Coach a rifle, but Coach won't take it and points at me instead.

"Don't you want to go first?" I ask.

"No. That wouldn't do," Coach says. "I see double most days lately. And right now looks to be one of those times."

But I threw him a pass as hard as I could and he caught it an inch from his head. "How'd you do it?" I ask him. "Catching that football I threw you last time?"

"Careful now. Homer's got his eye on that straw donkey, so you've got to make all three shots count."

The metal ducks go by and I aim for the tail of the first one so I can hit the second mallard square on the jaw. It clinks and Homer jumps up and down while I wait for Coach to answer.

"Whatever's furthest to my left is a wash," he says. "They're just phantoms. Things like goalposts at night or moving targets are tougher. Come on now, Red. You've got two more."

"Hit 'em good, Red," Baldo says.

I take the gun and wait for a pair of ducks to pass, then fire at the next two, knocking them flat.

Homer squeals with laughter.

"Is that the donkey you want?" I ask him, pointing to the pink sombrero sewn in between a donkey's ears. Homer nods and says, "Oh boy!" when Baldo hands it to him, then he jumps into Coach's arms.

Coach winces, keeping his eyes closed longer than he should. "You mind taking Homer for a while?" he asks.

I've never held a kid before, but Homer wraps his arms around my neck anyhow and tucks his head under my chin.

"Where's your girl?" Coach asks. "And don't tell me there isn't one."

"She should be in the Square about now," I say, thinking about Angie and that contest in the gazebo.

"Then let's go," he says. "What sort of things does she like?"

"Pearls," I say.

"Uh-oh. I built Eleanor a flower garden and her carnations have a tough time of it, but pearls take more than digging. They need the sweat of working for pay. That'll take you some time."

"She has to go out with me first."

"She will," Coach says, like he's sure about that, and I'm grinning again.

We pass the food stands and see Mrs. Featherhoff collecting money from a bunch of little kids who want a crack at that piñata with Father Pierre's cane. Father's showing the kids how to use it and laughing along with them. I remember when we used to do that, too.

When we get to the gazebo, Mr. Casillas is in front of the microphone. Rudy Kovacs is standing pretty near it on the curb, though I don't know why. Rudy's carrying a bottle and wearing his Muckers jacket, but he didn't earn it. He starts laughing at Tony's father. Holding the bottle lower, he tosses it at the gazebo. The bottle hits the lattice that's hemming the platform, and Mr. Casillas stops talking and blinks.

"You dropped something," I tell Rudy, standing close behind him. Homer's got his face buried in the straw donkey under my chin. I can hear him whimpering.

Rudy turns around and smirks, looking up at the sky and acting all innocent. Coach grabs him by the shoulder. "A bottle can get slippery in the heat of the sun," Coach says. "But it's time to pick it up and leave."

Rudy keeps looking at Coach sideways, tapping the bottle with the tip of his boot.

"If you want to set foot on the field again, you'll do it," Coach warns him.

Rudy finally snatches up the bottle and tosses it from hand to hand like he's juggling. Then he throws it in the trash.

Tony's father waits until Rudy's in front of him, then hollers, *"¡Viva Mexico!"* flailing the bell high above his head and ringing it like crazy until Rudy's halfway up the hill. The mariachis start strumming those fat guitars they're holding, and Mr. Casillas calls the girls up onstage.

They're all aiming to be Queen of the Fiesta, though I don't know why the others even bother. Mrs. Rodriguez shows the girls where to stand—half of them are the phone operators she's in charge of. But no one comes close to the kind of pretty that Angie is. When her name gets called and she comes up on that podium, I can hardly even breathe.

"Uh-oh. You're done for, aren't you?" Coach whistles. "Just like when I first saw Eleanor. She was already engaged, but married me instead. Left that big ranch her folks had planned on us living on to come up here." He's taking Homer from me, but I can barely feel it. "She's afraid of driving around these crazy turns," he says, "but even more terrified of the burros. She's so happy that I pulled through, she might even let Homer have one."

I'm not listening to what Coach is saying anymore. I can't stop looking at Angie. Her hair blowing soft against those bare shoulders. The red-and-green paper flowers tucked behind her ear. And I think I'm a fool for thinking that she'd want me. Only there she is, up on the podium in a shiny white dress, smiling and waving at me like I'm Robert Mitchum, or someone just as famous who walked off the screen at the picture show.

She's still smiling when Mrs. Rodriguez takes hold of her arm and looks where Angie's been looking; then that smile disappears with the wind.

I look at Mrs. Rodriguez, then back at Angie, where my gaze finally stays. I don't care if Mrs. Rodriguez is in charge of all the girls at the phone company—I can't stop looking at Angie.

"I've got a good feeling about this season," Coach says. "There's a whole lot of people in this town not wanting you to be with her, but I can see in your eyes that won't stop you. Remember that when the papers keep saying you've got no business winning on the field." He puts a hand on my shoulder. "Think how badly you want to. How badly you want her. And that you've got every right to both."

* * *

I'm halfway into the Barrio; most of the neighborhood's still in the Square celebrating, including Mr. V and Cruz, who hopped on that float with Tony after ditching his horn. Hoisted a few of his brothers and sisters up there, too.

Me, I'm aiming for the bottom of the Gulch. I saw Angie walking home with that crown. Not the big sparkly one they put on the Fiesta Queen, but the smaller one—they called it a tiara when they gave it to her. She's the queen's assistant, though I don't know if that's just a way of saying if the queen drops dead or gets polio, the princess moves up to take her place.

I step onto the Villanuevas' porch and it creaks, so that's taking another risk since I don't know who else is home. But I'll say I came to see Cruz if she doesn't answer. There's no reason for them to believe any different.

I knock on the door and Angie opens it, but I get so nervous I ask for Cruz anyway. "You know darn well he isn't here," she says, letting me come in. She's still wearing that crown but with a different dress now. They keep changing them on special days like this.

"Who did you *really* come to see, Red?" she asks coyly.

"I'm looking at her."

Angie smiles.

"You should've won Fiesta Queen," I tell her. "Not princess."

"You think so?" She blushes. "Sure, it would have been

nice, but it doesn't matter. And it wouldn't change things. I'm still who I am." Angie shrugs, then she slips her hand in mine. "I'm sorry they benched you," she whispers.

"That's behind me now. Over and done with," I tell her. "I'm playing Cottonville on Friday."

"So you're different now?"

"Not different, just confident."

Angie squeezes my hand and the little kids behind her start giggling.

"Good thing they don't know my name yet."

"Red!" the one without the diaper blurts out.

Angie pretends like she's gonna paddle him but purposely misses. "If you stay much longer," she says, "Mrs. Esperanza from next door will tell Papá. She's such a snoop. I know why she doesn't fix her shutters—so she can see into other people's business."

"In a week I'll be all business," I say as she gently ushers me outside.

"Sounds like Cottonville doesn't have a chance," Angie tells me before closing the door.

THE VERDE MINER

Twice-Weekly Voice of the Mountain

HATLEY, ARIZONA   WEDNESDAY, SEPTEMBER 20, 1950   FIVE CENTS A COPY

MID-WEEK EDITION

Rival Teams Set for Final Clash

The Cottonville Wolves and Hatley Muckers battle in their annual matchup on Friday, with Hatley winning the draw for home field. Both teams are bitter rivals and undefeated this season.

Roy "Runt" Studdard, Cottonville coach, says he'd be worried the confrontation could become a bloodbath, but says the Hatley players are too small. "My quarterback got his jaw wired a few years ago, but that was when their team had weight. I'm guessing they'll have to play nice when you look at their size."

The game will be the last time the teams face off. Hatley High will close its doors at the end of the school year and is expected to merge with Cottonville next year.

"What they don't have in weight my boys make up for in toughness, speed and finesse," Muckers coach Ben Hansen said. "Besides, it's not a weight contest. It's a test of grit and skill."

"It'll be nice to play more teams with grass fields," Coach Studdard said, on playing Hatley for the last time. "I know we got a slag field, too, but it doesn't have 60 years of tailings. I don't know what they put in the smelter back in those days, but razor blades wouldn't be any different."

One Blast Too Many: Ernie's All-Car Garage Slides into Gulch, p.2.

WANT ADS

Chapter 16
BAD BLOOD

"FELIX O'SULLIVAN, I'VE BROUGHT SOMETHING to fatten you up," Mrs. Hollingworth says, knocking on the wood framing of the screen three hours before the game. The last time I saw her anywhere near our house was a few months after they took Maw up the hill, so I don't know what to say.

"Mr. Mackenzie told me how much you enjoy my lemon meringue pie, so I baked you one."

I can see her blushing and I say, "Thank you, ma'am." She gingerly hands the pie over, like it could shatter into a million pieces, which would be fine by me—I'd just lap it up with a spoon.

"Now, make sure to eat it soon in case the meringue falls," she says. "It's true that we have to be more careful when we bake up here than those living down in Cottonville. But it should keep nicely in the Frigidaire until after you beat the Wolves . . . as per my note . . ." Mrs. Hollingworth's voice

158

trails off as I put the pie in the refrigerator and leave her on the porch.

"Unless you're not opposed to eating dessert *before* your dinner," she calls, catching me break a hunk off the pie crust. "You *will* beat Cottonville, won't you, Red?"

"We'll sure try."

"Good. Consider it a victory pie in advance, then," she says, "on behalf of all the ladies on the hill."

I wait until Mrs. Hollingworth gets to the cobblestones before taking a slice out of the pie. It's good not having to worry about being hungry and to focus on beating those Wolves instead. Then I lick the bits of meringue off the wax paper and read what she wrote in the note.

Dear Red,

It would give us a great deal of pleasure if you knocked the stuffing out of Cottonville one last time. So eat up and Fight! Fight! Fight! Ever since they took the smelter away from us, there's been nothing but talk of country clubs, mile-high soufflés, and flat roads paved with macadam. But none of that matters if you can't win.

Yours Truly, Mrs. Reginald C. Hollingworth

* * *

The bleachers are meant for Hatley folk. There aren't any for the opposing team and never have been. I think if they ever tried to sit on our benches they'd get shoved off. Leroy Piggett, the most obstinate resident of our town, would be the first to do it. And if it was a Wolf supporter who had the poor judgment to sit on our side, there might be a stone hurled at his head. Leroy smuggles them in with his picnic hamper, claiming he's got such a whopper of an appetite and that's the reason the basket's so burdensome. But everyone knows those aren't sandwiches wrapped in wax paper, but nugget-shaped weapons as powerful as an angry fist.

Leroy collects his artillery after a hit, too. And dates them. *Bloody Nose Fight, 1940. Busted Kneecap, 1945.* The sheriff just laughs when he sees Leroy hobble up the hill, letting him pass through the gate without much of a look or even the seventy-five-cent admission. The others don't make a fuss either. They've got rocks in their pockets and purses, too. And Mrs. Hollingworth and Mrs. Menary will tell you it's to ease the arthritis.

That's what Cottonville does to us.

We battle hard against every team, but it's different with Cottonville. The blood between us is just plain bad.

Cruz says the line was drawn the minute they took our smelter away and hauled it down the mountain, putting up a town so flat and lifeless that it resembled the snobbish South. I don't know how snobbish they really are, those Wolves and their low-lying brethren. We don't speak to each other or walk on the same side of the street. I know they like fountains. There's two in front of their country club.

We use our water for drinking. "Who pisses away water when you're livin' in a desert?" Pop likes to say. "Cottonville, dat's who."

Their effigy is coming up the side of the hill. A mock version of me on a broomstick is going up in flames and being flailed right and left by their captain, Gunnar Swensen. The Cottonville band is behind it, encouraging the image to burn. The rule is, it's got to be extinguished by the time they get to the ticket taker, or they'll have to pay admission for the dummy.

160

"Hey, whatcha got in those instruments?" Leroy hollers at their band. "Get that coal out of them tubas so we can really hear you play!"

That's what Cottonville people fight back with—lumps of coal confiscated from the heaps used to fuel the smelter, tucking them in their socks and maybe even under those caps the band wears.

They're marching across the field to the opponent's side, which butts up against the mountain, so there's not much room for more than their squad and a couple of coolers. You can fit maybe six, seven cars behind the end zone. They sit on the hoods.

Cruz is holding our effigy, with Beebe right behind him cheering. It isn't quite so charred yet, and he made the face look more like their hot-tempered coach, Runt Studdard, who's spitting on our field, his arms splayed over a good-sized paunch, and smirking with the Swensen brothers, though he barely reaches their shoulders.

They think we're like vermin just because they see daylight, working above ground in the smelter when we're digging underneath in the dark, or because we haul a bus across the slag. But I know every inch of this field and what it can do. I've worn it like a second skin. And this time I've got the plays etched in my mind. The what-ifs. We went through them a dozen times at practice.

Beebe takes the effigy from Cruz and he points to the Cottonville fans, making a fist like he's aiming to hurt somebody. And I know that can only ruin things, even give the Wolves a win.

"Damn gringos," Cruz shouts, looking at the effigy of me propped up in a truck next to the Cottonville band.

"I'm a gringo," I tell him.

"Yeah, but not a Cottonville gringo."

Coach is yelling pretty hard just to get our attention, with Wallinger flailing his hands to get us over. The game hasn't even started yet and already our spectators and theirs are taunting each other.

"I know you hate those guys across the field," Coach says as we gather into a huddle.

"Worse than hate." Cruz kicks at a loose piece of coal. "They're loco."

Alonzo musters a nervous laugh.

"That kind of thinking won't get us a win," Coach says. "You need to be wearing these uniforms a few more times, and I don't want them getting so torn up and bloodied that we won't recognize you. We need you. *All of you.*" Coach looks over at Melvin Sneep, who's got his eyes closed and is biting his lower lip, then at Rudy—but those two won't be playing much.

"Just play smart," Coach says, grabbing Cruz's shoulder. "That's the best revenge, boys. *Winning.*" Coach shoots an index finger in the air. "Remember, those Wolves have next year. We don't. You're faster than they are. They lumber and seethe and want to hurt you. Don't let them. You've got to outmaneuver their line."

Tony focuses on the Swensens, butting shoulders on the other side of the field. They're bigger than he is, only Tony's wider and can throw his body as fast as a bullet, trapping you in his human gunnysack until there's no way you can wriggle free.

We walk onto the field and a chunk of coal bounces off Cruz's helmet. A bigger one lands near my foot. Cruz reaches down and picks up the chunk. "Told you they're all loco," he mumbles, tossing it off to the side.

First play and I'm coiled tight as a spring, connecting with Cruz, who's like a rocket, sprinting past our chalk line for a touchdown, giving us the early lead. But it's clear Cottonville's out for revenge and aiming to hurt me. Next time we get the ball, the Swensen brothers—all three of them—walk onto the field. Lars, the oldest and biggest one, points a ruddy finger at me.

"What are they doing, putting all three of them in?" Tony says. "Lars never even plays when he gets that big and slow. Watch your back, Red," he whispers. "Must be seven hundred pounds all together."

They're huge and angry and I don't like how they're looking at me. I hand off to Managlia and he runs. Then I'm down on the ground, my cheek cutting into the slag long after the ball has left me—tackled by a Swensen, though I don't know which one. "That's where you belong, Mucker. In the dirt or under it," he spits at me, punching my gut. "Crawling around with all those worms."

My ear stings. My pinky finger's dangling limp and swollen.

"You okay, Red?" Cruz asks, helping me up. "I'll get open quicker."

But I get sacked two more times before we build up a 10–6 lead, and Tony's left eye swells shut. The referee finally blows his whistle and slaps Cottonville with a penalty for unnecessary roughness.

"They're cheating on every play," Cruz yells as we gather in the end zone at the half. "We're getting held, clipped, punched."

"You're letting them get to you," Coach says, motioning for us to settle down.

Cruz won't hear any of it and keeps shaking his head. "They think they're better than us because they're big and white and rich."

"That's what you believe," Coach tells him. "And you're wrong. The only way they can win is by throwing us off our game, and you're letting them." He punches at Cruz's chest. "You've got to stop it—all of you—because we just can't lose. Not even one game. If we do, the chance for the Cup is over. The only way we can get there is to go undefeated. Nobody'll give a spot to a little prickly-ass mining team unless we win every game."

My elbow's bleeding. Before we walk onto the field, another ambulance crawls up near the bleachers.

"What do we need two ambulances for?" Alonzo asks.

"You'll see." Cruz snaps a nose guard to his helmet. Tony puts one on, too, right above his battered cheek. Cruz points at me to get one, and I don't want it to be that kind of game, but it already is. Rough and bloody and littered with dirty plays.

"You can still bust your nose wearing that," I tell Cruz.

"Yeah, but it won't hurt as much."

We get on the field and I glance around at the others. Diaz, Torres, and Managlia look pissed and way too angry for us to lose. On the sideline Coach is staring up at the sky, then over at the field. He smiles. He actually squats down low and smiles, taking in the bloodied faces, the referees gathering up the rocks and the coal, tossing them beyond the field so we can play. Then he looks at me and mouths the word "win."

He's right. We have to win this. And I'm not gonna let them take this away from us.

"Muckers! Muckers!" the Hatley fans chant.

"Let's get 'em," I say as we line up. "First play."

Lupe runs the kickoff back to our thirty and I call the same play we scored on earlier. Cruz runs a quick square-out to the flat, then breaks long.

I roll toward the sideline and Cruz runs it perfectly. He stiff-arms the lumbering Cottonville defender, sprinting past him, and my throw is right on target. Cruz doesn't even break stride, hauling in the pass and running untouched to the end zone. The fans go wild. We race toward Cruz, whooping and jumping. And then we hear the referee's whistle and see the yellow penalty flag back where Cruz caught the pass. "Offensive pass interference," he says. "No touchdown."

"That was stupid," a Swensen laughs. "Guess you guys are breathing too much dust from our smelter."

"Can't play football inside a country club," Tony says, giving the lineman a shove. "The ceiling's too low."

Cruz is arguing with the referee. Alonzo and Quesada hold him back but it's too late. The referee tacks on an unsportsmanlike-conduct penalty. The taunts are deafening now, not just from the Cottonville fans but their players, too, with Runt Studdard yelling, "Get that wild man out of here!"

We huddle up and Tommy, the water boy, runs onto the field, handing us cups to drink. "Coach Hansen says stop taking the bait," he tells Cruz. "Or he'll pull you out of the game."

I dig my finger into Cruz's jersey. "You've got to settle down. That's just what they want. For you to get kicked out. And us to lose this game."

"We can't end it that way," Tony says. "As losers."

"You don't know what it's like," Cruz hollers at me.

"And neither do you." We glare at each other until Tony gets between us.

"So who you gonna blame, Cruz, if we lose?" I shout. "The gringos? 'Cause I want this, same as you."

"We all do." Diaz nods. Then Torres.

"Hit 'em!" the angry mob screams.

More pieces of coal rain down on us.

Those penalties set us back almost to our chalk line—just a few yards away from the Cottonville supporters.

"Make 'em pay!" a woman in a Sunday hat shouts, raising her fists at us.

I find Torres twice but the passes go incomplete, so I scramble forward on third down, but only gain a couple of yards. Now we're punting from the end zone, and they'll be coming at us. Our lead is still only 10–6. I grab Quesada by the front of his jersey. "Boot it all the way to their country club," I tell him. He's got to send this punt farther than he's ever kicked before.

His punt spins toward the sideline, low and short. Their return man scoops it up and barrels all the way to the fifteen-yard line. A Cottonville receiver makes a diving catch in the end zone on the next play, colliding with our linebacker, Rico Verdugo, who's on the ground, knocked out by the impact.

The crowd gasps. For the first time in the game there's silence. Verdugo should have been up by now, or at least moving. But he's still lying on his back.

"Get up!" I yell.

"Fight it and get up!" Cruz says.

I don't think Verdugo can move his neck. Coach sprints over, kneels beside him, and starts talking. But I can't see Verdugo talking back. Coach calls for the ambulance.

"Is he moving?" Alonzo asks me.

"Not yet."

"I don't wanna be a Wolf next year," he sniffs. "They'll kill me, too. They already said so."

"You'll never be a Wolf," Cruz says. "And they'll never close the mine. Muckers don't die. They just find more ore."

Verdugo is being hauled away on a gurney. He lifts one arm slightly and we cheer. I don't know why. It looks like this could be something bad.

Cottonville kicks the extra point to make things worse. Now they're up 13–10.

"Time to shove that ball down their throats," Cruz says in the huddle.

"Just play smart," I tell him, "like Coach said." The blood's dried up in my ear, plugging some of the sound, but I know we can't lose. Even if it means getting torn up some more.

We reach the Cottonville twenty. There can't be more than a minute left.

"Gotta get a touchdown," I tell them. A field goal would tie the game, but that wouldn't help us get the Northern Crown.

"End-around," I say. We haven't called a bootleg yet this season.

I drop back to pass and feel the pressure from the Cottonville linemen, the burly Swensens hungry to defeat me. But I deke and turn, flipping the ball to Cruz. He circles past me and is hit hard, taking a shot to the face. He pivots and yanks at the lineman's helmet, throwing him to the ground. And then he's gone, racing away like a lightning bolt.

Cruz eludes another tackler and dives over the line, hitting pay dirt. We all rush on top of him. We're back in the lead. He wipes his fist under the nose guard and it comes away covered with blood.

"I'll never be a Wolf." Alonzo grins. "Rather move."

Three plays and they get nowhere. Tony and Alonzo make sure of it. The final gun goes off and the game is over. We won it, 17–13.

Cruz jumps in the air and points at Coach Studdard, who's throwing a fit on the sideline. But I didn't anticipate what comes next. The Swensens start attacking Cruz, knocking him flat, and we all come running, barreling over their burly bodies. Me, Tony, Alonzo, Managlia, and the rest of the team. Then the Hatley folk tumble onto the field, adding to the mound, and it's hard to know who's who. Someone's on top of me punching my shoulder. I cover my face with my hands until Coach Hansen hauls me up. He's yelling at us to get home before it's too late and to stay out of it. That we're already bloodied up enough.

The referees try to break things up but Cruz keeps slugging at the Swensens. Then the siren goes on in the sheriff's car. Sheriff Doddy drives onto the field, yelling, "Go home or face arrest!" into his bullhorn. Then he shoots his gun at the sky. Mrs. Hollingworth screams, covering her mouth with a bloodied lace glove, and the Cottonville people flee, clambering down the hill in a hail of pummeling stones. The Swensens are close behind, getting hauled away on the bed of their father's pickup.

Leroy Piggett refuses to leave until he's collected all his rocks.

"The ambulances are full, Cruz," Hap, the driver, tells him, "but you'll need to get that stitched."

Cruz's face is scraped up pretty good. It's so bloody he can barely keep his eyes open.

"That's okay. I'll walk up." Then he comes over, feeling one of the cuts above his eye. "Did you see the look on their coach's face when I gave him the finger?" Cruz says, beaming, the blood dripping off his nose.

"You're an idiot," I tell him. "You almost cost us the game."

Chapter 17
CAUGHT

I WOKE UP EARLY AND waited in bed for the sun like I usually do, so the day wouldn't get ahead of me and I could savor the win. I know you can't stop time, but when it's this early in the dawn, it seems that I can. Sometimes I spin it backward and Maw isn't sick anymore; she's singing her warbly notes in church, holding my hand, and me covered in lilacs from her Sunday perfume.

Or I'll keep unraveling it until I'm not alone in this room. Bobby's here, too, in the twin bed across from mine sleeping on his stomach, the pillow curled up in a ball under his throwing arm with him facing me, breathing life into the dark. I tell him about the games we've been winning, especially how we beat Cottonville and that we're still undefeated, no thanks to Cruz.

But today I decided to spin time forward since I was thinking about Angie.

I closed my eyes and there she was, lying next to me real

170

quiet and me telling her about the dawn—how I can make it my own—and her understanding.

I didn't want to do anything with time right then except let it float. But then Pop came home—it was well after four—and was he in a mood. He hasn't stopped drinking since news of the raise. And time got hold of me again, throttling up to full speed, with Pop chopping away at the chilly air with his drunken snores until the dawn climbed out my window and Angie along with it.

I slide down the banister bare-toed and sneak onto the back porch, trying not to wake up Pop. Whitey, the neighborhood burro, is on the hickory settee having breakfast. I can see his silhouette in the twilight, pale and hairy against the navy sky, his hooves curled up like a pile of bones bleached by the desert sun.

"Brought me a banana, huh?" I whisper, grabbing one from the rotting bunch hanging out of his mouth. My pinky finger starts throbbing as he wrestles me for it with his brown teeth until the banana rips off and he sees he'll have to move to get it back.

"Shite!" Pop wails, slicing the day open with his angry spit of a cry. He's hit his head on the iron bedpost again, rushing to work the early shift.

Whitey stops chewing and I dash into the kitchen, knowing there's just enough time to grab my shoes so I won't have to make Pop something out of nothing and get accused of eating what's not even there. But my shoes aren't on the step stool where I'd left them. Pop hobbles down the stairs and I'm caught.

"Make me an egg," he grumbles, standing there buck naked and holding my shoes in his hands. He hurls the left one at me but I duck just in time. "Then you'll get the other one," he says, sitting on top of it—in Maw's chair—with those bare-ass cheeks.

There's no use arguing. It won't get me the other shoe. I need to come up with an egg. I take my helmet and head into the raw morning down the streets along the Hogback.

The cobblestones are sharp and slippery cold against my bare soles, and I have to clamp down on my lower lip so I won't react and get found out. There's a skunk crossing the street after a night of scavenging, and it ducks under the Rakoviches'. I'm headed a few streets over, down to Second and a little brown house. Not a house, really (it's not much bigger than the ovens). More like a lean-to sprouting up from the dust, and the color of a shaggy old juniper trunk in the waning darkness. I hurry over to it and huddle down.

They're clucking inside, those broody hens, while the sky changes. A band of orange skims the rim of the Black Mountains, swirling and churning under smoky clouds. Then the sun pushes through and rises red and the desert isn't dark anymore. Its color reaches clear across the henhouse, where the door's half open.

Mrs. Palermo left the latch undone and my stomach tightens. I wonder if she's been out collecting already and there won't be any left, or if she's about to and I'm bound to get caught. I'm not proud of what I'm going to do, or coming up with the idea in the first place. But I can't see another way. She's given me enough eggs already, and I just can't bring myself to ask—no one needs to know about Pop and the things he does. I guess I'd rather steal.

A rooster finds me and I teeter a bit, then kneel still. He juts his angry neck at me, then lifts his legs high and walks away. The wooden door creaks as I open it more, but then the rooster crows, covering up the sound. A few hens screech and flail their wings, losing some feathers as I slip in, scanning the rows lined with hay. I pick a hen that looks the quietest: a little russet one near the window with her eyes closed, bathed in the orange glow. Not sleeping, but looking serene, like she was praying. I reach under her and she blinks, scratching my wrist with her claws. I put the warm egg in my helmet and crawl behind the house until the chickens settle. Then I take the long way back so Mrs. Palermo won't see me.

The chicken got me pretty good, but I deserve it. I lick the scratches to try and stop the blood and walk up Main Street. Town Hall's shiny as a copper pot—that whole side of the street is—and I can't help but stare. It's the only time the town looks pretty and not bandaged up; taking on the light of the orange sky with the moon higher up and Venus right near it, hopeful and brighter than any of it.

The egg wobbles in my helmet as I dip down to First Street. I clutch it, thinking, *Why didn't I get two? Mrs. Hollingworth's pie is long gone.* That's what my stomach's making me think: *Stealing is stealing; what's one more?* with the rest of me glad that I didn't, whispering, *You shouldn't have taken it in the first place.*

Pop's still sitting there in Maw's chair, sleeping. He blinks when he hears me and comes into the kitchen, then leans over the sink and splashes the water jug over his head. "Not too runny," he murmurs, scrubbing his ruddy face with his hands. I get out the frying pan and he climbs the stairs to get dressed.

This day was supposed to be mine. I woke up early enough to stake a claim on it and left plenty of room for slaps on the back from the people in town. "Good goin', Red," they'd tell me. "I knew you'd win." And all those smiles from the mothers mixed in, too. But Pop's got a way of spoiling things you thought would matter a whole lot.

I crack the egg on the iron rim and wait, taking the fork with me to the living room. It's lying there on Maw's chair—the right shoe—splayed out and flattened like a tire ran over it. I can get it and leave, but what would it matter? I can't take the egg back to Mrs. Palermo's henhouse and put it under that bird. And I don't feel like going into town much anyway. I'm no hero. I'm a thief. A hungry thief who swipes eggs from his friend's mother. What would Rabbit think about that? Me preaching to him about what's right and not going to war, while I'm stealing eggs right from under his mother's nose.

"How's that egg?" Pop hollers.

I bet Rabbit's probably shooting targets on a mountain somewhere in Japan, getting yelled at, too.

"Done," I say. I scrape the egg onto a plate, then go get the shoe. Whitey's still on the settee. He doesn't even look as I go by. Maybe I deserve getting yelled at. And I don't even have a job anymore now that Ernie's garage is gone, so how am I going to get that money for Bobby's pew? If somebody tries to be nice to me today, I think I just might puke.

* * *

September 23, 1950

Dear Rabbit,

How are you doing? Are you overseas yet? I thought I'd write to you now since it can take a while for a letter to get over there. It took nearly a month for Bobby to receive ours. I suppose you could still be in boot camp. I guess if you didn't happen to make it through, we would have heard about it by now.

174

You sure seemed glad to get out of Hatley and be a soldier, but to tell you the truth, I'd rather have you here. I know Cruz feels the same way, though he'd never admit it. And you have every right to be sore at him. He told me to tell you how we beat Cottonville, but he nearly screwed the whole thing up by acting ornery. He got his nose smashed in fighting those Swensen brothers and his forehead's stitched up, too. Me? I suppose I just went along for the ride. I didn't do anything flashy to win.

And I do, too, know what it's like not to count. Remember how you were saying that up on the hill? How's this for not counting? Maw still looks straight at me and doesn't see me. It's because of Bobby. I'm not saying I could ever make the hurt go away, but I'm a part of her, too. And Pop. I know every time they look at me it reminds them of what they've lost, but I lost him, too. I know if I wasn't here Pop would be at a bigger mine already, getting more pay.

Pop can go to Mexico for all I care, except he won't, because there's football. The stakes are too high. We're undefeated. Can you beat it? If we take Kingman, the game against Flag will be for the Northern Crown. Pop says it's 50 to 1 that we don't. Flag's averaging a foot taller than us, and Verdugo's got a broken collarbone courtesy of those Wolves. But the last time we checked we were so gunned on winning I don't think a foot would stop us.

We're gonna win. First the Northern Crown, then the state championship. Even if it kills us. Funny,

(Over)

me saying that and you being the soldier, when all we get over here are explosions from the mine. But we really believe it. Cruz says if his face gets smashed again and he's left for dead he'd be okay with it, if it meant winning the Yavapai Cup once and for all.

Any chance you'll be home to see it? Benny's selling the Phoenix newspaper again at the diner, now that we've got Korea. It says things are going good since Inchon. We'll go to Benny's after we win and you'll be the only one in uniform. Won't that be something? That'll shut up Cruz for once.

Your friend,
Red
Red O'Sullivan

P.S. I stole an egg from your mother's henhouse.

THE VERDE MINER

Twice-Weekly News of the Mountain

HATLEY, ARIZONA   SATURDAY, SEPTEMBER 30, 1950   FIVE CENTS A COPY

WEEKEND EDITION

Muckers Swamp Kingman, Will Play for Northern Title

Quarterback Red O'Sullivan was the man of the hour, passing for three touchdowns and rushing for another, as the undefeated Hatley Muckers mauled Kingman, 33–6, Friday night.

In the scrappy game that saw plenty of smash-up plays and cut-up players, O'Sullivan completed lightning-precision scoring passes in the second quarter to Peter Torres and Cruz Villanueva. In the third, O'Sullivan connected with a battle-scarred Villanueva again on a 77-yard scoring play, then ran for a razzle-dazzle 13-yard tally of his own.

Defensive tackle Tony Casillas closed out the scoring when he scooped up a Kingman fumble and rambled 26 yards for a touchdown.

"Our whole team got in on the scoring," said O'Sullivan as he boarded the bus for the long ride back to Hatley. "This win proves that we're ready for anybody."

The win raises the stakes on Hatley's final regular-season game—a visit to Flagstaff in two weeks. Flagstaff, the big, bruising team in the North, gave notice last night by trouncing Winslow that they'll be gunning for the Northern title and continuing their undefeated record. Whoever wins in this much-anticipated tilt will draw home field to play against the Southern champs—whoever they may be—for the state title and the Yavapai Cup.

MacArthur to North Korea: "SURRENDER OR DIE," p.2.

Chapter 18
NO WAY OUT

SATURDAY, SEPTEMBER 30
4 : 58 P.M.

THEY'RE PLAYING *No Way Out* at the matinee, and I'd sure like to be sitting next to Angie. But Bigsby said if he gave me a private showing—even if it was in the middle of the night and I promised to fix his flats forever—he'd still get fired if Mr. Ritz caught wind of it. That he couldn't take that chance. So I have to be content sitting in the last row, looking at those two injured crooks on the screen and at the back of Angie's head four seats in front of me. She's with her sister, the one who's in eighth grade.

"*Just hold your head like this,*" the doctor tells Johnny Biddle.

"*Don't do it, Johnny. Don't do what he says,*" Ray Biddle hollers, punching the doctor in the arm.

"*Look, I'm trying to help your brother. Why don't you just shut up?*"

"*You watch yourself, black boy. Watch how you talk to me.*"

Angie jumps a bit when the shouting starts and her hand lingers in the popcorn bag that's on her knees. Maybe it's because she can't believe how Ray's treating that doctor either, blowing smoke in his face and spitting at him when he's only trying to help.

I want to ask her if it's okay for me to come over there, not knowing if her sister's a tattletale or what, so I toss a popcorn kernel at Angie's head and it gets stuck in her hair. She brushes it away and hardly even moves. Her sister laughs, though, and turns around and smiles at me like she knows something, although I don't know what that's supposed to be. Are you going around with someone if you can't tell anybody about it?

I start walking down the aisle to ask Angie face to face, because all this hiding is really stupid—like how Ray's telling Sidney Poitier, who's playing the doctor, to keep his black hands away from him—and me not supposed to be with Angie because her skin is brown. As if how you're born is all wrong just because somebody says it's not the right color, and all you deserve is to be pinned into a corner without any choices on who to love.

But then Dell Bruzzi comes running in, and before I can do anything he's standing in the middle of the aisle yelling, "The dynamite truck's about to explode!"

Angie's sister screams and everybody starts climbing over the seats to get to the exits, dumping buttered popcorn all over the place, not acting neighborly at all, pushing and shoving each other aside even though the theater's half empty.

"Angie!" I grab her elbow a few feet from the door.

"You go ahead, Theresa," she says to her sister, ushering her outside. "Now go straight home!"

The beam from Bigsby's flashlight passes over us as he leads Mrs. Ramsey and her bad knee to the exit. I shove a mess of buttered popcorn aside with my sneaker so she won't slip on the floor. Then I whisper to Angie, "Stay here with me."

"What?" she says. "The whole town's ready to explode and you want to stay here?"

"It's always been that way—the town about to blow," I say. "This is as safe a place as any."

Bigsby swings the exit door shut and there's nobody left in the theater except Angie and me.

"Now I know you're crazy," she says, "waiting to get blown to high heaven."

"You can go if you want to."

Angie hesitates, then cracks the door open a few inches.

"I can't make you stay, but I'd sure be glad if you did."

She keeps looking outside.

"Anything blown up yet out there?" I ask.

Angie shakes her head. "The dynamite truck's on top of the hill, but nobody's near it. The fire trucks wouldn't even take a hose to those crates of explosives."

"They would've gone off by now if they were set to blow," I say, reaching for her shoulder. "And now the sun's behind the mountain, so things are bound to cool off."

The door swings shut and Angie turns to face me. "Aren't you afraid of anything?" she asks.

I don't even have time to think. She comes closer and takes my hand.

"I may be on a lucky streak," I say.

Then she kisses my hand real soft, as if it could be precious, like gold or something. "Anglos aren't supposed to be superstitious. Just Mexicans."

"Well, now you know. Hey, Bigsby's left the movie running; it would be a shame not to see how it ends, don't you think?"

"Can't you guess?" Angie says.

"It might have a happy ending." I take her hand and we walk over to the concession stand. "I told you I'd get us a private showing."

"So it was you who planted that shoddy dynamite on the truck!" she says, throwing me a wry grin.

"No way. But if that's what got you here alone with me, I'll take it."

Mrs. Ramsey's left the popcorn going. It's crackling and coming up like crazy. "Hey, grab me some paper bags," I tell Angie. She gets a couple and starts scooping the popcorn.

"I can't figure you out," she says as we make our way to the center row. "I didn't think you'd be so daring. I mean, you say hardly anything in school, but you're hopping on trains and holding me hostage in a movie theater. Is this what it's like to date a gringo?"

I just smile. Angie told me all I need to know. *We're dating.* And I'm feeling hopeful for Sidney up there on the screen, even though the brother didn't make it and Ray's steaming, looking for revenge. I'm thinking Sidney's in the clear because of the autopsy, only Ray's just knocked out the cop who's guarding him, stealing his gun. And I have to admit, it looks pretty bad for Sidney.

Angie covers her eyes as soon as Ray points the gun at Sidney.

"It's hard watching a movie like that, isn't it?" she says, wincing. "It makes me so sad that I want to hurry things up so change can come. But sometimes I wonder if it ever will."

"I'm here with you, aren't I? It's a start, isn't it?"

"That's because nobody can see us."

"Then no more hiding," I tell her. "I mean it. Next time I'm taking you to the eight o'clock show. *On a date.* They can gawk all they want to. I don't care."

Somebody opens the front door. It's Bigsby. "Sorry, Red,"

he says, "but I gotta stop the movie. We're closing up until tonight's show, since the town didn't get blown up after all."

The streets are empty when we get outside, and the dynamite truck's gone.

"I'll walk you home," I tell Angie.

"Just to the top of the hill," she says, "so Papá won't see."

We've lost the heat of the sun. It's behind the mountain already, acting the way a lightning rod does, splitting open the sky. I can see its jagged pieces of red and gold reaching for the horizon—right next to Angie's brown eyes.

We get to the top of the hill and Angie pauses. She looks up at me for a while, staring into my eyes, searching for what I already know: *I belong to her.* No matter which way she feels. And so I kiss her. Right out in the open. Long and hard. Her lips, telling me she's hungry for me, too, repeat everything mine do. Then she pulls away, eyeing me like a startled fawn, and before I know it, she's heading down the path into the Gulch.

"I mean it about the picture show!" I say, watching her pass one of Carl Purdyman's cows. "I'll take you next Saturday night. And I don't care who sees."

Angie turns and signals me to hush. But even though it's dusk, I can tell there's a smile behind her fingers.

I keep watching as she descends deeper into the Gulch, heading for the Barrio, the desert wind toying with her hair like it's a kite. She's barely a speck now, but I don't lose sight of her. Then the Gulch closes in and takes her from me, until there's nothing left but the night.

The six o'clock bell sounds and the miners shuffle out, tired and hungry and anxious to get home, the dynamite truck long forgotten. There's smoke coming from the chimneys dotting the hillsides, carrying with it the smell of supper—meals that take longer to make than something you cut out of a can.

I keep standing there, taking in the smells. There's beans and maybe sauerkraut. With kielbasa, I think. Definitely pork.

I watch the juniper tips cornering Loco Francisco's little garage give in to the wind as he lights a match to heat up his supper. Then the sound of pure laughter, untouched by sorrow—from those little brothers and sisters—comes to me from the belly of the Barrio, and I know Angie's home.

Chapter 19
CUT OPEN

TUESDAY, OCTOBER 3

3:35 P.M.

CRUZ GOT HIS STITCHES CUT open in our win over Kingman. His nose is busted, too. There's a piece of brown tape on his forehead and a white one across the middle of his nose that he keeps running over with his thumb, waiting for practice to start. He's staring up at the sky as if there might be something in the clouds he should know. Then he catches me looking and his expression changes. It puffs out again and gets all proud, the same way it always does before a practice or a game. As if this one's no different. As if the town's the same and its very existence isn't being choked off by this morning's announcement: the mine is closing.

But no matter how big Cruz tries to make himself feel, he looks small against the open pit, like a chipmunk clinging to the highest branch of a piñon tree with nowhere to go.

Pop's down there in that hole. I can hear him yelling at the crew, and he shouldn't be doing that. There's only two weeks until the mine shuts down.

184

"What's the matter?" Cruz says. The football hits me in the head (he knew I wasn't looking), and I'm pissed because it stings. "Never seen an open pit before?"

"Not when it's about to close." I shoot the ball back, aiming for Cruz's throat.

"Ruffner's just trying to upend us," he says. "Since all the town cares about is football now that we're winning."

I study Cruz's face, searching for something that might go against what he's saying, like the look he kept giving those clouds. But he comes over and glares into the pit, acting all annoyed and shaking his head, as if what's posted on those signs they hammered into the slag means nothing. Or something temporary, like WET PAINT or DETOUR.

"You know when the mine closes ahead of schedule, it's permanent," I tell him. "It means there's nothing left."

"Bullshit. It means Ruffner's sore that we're gonna be champions and he's got nothing to do with it. You know what I'm gonna do after we win? Lean over and piss right into that pit."

"Just be happy you won't have to be a miner," I say.

Cruz lets the ball spill out of his hands and dribble onto the field. "What are you, some kind of gringo idiot all of a sudden?" he says.

"You could go to college. Get one of those football scholarships."

He grabs the neck of my jersey and throws me down.

"Now who's the dumb one, huh, Ugly?" He spits it into my ear. "Scholarships don't go to greasers. They go to you. Don't you get it? I'm always gonna be a mucker, on the field or in the pit. It doesn't matter where. And when Rabbit gets home, he's gonna bake bread. Some of us know where we stand right from the start, but it's different with you." He shoves me closer to the ledge. "You can get out of here. And if you don't I swear I'll kill you." Cruz thrusts my cheek into the dirt, forcing me to glimpse the bottom of the pit a thousand feet below. "'Cause I couldn't take becoming my father and watching you be yours, knowing you didn't have to, only you stayed because you didn't want to go leaving your dead brother behind."

Cruz finally lets go of me. His stitches have popped open again, and blood starts oozing out of the edges.

"Jesus, how often do I have to get this thing stitched up?" he says, tearing the tape off his forehead and tossing it into the pit.

The whistle sounds below and you'd think there'd be cheering. There always is at the end of a shift. I can see Pop down there, no bigger than an ant, sitting in the crusher, not moving. And Santiago, who hasn't let go of the jackhammer yet, the bandanna over his mouth coated with dust as he hangs over the handles. I suppose Bobby would've been down there, too, if he'd come back. And that would've been a waste.

"There's no way I'm ever working in a mine," I tell Cruz.

"Yeah, well, you wouldn't last anyway," he says, getting his helmet out from the duffel bag. "I've seen how many times you get sacked."

Coach backs up the school bus, then motions for me to get out the tackling dummy slumped over in the first row. He has that surly, you-think-you-know-what-you're-in-for-but-you-don't grimace on his face. The muscles on his neck widen, flaring out beyond the collar of his T-shirt, and I don't know where he gets it, or where any of us do. He's been working us harder than ever, but plays right alongside us, spitting out encouragement.

The only one who gripes about it is Rudy.

I get on the bus and just about jump two feet, thinking the dummy's the one who's talking, but it's Managlia sitting in the back, his arm in a sling again, though it's been almost two weeks since the Cottonville fight. Both eyes are ringed the color of a shiny plum, and the black and purple are too fresh to be from the game.

"I can't play, Red," he says, crying through those puffy slits.

"You just reinjured it against Kingman," I tell him. "It'll heal up in time for Flagstaff."

"It's not the arm. It's my pop. He's getting transferred to Ajo and taking me with him. Tomorrow. Doc told Coach it's a dislocated shoulder, but it's really just a sprain. I tried to reason with my pop, only . . . it's just me and him." Managlia coughs up some phlegm and presses a finger against his bottom lip, which has started bleeding. "If anyone knows what that's like, it's you, Red."

I look at Managlia's swollen face, the busted lip trying to form a broken smile. He doesn't even bother to paw away at his tears or tell me he fell down the stairs or slipped running sprints up the hill, so I know he's more afraid of his pop than I've ever been of mine.

"We're gonna win," I tell him, throwing the dummy over my shoulder.

Managlia doesn't say anything.

"You coming?" I ask. "You're still a Mucker."

He holds the sling tighter against his stomach and looks out the window. "I'll watch from here," he whispers.

Coach blows his whistle and we group around him in the center of the field. He looks at Wallinger and hands him the clipboard, then Coach folds his arms firm around his chest.

"Rico Verdugo got out of the hospital today," he says.

"Is he comin' here?" Alonzo asks.

Coach smiles for a split second then shakes his head. "Verdugo's out for the season. His football days are over and I'm sorry for that. But we still have ours. There'll be some changes. Managlia's out, too, with a dislocated shoulder."

"I thought it was just a sprain," Cruz says.

"Misdiagnosed. Torres moves from end to fullback. Rudy Kovacs moves up from second string. He'll take over Torres's position."

None of us says anything. Tony keeps wrapping his fingers, then cuts off the end of the tape with his teeth. I never thought one of us would get too hurt to play. Now we only have one sub left. And the person who should've never made the team is going to play.

"Come on now, right side first," Coach barks as Wallinger divides us up for the drills and Rudy puts on his gloves.

I strap the dummy onto its hinge for the one sub we have left—Melvin Sneep. I think Tommy, the water boy, could give it a better going-over. But if Rudy's face was on it, there wouldn't be anything left of it. The stuffing would be shredded pretty good, since we'd all take a shot. Rudy and his stupid gloves. He wears them on the field so he won't have to touch any skin that's darker than his. But there isn't anybody on the team Rudy likes and the feeling runs both ways.

He takes his position, but as soon as Coach blows the whistle, Lupe Diaz switches with Cruz, who lunges into Rudy hard, tossing him to the ground.

"What's the matter, can't grip anything with those gloves?" Cruz says.

"Your days are numbered," Rudy says. "We just shut down your mine."

"Settle down, boys," Coach tells us. "Practice just started."

"Then get those wetbacks to lay off me," Rudy shouts.

Cruz sucks in his breath. "What? You'd rather have a bohunk mow you down?"

"I won't have that kind of talk on my field," Coach yells. "We're above all that." Coach is eyeing Rudy, but Rudy won't look up. "You've all chosen to be on this team, and we have the same goal: to win," he says. "You can't buy it or mine it. You have to earn it. And you can't win it on your own. We need each other. The Slavs need the Mexicans, and the Mexicans need the Irish and the Italians, so we're all equal, aren't we? Now come on, let's get set to do the drill on the left side."

But Rudy won't get into position. "You're wrong, Coach," he says. "We don't swim with them and we don't eat with them. And when this is all over, my father won't let you anywhere near a white player. You'll be lucky to be coaching at the Indian school up in Flag."

We all aim for Rudy, who's swinging at any of us before Coach gets in between yelling for us to stop. Rudy's still thrashing and he butts heads with Coach. Both soar into the air like elk bucks sparring during a rut—Rudy's helmet lashing Coach in the forehead. Coach lunges backward. His head bobs twice as he lands, then his body goes limp as a rag doll, his face moist and pale a few feet away from his cap.

My stomach freezes but I start to run, not waiting to see if Coach might be okay. The wind slaps my face, drowning out the yelling and screaming behind me as I sprint toward the icehouse to get to a phone. If the door's locked I'll smash open the window. I don't care about my hand. But then Gibby walks out of the icehouse.

"Ambulance!" I scream.

He looks at me, puzzled.

"Call an ambulance!" I shout, louder this time. I run past him and head for the hill, refusing to let the elevation slow me down. When I finally hear the siren up top, I sprint even harder, picking off street after street. I have to get ahead of this day and what it might look like tomorrow. As I round the bend for Company Ridge, the pitch catches my stride, forcing me to push even more. I pump my arms harder, but I'm only punching at the wind. The last incline gnaws into my calves until, finally, it beats me, and I collapse on the side of the road.

The ambulance passes me, throwing a halo of crimson over the darkening hillside as Hap drives it to the field. And I hope that siren's still going when they come back up the hill.

THE VERDE MINER

Twice-Weekly News of the Mountain

HATLEY, ARIZONA   WEDNESDAY, OCTOBER 4, 1950   FIVE CENTS A COPY

MID-WEEK EDITION

Mine to Close October 17, Workers Notified by E.C.

Permanent termination of mining and smelting at Hatley and Cottonville was announced Tuesday morning by the Eureka Copper Mining Company. Notices posted at the smelter and mine read: "To employees: the company regrets to announce that due to the depletion of the ore reserves, all smelting and mining operations at Hatley and Cottonville will permanently terminate October 17, 1950."

No figures were released by the company, but it is estimated that 500 employees will be affected. Some are being offered similar jobs at other E.C. operations. Though closing of the mine had not been unexpected, definite setting of the date did not come easy to many veteran workers. Transferred or otherwise, it won't be pleasant to be uprooted from the place they have long known as home. Some have records of 35 years or more, dating back to the boom days.

WANT ADS

HOUSES FOR SALE—Bid for purchase of nine houses located in Hatley to be accepted at Eureka Copper offices, care of H. W. Elton, by 10 a.m. October 30. Bids may be made on any one house or entire group. Successful bidders agree to raze, tear down, or remove said houses from their present sites within 45 days of contract.

COME & LISTEN—Selling a portable, mechanical phonograph with 15 popular & western records. $14. Contact Tuffy Briggs. Miners' Hospital.

REAL PEARLS—Nicest pearl necklace you'll ever see. Must sell by end of the month. Call Red O'Sullivan. 869-H.

Ritz Theater Closed Until Further Notice. Buddy Ritz Missing in Korea.

Chapter 20
RUNNING INTO THE PIT

I'M NOT THE ONLY ONE when I get to the field at midnight—there's Cruz and Tony standing around Mr. Mackenzie in T-shirts and shorts same as me, their football shoes already laced. Alonzo Cushman, Lupe Diaz, Ricky Sanchez, and Marty Quesada are here, too. Pretty much most of the team. Except for Rudy and Wallinger.

"I called you all here," Mr. Mackenzie says—he's wearing a miner's helmet and the carbide lamp shines over us like bursts from a meteor shower—"because I know you can keep quiet about what we're about to do."

"Where's Wallinger?" Cruz asks.

"He's in Prescott for a job interview I arranged," Mr. Mackenzie says. "He'll be back tomorrow afternoon in time for practice. He's still the interim coach while Coach Hansen's recuperating in the hospital."

"Hank Wallinger can't help you win." It's Pete Zolnich talking. He's been sitting in the bleachers where there's no

192

light. We all turn and watch him come over. "Wallinger's from Cottonville, and he's as selfish as they come," Zolnich sniffs, turning on his carbide lamp.

"Peter's able to be here with us because, well, we've decided to take matters into our own hands," Mr. Mac explains. "So Sheriff Doddy has issued a special dispensation for him to be released from jail until the football season's over."

"Since it's an emergency." Zolnich smiles. "The sheriff was a Mucker in twenty-four, too, when we won the Northern title against Flagstaff, like you're gonna, though I wish Sims could be here, too."

"The English teacher?" Tony asks.

Zolnich shakes his head. "Not that whiny nut. His father."

"Tuffy Briggs will be keeping time during the drills," Mr. Mackenzie says.

Cruz's brother Manny comes out from behind the bleachers, still looking fit and towering over Tuffy's wheelchair, which he's pushing onto the field, and I haven't seen Tuffy come out of the miners' hospital since Maw's been there.

"That's right." Tuffy holds up the stopwatch he had tucked in his wheelchair.

"But there's no train to race at this hour," Tony says.

"You won't be racing the train," Mr. Mackenzie says. "You'll be racing against yourselves."

Zolnich starts taking out helmets from a net bag and lines them up on the field. "You want to win, don't you?" he says.

"But the town's dying," Melvin Sneep murmurs.

"You never die if you win," Manny says. "And if you win this time, it'll make going under in that big hole bearable." He points to the open pit. "No matter where the mine is you get transferred to."

"That's why we can't lose," I say.

"No way we'll lose," Cruz says. Tony and the others agree.

"We'll show you how to win," Zolnich says. "Like we did against those Flagstaff Warriors."

"Slag and rocks weren't enough," Mr. Mackenzie adds. "You need the endurance of a miner. Ready, Tuffy?"

Manny wheels Tuffy to the edge of the pit.

"Follow me, boys," Mr. Mackenzie says.

"Are we getting thrown into the pit?" Melvin asks.

"We want you to be stronger to win, not dead," Zolnich tells him. "You need to build strength to beat the Warriors. They're twice the size of you."

"Now take a helmet," Mr. Mackenzie tells us, and I realize those aren't football helmets on the ground, but miner hard hats like the one he's wearing.

"We're going down there?" Alonzo asks.

"Might as well get used to it," Lupe says. "For when we get to Ajo. Nobody's fitter than a hard-rock miner."

"Coach Hansen trained us on these ledges," Manny says. "So that we'd be strong enough to play both ends once we got to Flag."

"Took it right out of Coach Kerr's playbook from twenty-four," Tuffy says. "It worked."

"Go single file running down the ledges, then sprint back up once you get to the bottom," Mr. Mackenzie explains. "And make sure your light's on. After three nights of this you'll be faster on the way up, I can assure you." He eyes Melvin. "That's the goal anyhow. Who wants to go first?"

I put on my helmet. "I will."

"You've never been down there before, Ugly," Cruz says. "Sure you don't want me to go first?"

"Not this time."

"I'll be right behind you, then."

Manny makes his way down and says he'll meet us at the bottom.

"How do we stop ourselves from slipping?" Melvin asks.

"If it can hold a hundred-ton shovel, it'll hold you," Zolnich says. "Just don't look into the pit, and stay on the wall side. Now get going."

I run into the darkness with nothing but a narrow beam from my lamp to show me the wall. The ledges are hard-packed and not too steep, but Melvin's right: the footing's slippery and it's hard to get a toehold, especially once the first ledge quits. The only way to the next one is by side-stepping into a sharp slide down a path that's a vertical drop.

Nobody's saying anything behind me as we go deeper, trying to miss the unseen divots that could trip us up, hidden in a surface no wider than a pickup truck, and there's no sign of Manny up ahead.

"Keep your knees up high," Cruz shouts, nearly clipping my heels. He seems to know what it's like down here pretty well, running sideways—even off the slopes—and could overtake me if he wanted to.

I run down another ledge, snatching a glimpse skyward to where we came from. But I can't see Mr. Mackenzie or Tuffy or Zolnich, and it seems impossible to make your way out of here when you're in this deep, like being trapped inside a box made of stone with the lid barely open—just enough to see the stars and how far away they are from down here.

I catch sight of the burning pyres of ore to my left down below as I slide into the final ledge, where the air thins out—though that doesn't make any sense—collecting in the middle of the pit like a smoke signal. It's sour and stronger than the sulfur that hits us by the time it gets to the school after a blast, and I don't know how Pop's done this all these years.

Some of the guys start coughing and I try not to breathe it in, but I'm winded and it stings going down.

"The last ledge gives out in ten paces," Cruz says.

He's smiling at me from above like he's enjoying seeing me sweating and feeling trapped. Cruz never seems to feel that way.

Then another voice calls out, "First time you've ever been down here, huh, kid?" I see the carbide light before I can make out who it is as I hit the bottom of the pit. I thought we'd be alone somehow, with just Manny waiting for us when we got here, but there's a crew of about a dozen miners, eyes wider than ringtails' and lined with soot, looking at me, grinning. They start clapping, then somebody yells, "Good goin', Red. Your pop never thought you'd be down here."

"Welcome to the jungle," Manny says.

"Don't get used to it," Cruz says when he reaches me.

"I won't."

"Time for target practice." Manny points to me as Diaz and Quesada make it down. "The rest of you guys start heading back up."

Manny's lined up ten footballs on the rocky floor about forty feet from the shovel and the rail track it's mounted on. "That's how Coach Hansen got Bobby ready for Flagstaff," Manny explains, looking up at the dipper stick of the bucket. "Shovel precision. Nothing like it to get your throws higher and away from those Warrior fingers.

"You've got ten shots and thirty seconds to hit the bucket where I put it," Manny says, tossing me the first ball. "I can still throw, you know, even if I'm missing a few fingers. Your body adjusts. Sometimes faster than anything else does."

The rest of the shovel crew gathers around me, pointing their carbide lamps at the shovel as Manny climbs up to the controls. I focus on the mouth of the bucket, thirty feet up, and its row of bottom teeth. I can see the arc of its swing in my head and shoot for where I think it'll go, and I connect on the first try. The miners clap and start yelling, "Do it again," and I do—over and over—just like I did with those ducks at the fiesta. Then the shovel rotates and lurches low to the ground and I hit the boom instead, so Manny bobs it up and to the short side. I nick both the dipper stick and the bucket.

Manny puts up his eight fingers. "Eight out of ten. Not bad, Red."

I look back and Tony's putting Melvin on his shoulders. "For balance," Tony says, laughing, as he turns to go back up. "What you got, rocks in your pocket?" Tony asks him.

"I gained twelve pounds since the season started," Melvin says. "I guess all that fighting with the bus helps."

"Tuffy's still timing you," Manny tells me. "Better get back up there."

The rest of the miners collect at the base of the ledge and shine their lamps along the path to help me see—their eyes hungry for what they believe I can do. I start racing toward the sky, away from the burning ore and out of this box, ignoring the sting in my own body, the sweaty ribbons of sulfur smoke whirling all around me. I pass Tony, and Melvin waves, but I focus on the faces of those miners, coated in soot and hopeful, and on how Bobby must have done the same thing, racing up these ledges and feeling the need like I do right now, wanting to make them feel puffed up and proud.

"Six minutes and nine seconds," Tuffy tells me when I get back up to the field.

"You're bleeding again," I tell Cruz.

"Bleeding's good."

Tony drops off Melvin next to Tuffy.

"You'll be doing the same drill twice more," Mr. Mackenzie says. "Saturday and Monday at midnight. That should make you good and ready to take on Flagstaff."

"How'd you get permission from Ruffner to stop a shift from running for an hour in the first place?" I ask.

"I didn't get permission from William Ruffner," Mr. Mackenzie says. "I got it from your father."

Chapter 21
NEXT TO NO SHOT

WE COULD SURE USE RAIN, it's been so dusty around here. Every time I shoot the football through that tire and it lands on home plate, it churns up a dust storm and I have to wait for the clouds to settle before throwing again. I know it's too early for anyone to be at the school except Charlie, but I can see the sidewalk from here, and Mr. Mackenzie should be walking across it anytime now. I'm hoping he'll know something more about Coach.

It only takes two more throws before I hear Mr. Mac as he comes around the corner in his pin-striped suit. He sees me right off and walks over, saying "Good morning," dropping his cane in the coldenia behind the fence, and lifting up the tire to forty-five degrees. I'm trying to figure out if the "good morning" is really a good morning like things are going well, or if it's a good morning like you have to grin and bear it because if you don't, you just might start welling up not knowing if the tears will stop when you want them to.

"Any news about Coach?" I ask, hurling the ball through the tire. It goes through without skimming the sides and Mr. Mac looks pleased.

"You're looking much stronger, Felix, just in time for the game with Flagstaff. Looks like all that ledge work helped."

"That and Faye Miller bringing me all those casseroles."

He nods and holds the tire up a notch higher.

"I've seen her little boy," I say. "It's good she . . . kept going. With her life, I mean. Got married. Do you know her husband?"

Mr. Mackenzie lowers the tire and scoops up the football. "No, I don't, Felix. But her son, Samuel, he's really taking to the school and he sure loves football." He tosses the ball back and I aim for the tire again.

"I remember the first time Ben Hansen saw this town and this tire," Mr. Mackenzie says. "He asked if we were supposing there'd be a flood and we'd all hang on to that tire and go swinging over the baseball field. I brought him here, you know. When nobody thought the T formation would work or a coach from the Midwest for that matter. And you know what? He loved it here. 'This is home, Edward,' he told me after only a year." Mr. Mac holds the tire up higher and I rocket it through again easy, then wait for him to collect the ball.

"Is the hospital letting him take visitors yet, I mean . . . other than his family?" I ask.

Mr. Mac puts his hands in his pockets, then kicks up some dust with his wingtip. "There's a good chance we're gonna lose him, Felix. And if we do, it will be a sad day."

My heart and my mind go racing for the right words but they won't come.

All I hear is Mr. Mac saying how he knows how fond I

am of Coach and that he and Coach are friends—just like me and Cruz—and I don't know what I'd do if Cruz was in that Cottonville hospital right now with nearly no shot at making it.

"Everybody thinks a coach just wants to win for himself and some people think that about Ben Hansen, too, he's so driven," Mr. Mac says. "But that's never been why Ben does all this. You know what he told me just last week? He said, 'Isn't it funny how they've saved me the best team for last? We're gonna take it, Edward—the state championship. You know what that would mean to the boys if they won it? How different they'd feel for the rest of their lives? That's what I can see for them. I can taste it, Ed. That Yavapai Cup trophy's been earmarked for them.'"

THE ARIZONA DOMINION
THE STATE'S BEST NEWSPAPER

Phoenix, Arizona   *Friday, October 13, 1950*   *Five Cents*

SPORTS CENTRAL
Phoenix-Flagstaff Gridiron Showdown Expected

The reigning state football champions, the Phoenix United Coyotes, are one victory away from getting a chance to defend their title. The undefeated Coyotes host Mesa on Saturday in what is expected to be a rout.

In the North, Flagstaff seems certain to take it all, with only a scrappy but undersized Hatley team standing in their way. Those two face off in Flagstaff tonight. The likely Phoenix-Flagstaff state championship game would be Oct. 21 in Flagstaff.

"We're not looking past anyone," said P.U.

coach Pug Johnson, who admitted that his players have been studying film of Flagstaff's most recent games. "We beat Mesa by 35 points last year, so we're confident. And Hatley's the smallest team in the state, so don't expect much from them."

Chapter 22
BITTERSWEET

FRIDAY, OCTOBER 13
8:40 P.M.

THE LAST TIME A MUCKER team beat Flagstaff, Bobby was quarterback with Manny his top receiver, and every lineman on that '41 squad as big as Tony.

We've held the Warriors scoreless for half a game instead of letting them run roughshod over us like the papers predicted. It's been a physical game and not very clean—two unnecessary-roughness penalties against Flagstaff and one on us. Cruz let his temper gallop onto the field again and hit a receiver about five yards out-of-bounds. But none of that is the same as beating them—we haven't scored yet either.

But we've run the ledges, same as Bobby's team, and Mr. Mackenzie says we're faster than they were. Manny does, too. They both drove up to watch us play. Zolnich isn't allowed to leave town or he'd have been here, too. And if the mine wasn't closing, we'd have a whole lot more people rooting for us under these pines. Must be at least three thousand Warrior fans in the stadium, which is the biggest we've played in

203

all year. Most of them are dressed in Warrior colors—green and white—like Christmas candy.

We're sitting in the locker room—which is the size of our auditorium—waiting for Wallinger. He's been in the john for the entire halftime, he's so nervous. The folding chairs are cold as icicles and start vibrating with the sound of those Warrior cheers, so I get up, clench a fist, and punch it into my palm.

"Wonder what Coach Hansen would tell us right about now?" Lupe says.

Cruz lifts my throwing arm up high. "He'd say that we've got the O'Sullivan magic! Isn't that what Coach told us when we first started this season?"

"And that we're Muckers," Tony says.

"What do Muckers do?" I start chanting. "Muckers fight!"

"No matter what pit you're in," Cruz adds.

"Remember the ledges?" I tell them. "All that running up and down?" I start pounding on the seat of a chair. "Flag kept bringing in subs the first half, but they couldn't wear us down. The second half belongs to us."

Wallinger finally comes out of the john with a cap on like Coach Hansen's and barks, "Let's get out there and win." But there's no way he could ever be like Coach, or we could be like Bobby's team—we've got to be even better.

* * *

"We're throwing the ball this half," I say to Cruz. "Get open."

He slips past his defender and I send him a long, high pass on the first play, like I was aiming for the bucket of that shovel. I get hammered to the ground, but by the time I get to my feet Cruz is all the way to the ten-yard line. Next play I find him in the end zone, and we're up 6–0.

The passing seems to loosen up their side, too. Flagstaff marches right down the field in about six plays and takes the lead, 7–6.

I get sacked on our next possession, then take a vicious hit on an incomplete pass. My nose smashes against the turf and the lights blind me for a second when I turn, making me think about Coach. "The lowly Muckers"—isn't that what he'd told me?—"against the mighty Warriors . . ." I catch a whiff of the grass and shake my head clear.

"No penalty?" I ask the ref. "He hit me five seconds after I threw it!"

The referee just shakes his head. The Flagstaff tackle—built like the ponderosas lining the stadium—points a finger at me. "Get used to it," he says.

Early in the fourth quarter I find Cruz with a bullet in the center of the field. He breaks a tackle and crosses midfield before they bring him down.

As we huddle up, I see Cruz's forehead is starting to bleed again. But at least six of us are bleeding, so who cares? I've got a cut above my thumb and a gash on my shin.

"They're winded," Cruz says. "Keep up the pressure!"

I hand off to Lupe, but he's stopped before he reaches the line. I pitch to Cruz for an end-around, but they maul him after two yards. And then I throw an incompletion with too much pressure from their line.

Fourth down. Wallinger is signaling for us to punt. I ignore him.

"Tony, Alonzo, hold the line!" I say. I call another pass play and stare straight at Cruz. He scowls and says, "Just get me the ball."

But Cruz is covered tight and our guys can only hold the line so long. I scramble toward the sideline, then Lupe throws a block—it's beautiful, and one that Coach Hansen would be proud of. I've got daylight ahead. I streak down the sideline with everything I've got, and Cruz comes out of nowhere to cut down their safety and set me free to score. I hit the twenty then the ten and keep going for the longest run of my life—forty-six yards—and suddenly we're back on top.

They block Quesada's extra-point attempt, but we've got the lead and the momentum. It's 12–7.

Flag starts rolling up the yardage after the kickoff. Nothing big, just a steady stream of four-, five-, six-yard runs up the middle. Alonzo is wearing down. Lupe drops to one knee and stares at the sky between plays. Cruz curses under his breath.

Their size is getting to us. "Remember the ledges!" I yell.

The clock is ticking down and we might never get the ball back. All Flagstaff needs is a touchdown to win the crown.

They're at our seven-yard line and the quarterback is barking signals. I inch toward the line, expecting another running play, but he drops back to pass.

Their receiver has a step on me and he's sprinting toward the end zone. I hear a crash in the backfield and look over. Tony's broken through the line and laid out the quarterback. The ball pops loose. Players from both sides dive for it and I can't tell who recovers.

Alonzo leaps up from the pile, holding the pigskin. I shake my fist and race toward him, smacking him on the back.

I try to catch my breath as we huddle. We're backed up near our goal line and need to get out of here. I call for a simple handoff to Lupe. He never fumbles. But he loses a yard on this one.

Cruz grabs my jersey. "Throw it," he says. "I'll get open."

I drop straight back and look for Cruz, but two defensive

linemen are on top of me in a second. I dodge past them and fire a short pass over the middle. Cruz grabs it on the run and angles toward the sideline. I sprint upfield, too, hoping to throw a block.

Two defenders crash into Cruz, and almost without thinking I yell, "Over here!" I'm in a full sprint as Cruz flips the ball to me, and suddenly I'm in the clear again. There's no one within ten yards of me as I race full throttle until I hit pay dirt.

That should seal it. Less than two minutes to play and we're two scores ahead. The Flagstaff fans are dead quiet. Our guys are going nuts.

"Nice run, Ugly!" Cruz says, smacking my helmet. "Northern champs!"

"Not yet," I say, dizzy and puffing. "Play defense!"

It gets even rougher, but we don't break. I'm still out of breath as the final seconds tick away, but I'm so excited I don't even care. We're Northern champions. We run off the field holding our helmets in the air.

* * *

12:30 A.M.

The stadium went all quiet after the final gun sounded, and I thought somebody had been shot. First time I thought that in all the time I've been playing. And I closed my eyes, hoping Coach was still alive. They still won't let anyone see him except his wife. Cruz says that means he's going to die, but Coach nearly died a few times before in combat and made it through. Worst thing about it is, he's in Cottonville, since the miners' hospital isn't equipped for operations anymore. But I can't imagine him missing the championship game. Looks like we'll be playing Phoenix.

The bus ride home's been quiet. Mostly the guys are sunk

into their letterman jackets, dozing off in the seats and looking pretty beat up. Rudy's near the front by himself, making
conversation with Wallinger, who's driving with a stupid-ass
grin on his face, like he's the new coach or something. They
should've suspended Rudy for what he did to Coach, but
they said it was an accident and we only have twelve players
left on the team.

I look over at Cruz, who's sitting in the row ahead of me
staring out the window. But it's dark and you can't make
things out, especially through the frosty parts of the glass.
We're too deep in the mountains to see any stars.

"One more win," I whisper to him. "And the town'll go
wild." I know that's what he'd want me to say, so I say it, trying to get back to how things were before that practice, and
maybe even before Rabbit left.

"Do what you did tonight, and we could beat Phoenix
right now," Cruz says. He can barely see through the eye
that's puffed up blue. "Then my father could be there." Cruz
makes an effort to smile, pounding his bloody knuckles
together. "His shift starts the day after next, so the whole
family's leaving for Ajo tomorrow. Except me and Manny.
Guess I'll go when I graduate," he whispers. "Unless things
change."

"So, just you guys and Angie are staying?" I ask.

"Uh-uh. Just Manny and me for now. Angie's going, too."

Angie...leaving? This bus is going too slow. If I could, I'd
jump out the window, sprint all the way home, and find her.

"Hey," Lupe says. "Look at all the candles." The rest of
the guys come over to our side of the bus and Cruz clears a
circle on the window, then points to our mountain. Hundreds of lights, flickering red and orange, are sprinkled
across the Barrio.

"They're doing everything they can to make Coach live," Cruz says. He and Lupe make the sign of the cross, pressing their fingers against their lips.

She never told me she was leaving. I was counting on her staying. And I don't want to think about what's left for me after Angie's gone. I look out the window at the candles and hope that Coach will make it. But a part of me feels like it's me who's already dying.

* * *

1:05 A.M.

Cruz said Angie's working the graveyard shift at the Exchange, so I go to the booth across the street and dial the operator as soon as the bus pulls out and the rest of the guys have headed home.

"How may I direct your call?" Angie says.

I didn't think I'd get her straightaway. I thought for sure it would be Mrs. Rodriguez. "Nowhere," I mumble, hesitating. "I mean, not to somebody else. To you."

"Who's this?"

"It's Red."

There's a pause, and I get this panicky feeling like she might hang up on me.

"And you don't want to call anybody?" Angie says.

"I'm calling you."

"Red, have you been drinking?"

"No."

"And this isn't some sort of dare?"

"Course not. I'm in the phone booth across the street. By myself."

I look up at the window and Cuca Hernandez's face is pressed against it. Angie's right behind with her headpiece on, all flustered because she's trying to open the window, only it's locked.

"I need to direct the call," Angie hollers at me after getting the window up. "It can't just stay here. It has to go somewhere else."

"How about here?" I quit talking into the receiver and open the booth door. "I could hang up," I yell over to her, "and you can call me right here."

Cuca sticks her head out the window. "Hey, Red," she yells. "Nice going! Heard you beat Flag. But don't stop there. Maybe we'll get that state championship yet. Won't Phoenix fall over!"

"We won," I tell Angie, trying to make her smile.

"Is that what you called me up for? To tell me you won? Don't you think I know that? It's all the Valley's talking about on every line."

"'Cept you."

"Uh-oh," Cuca says, dipping her head back in.

"When were you gonna tell me, Angie?"

"Tell you what?"

"That you're leaving."

"Red, we shouldn't be talking like this."

"You're right." I hang up the phone, climb those stairs to the Hatley Exchange, and knock on the door.

"It's him," I can hear Cuca saying. "Better get that, Angie. I know it's not for me."

"I can't talk now," Angie says, opening the door a crack. "I'm working."

"Don't you get a break or something?"

"I already took it."

"I'll cover for you," Cuca says, opening the door wider. "I wouldn't miss this for the world."

I follow Angie down the stairwell and through the alley-way onto Main, feeling like there's a million miles between us and I don't know why. When we get to the pool, I open the gate and Angie looks back, surprised that I'm going in there.

"Come on," I tell her. The pool's still filled—they won't drain it until Armistice Day—and I lean against the ladder to the high diving board, trying not to look into her eyes or I'll start fumbling, forgetting what I came to say. "What were you gonna do, just leave without saying goodbye?"

Angie starts biting her lip. "I was going to tell you," she says, folding her arms.

"Oh yeah? When? You're leaving tomorrow."

"I thought you'd be happy for me. At least, I won't be in Hatley anymore, stuck in the Barrio. Any place is better than here."

"*I'm* here."

"What am I supposed to do, Red, wait for you until they say it's okay for us to be together? I don't want to sneak into the movie theater, and it's too cold to swim in the Verde."

"We're at the pool right now, aren't we?"

"Yeah, and it's past midnight. Nobody can see us."

"I can change that. *Hey, everybody! Look! I'm with Angie!*"

"Shhh," she whispers, tugging at my arm. "I nearly got fired when Mrs. Rodriguez saw me looking at you at the fiesta. Now she can't decide if she'll give me a reference."

"I don't care, Angie." I reach for her chin, but she turns away and I can't see those eyes. "Come on, can't you stay until the championship game?"

She shakes her head. "Papá's shift starts Monday. You'll just have to win without me."

"I don't want to."

Angie finally turns to me and her lips start quivering. "We can't always get everything we want, can we?" she says. "I'll be in Ajo. Besides, two years is a long time to wait."

"A heart doesn't go changing all of a sudden and falling for someone else," I tell her.

"Who says I've fallen in the first place?"

I have to take a seat on the low diving board after that one; the wind's knocked out of me, and it feels worse than a punch in the gut.

Angie sits on my lap, stroking my hair like you would a puppy dog stung by a scolding. "At least, I'll never be a Wolf," she says, kissing my ear.

If it meant her staying, I sure wouldn't mind.

"It hurts too much," she whispers, "when you know you can't have what you want and even if you could you still can't. Not really. They'd make it so it wouldn't be right, somehow."

"If we really believed that was true, then we'd never even be here—me and you—and there wouldn't be a championship game on our field next week."

"And what happens after that, Red? What will you do?"

Wait for you is what I want to say. I'd wait a hundred years for her and even then I'd float above her somewhere—and wait some more. But the fact is I don't even know if Angie wants me.

"I have to get back," she says, rushing out the gate.

And I let her.

I lean back against the diving board and just lie there, looking at the stars, feeling dazed, until the old velvet box slips out of my jacket. The one with Maw's pearls in it that I've been carrying for a while, and I wish I could give them to Angie. It's getting awful crowded in my head and I don't want to think anymore. I guess I don't feel much like looking past winning either, if losing her hurts this much.

THE VERDE MINER

Twice-Weekly News of the Mountain

HATLEY, ARIZONA   SATURDAY, OCTOBER 14, 1950   FIVE CENTS A COPY

WEEKEND EDITION

BREAKING NEWS: Muckers Upset Flag to Win Northern Crown.
Going for State Title. O'Sullivan hero of the game. **Full story in next edition.**

Weekly Roundup: Cases Give Sheriff Busy Week

"This was the busiest week I've had since I've been in office," Hatley Sheriff Web Doddy said. Cases brought before him ranged from rape to a shooting.

—On a charge of rape, **Len Harper** of Hatley was bound over to superior court. The act was said to have been committed Friday night near the path up from the Gulch. The young Cottonville woman, unmarried, claimed she was forcefully taken into the mesquite brush.

—**Mr. and Mrs. Lloyd Pratty** received treatment for gunshot wounds after their neighbor, **Dell Bruzzi**, allegedly fired the shots. Bruzzi is being held in the county jail. Returning from a Bisbee trip, the Prattys found jewelry missing. Going next door, Mrs. Pratty accused Bruzzi's young daughter of taking it. Bruzzi warned Mr. Pratty not to come into the yard, which he did, and shots were fired, though Pratty's gun did not leave its holster. Bruzzi, who was a conductor at Eureka Copper's depot but not offered a transfer, was found hiding in the Gulch by Sheriff

213

Doddy. No jewelry was located in the Bruzzi home.

—Mine superintendent **Harold "Wimpy" Elton** posted a $500 reward for information leading to the arrest and conviction of the persons responsible for siphoning gasoline from Eureka Copper company vehicles. Sabotage with intent to cause a fatal accident was also indicated when sugar was found in gasoline left in a masher tank.

* * *

Monday, October 16, 1950

Dear Red,

Bet you'd never believe I'd be in Korea by now. Well here I am. They put me in a mortar company when they heard about me being from Hatley and all that dynamite we use to blow up the mine. I didn't exactly tell them I came straight from school. There's plenty of guys younger than me in this outfit and a Korean orphan boy who just won't leave us.

There's mountains everywhere. We're hiding out in them. When I first saw them it reminded me of Hatley and they've got the mud too. I changed my mind. It's gotten so cold you can barely think and there's only two pair of socks between Leo and me. Plus the pair he just found. Leo's from Louisiana so he's even colder. He's a Negro. Must be seven feet tall, I swear and real polite, offering to put the wet socks against his skin to dry overnight. I know where he got them. Off a dead soldier. But the Commie gooks stole the army boots and the socks looked big enough for Leo and were dry with no holes in them or anything. That's what they call the enemy out here. Commie gooks. They attack at night too,

214

blowing horns and making more noise than Crazy
Zolnich does when he goes after the drunks.

You beat Cottonville yet? Tell Coach Hansen I'll
write about it when I get home. Guess who's lighter
I'm using. You have to smoke just to keep your
fingers warm enough to fire.

Yours truly,

Rabbit

Pvt. Salvatore G. Palermo

Chapter 23
CHURCH MONEY

THE LATE-DAY SUN CAN BARELY cut through the stained-glass windows in the rectory as I kneel to get out the envelope from my gym bag, watching the trail of dirt from my cleats cake onto the carpet. Mrs. Robinson ended up buying Maw's pearls for the jewelry store, so now I can pay for the pew. There's no way Father's taking Bobby's nameplate away from us.

I didn't expect anyone else to be here, but there's a younger priest sitting beside Father Pierre in the front pew. I keep kneeling and listen to what he's saying.

"I'm afraid there won't be any money allotted for the leaky roof," he says. "Not with the mine closing. As difficult as it is, Father, you have to accept that this town is dying."

"You're wrong!" Father says in a harsh tone. "The people in Hatley depend on this church. That's more important than any mine."

"I'm sorry, Father. But with so many parishioners leaving, the diocese has to consider how long the parish should remain open."

I start coughing and they look my way.

"I brought the money for the pew," I tell Father Pierre. But he's distracted. "Leave it by the statue of Mother Mary, where it will be blessed," he says. Then he looks at my uniform and frowns. "You're still playing without a coach? What for?"

"Because we're gonna win the championship."

Father Pierre shakes his head. "See how my work is needed here with such cockiness?" he says. "When the town believes in football instead of God?"

The young priest smiles. "I think they call it spirit, Father. Team spirit." Then he turns to me. "You said the money's for a pew?" he asks.

I nod.

"No one pays for going to church anymore, son," he says. "There's plenty of room. You don't have to worry about leaving money for your pew."

I almost feel sorry for Father Pierre, looking so stunned, except he's so self-righteous. Even when his church is crumbling.

"You should be at the game," I tell him, but I don't stay and wait for his reaction. I know Father Pierre's hold on this town is slipping and it's got nothing to do with football.

THE VERDE MINER

Twice-Weekly News of the Mountain

HATLEY, ARIZONA   WEDNESDAY, OCTOBER 18, 1950   FIVE CENTS A COPY

MID-WEEK EDITION

Hatley Coach Ben Wylie Hansen Dies

Ben Wylie Hansen, head coach and director of physical educa-tion of Hatley schools, passed away yesterday in the Cottonville hospital where he was taken after suddenly becoming ill earlier this month. A meningitis infection aggravated by a condition resulting from a head injury received while in military service was said to be the cause of death.

Services will be held tomorrow afternoon at 2:30 in the Hatley High School auditorium. Father Pierre LaSalle will officiate.

Coach Hansen was born March 4, 1917, in Missouri. He was graduated from Springfield Union High School in 1934 and attended Southwest Missouri State Teachers College, where he received a bachelor of arts degree and a master of arts degree. His first assignment as a coach was in Fort Apache, Ariz., and in 1940 he came to Hatley.

On leave in 1943 to enter service with the U.S. Infantry, Hansen received severe head injuries when a gasoline motor on a moving target exploded at Fort Benning, Ga. He returned to his coaching duties at the Hatley schools in 1945.

Survivors include his wife, Eleanor; a son, Homer Wylie, age 4; his parents, Mr. and Mrs. R. O. Hansen, Springfield, Mo.; three sisters and a brother.

Mine Closes. Last Copper Ingot Poured

For the first time in 20 years, no dense plume of white smoke arose from the smelter stack at Cottonville, and the shovels were silent in Hatley's open pit. The last charge of copper was poured at the end of the day shift at 3:30 Tuesday, the oil flow to reverberatories was stopped and fires were pulled at 6 o'clock. Approximately 500 Eureka Copper mining employees will be transferred to Ajo or Bisbee, with Cottonville schools set to close also. **Full story, p.2.**

WANT ADS

STILL LOST—Black-and-white hound branded T over C on right rump. Last seen at Carsen's Lumber near Bitter

218

Creek. Has Casillas on brass plate of collar. Does not bite. Answers to Chalupa. RE-WARD. Phone 186-H.

PIANO TO TRADE— Willing to trade nearly new spinet piano for sewing ma-chine or comparable trade. See Mrs. Featherhoff. Upper Main, Hatley.

CHEAP—Extra-good 2-wheel trailer, or will swap for firewood. Vince Palermo. Hogback Bakery.

STATE CHAMPIONSHIP FOOTBALL
THE NORTH VS. THE SOUTH
HATLEY vs. PHOENIX UNITED

• *Arizona's only undefeated teams* •
SATURDAY, OCT. 21 | KICKOFF AT 3 P.M.
— RUFFNER FIELD, HATLEY —

Chapter 24
TEARS WON'T COME

THERE'S NO WAY THE SACRED Heart of Mary could have held us. As it is, folks are leaning against the sides of the bleachers in the auditorium, clinging to their kids and telling them to hush.

Cruz is beside me, staring at his knees. Tony's on my left, too wide for the chair. He's leaning forward like he's set for a tackle, only his knuckles are clenched and he's wearing a collar so starched it's cutting into his neck and chafing it red as chopped meat.

We just mumbled "Sorry" to Mrs. Hansen when it got to be our turn and watched Homer squirming around her ankles, his hair combed and spit-polished in place, while he played with his football until his grandmother took him away.

Now we're in the front row—they've kept it open for the team—and it hurts even more watching Mrs. Hansen from here, standing there alone, the black veil covering those swollen eyes and her bottom lip trembling as her hand gets shook by the steady stream of newcomers. Some of them were supposed to be in Ajo already. And then there were the Cottonville Wolves, and coaches who traveled a whole lot farther than from Flagstaff to pay their respects.

"Look who's here," Lupe Diaz says from a few seats over.

Rudy. He's in line like everybody else, with Mrs. Hansen about to shake his hand as if he wasn't a murderer and didn't kill Coach.

"No way he should be here," Cruz says, grinding his teeth.

How could Rudy show up for this?

He walks past us looking for a seat and I stare him down. Tony pounds his fist on the empty chair beside him and Rudy's face twitches. He goes around and slips into the row behind us.

Francisco comes up with Paradiso and sprinkles the coffin with his holy wand. "Darn mule," Mrs. Dearing sniffs, saying it shouldn't be allowed. But Francisco's never hurt anybody, and he won't go anywhere without Paradiso.

Homer runs up and gives the burro a hug. He starts crying pretty hard and won't let go of Paradiso's peppery mane until Francisco hands him a few pecans to feed the burro. "It's my birfday next week," he tells Francisco. "I'm gonna be five."

Faye Miller's behind them with her boy. "I'm seven," he says.

"Silly goose, you're not that old." Faye blushes, rubbing his curly head.

Francisco nods at Faye and gives her a slight smile.

Then Father Pierre steps from behind the stage curtain and lowers his palm for the band to be seated, and I want to cry, but the tears won't come.

Bobby's coffin was closed, too. Coach is too beat up for us to see, I know that, and he'd never want us to, not looking that way. But with Bobby everyone knew he wasn't inside. That his *remains* were never recovered. Manny said that meant he was either blown to smithereens or stuck in a cave they couldn't get to without burning up and dying.

Why'd they have a coffin anyhow? I'd kept asking Maw. *Bobby never came back.* But all she told me was to sit up straight, and that Father Pierre knew what was proper. And I suppose it was there for something to look at, to make it seem real for us, and everyone behind our pew feeling sorry, but mostly glad they weren't O'Sullivans.

I'd come home from school and found the screen door wedged open and Cussie's mom crying inside while Father Pierre stood over Maw, her head lying sideways on the kitchen table like it wasn't part of her anymore.

He's the one who told me about Bobby. It came out all echoed, like the Father wasn't really talking to me or about Bobby, the syllables passing over my head then floating up to the ceiling. *Haven't millions of soldiers gone to war?* That's what I could really hear, the voice inside my head, telling me how common the names *Robert* and *O'Sullivan* must be and how could they know for sure? But then the words *killed* and *dead* ricocheted off the tin, slapping me in the face so hard and sudden my knees buckled.

Cruz was there. He took my shoulder and walked me down the Barrio to his house. I must've slept awhile on the little cot by the fire, because when I came to, Francisco was smiling at me with his corn-kernel teeth.

And Mrs. V, she fed me soup with golden noodles. That got my tongue all fiery, and Cruz's brothers and sisters laughed, especially Angie, who said my hair must be made of carrots. I didn't mind any of it. For the first time since they'd told me about Bobby, I'd felt something.

They found me a black coat, wrapped a cross around my neck along with a medallion of Saint Christopher, and hoisted me up on Paradiso.

Francisco led the procession up Gulch Lane to my house, the Vs on either side of me, stopping only to let the women with their rosaries add sacks of food to my burro. Then a man called out, *"¡Viva Roberto!"* and the cavalcade raised their candles or pictures of Bobby with their sons and grandsons holding up the Northern Crown.

They left them on the steps while Francisco gave our house a good splash with his holy water. When Maw came to the door, Mrs. Villanueva handed her a loaf of warm bread covered up in a towel. "Thank you for coming!" Maw said, smiling the way paper dolls do, like she was having a party or going to the Elks Ball at the Lodge, back when Pop was the Exalted Ruler. And I wanted to go back to the Barrio with the others right then, to that little house flickering with candlelight, where it was safe and warm and alive. Where they talked about Bobby like he still mattered without going into hiding or keeping anything in.

"There's a bounty on Rudy's head," Cruz whispers. "It wasn't no meningitis that killed Coach. It was Rudy. If he steps one foot in the Barrio, they'll shoot him in the heart, I swear."

Tony leans back and tilts his chair toward me. "He can stay up on the hill but he can't hide," he says. "And there's no *santos* who will save him."

I glance over at Melvin, pale and scrawny, sitting next to Verdugo and his broken collarbone. If Rudy doesn't play, we'll have to bring Melvin in, or we forfeit the championship. But Melvin Sneep could cost us the game.

"It'll be a waste if we don't win it," Cruz says. "May as well be in that coffin."

I tell Cruz that we'll win because we have to. There's no way Phoenix United's got the same kind of pain stuck inside. Our speed will carry us, and we can work the slag to our advantage. It's what Coach wanted for us.

Angie, too.

I found a note from her in my locker this morning. I don't know how it got there. "Win or lose," it said, "you've given Hatley hope." She said Ajo isn't so far, just a hundred miles past Phoenix.

Hope. That's what you need to get through the pain.

Homer's still burrowing his head into Paradiso, and I wonder what it'll be like for Coach's boy. He's got a good mother. I suppose she'll move on, too.

I try to get a picture of Bobby back in my head, but his face changes into Coach's and then Angie's, and that's not supposed to happen at a funeral.

Homer finally lets go of Paradiso. He throws his little football and it hits the coffin. Father Pierre stops then stutters, adjusting his glasses as Homer runs into his mother's arms and buries his face in her bosom.

* * *

Faye Miller's on the porch when I get home from the funeral and the pot roast she's holding is just about the best thing you could smell. Her boy Samuel's on the settee petting Whitey—the side of his suit jacket's covered in fur.

"I thought Whitey would have bit the dust by now. Must be the oldest burro left in Hatley." Faye smiles, trying to keep her purse away from Whitey's gums. "Why don't I put this roast in the Frigidaire before Whitey gets it."

"I want a burro," Samuel says. He giggles as Whitey nibbles at his curls.

"Careful, he just might follow you home," I say. "That burro's too stubborn to leave Hatley—he's got the grazing rights to the whole town."

"Well, stubborn's okay," Faye says. "It helps you keep track of what's important in life."

"Do you and Whitey eat my mom's food all by yourselves?" Samuel asks.

"Well, I got a pop who lives here. But to tell you the truth, I don't always know when he'll show."

"Is he up in heaven, too, like your coach?"

Faye blushes. "Samuel, hush."

"Naw. I had a brother. He's with Coach."

Faye strokes Samuel's hair.

"Does he have orange hair, too?" Samuel asks.

"Yeah . . . but he got all the looks."

Faye comes closer and rests a hand on my shoulder. "Bobby would be so proud of you," she whispers. "And . . ." She hesitates.

There are things I want to ask her, too, like where her husband is, but I don't.

"I brought something else," Faye says. "I think it belongs to you." She takes a box from her purse. It's from Robinson's. "You ought to save these pearls for someone special in your life, Red," she whispers. "And when you do, don't ever miss a chance to let her know how you feel."

"I wanna see the trophy you get for winning the game," Samuel says. "I bet it's bigger than Whitey."

"We'll have to find out, won't we?" I say.

Faye takes Samuel's hand. "We'll be at the game on Saturday. Win or lose, it's just about the greatest thing to happen to this town."

225

Samuel gives Whitey a kiss before leaving, then Faye turns back and looks at me. "I'm proud of you *for* Bobby," she tells me. "How's that?"

"That's just fine," I say softly, putting the box from Robinson's in my pocket and holding on to it—tight.

Chapter 25
GOLDEN WINGS

FRIDAY, OCTOBER 20
5:57 P.M.

I COULD STILL SHOWER IF I wanted to; my locker's not far from the stalls. But I'd have to pass Coach's office, and that doesn't seem right with him not being here. None of the guys felt like doing much after practice, so they headed home to get some rest. Even Cruz. He kept going on about having to wash his car but he did that yesterday. I think he needed to be alone with his thoughts, and I suppose that's true of me, too. Funny how this jersey itches like crazy once the sweat gets into it, but I don't want to take it off just yet and keep looking at the trophies in the case across from my locker.

Somebody put our Northern Crown on the top shelf. Not in the center, but off to the left a bit, like whoever placed it there's saving a spot for the Yavapai Cup. It wouldn't have been Wallinger, that's for sure. He doesn't care enough, and there's no way he feels what we're feeling. It had to be someone who wants that Cup as bad as we do, or who understands us wanting it that much.

I try looking at that Northern Crown one more time from another angle, thinking it might be a split in the glass or something, but it's different from Bobby's from this side, too. The guy punting the ball is kicking it up a vertical line, same as on the other trophy, but he's made of copper, like my coloring, instead of bronze. By the time the copper reaches his forehead, though, it's turned the complexion of Cruz and Tony and most of the guys on the team. And I wonder if the fellow who made it knew what he was doing, and if he figured on the face of that punter burnishing brown like a Mexican Mucker's.

"Careful, if you stare at them long enough they just might come to life," Mr. Mackenzie says. "Seems like neither one of us is ready to leave for the night, are we?" He's lugging a box that looks heavier than a typewriter, and rests it next to my locker before coming over. "Charlie put the Northern Crown in there. Cleaned the rest of them, too, in case you were wondering. He told me he saw you pining over them, looking so forlorn that he went through every key in those stacks of lockboxes until he found the one to get it open."

"Charlie." I nod, leaning my hand against the glass in front of the Northern Crown as if I can touch it. Then I look over at Mr. Mackenzie. "We still don't know where these are going yet, do we? When the school closes."

"I'm afraid not," he murmurs. "I wish I did." He pulls his suit trousers up at the knees and sits on the box. "But what I do know is that it already comes polished. *The Yavapai Cup.* It's at least a foot taller than any of these trophies, and is bronze and copper with golden wings on the soles of the kicker. Like he just sent his dreams soaring into the sky and when they finally landed on the field, they'd come true."

I move my fingers along the glass slowly, to the center of

the top tier where the Cup could be, and I don't know if it's my imagination or the light or what, but it gets really warm. I try to imagine the outline of that trophy. Those wings on the kicker's shoes. "And if we win it, it belongs to us, right?"

Mr. Mac sighs. "Mr. Ruffner owns the property and the school."

"But he wouldn't have earned it."

"No, he wouldn't have." Mr. Mackenzie runs a palm across his face and closes his eyes. "This is my last day at this school, Felix."

I take my hand off the glass and think he's got to be fooling. "What do you mean? Won't you be at the game on Saturday?"

"I would never miss that," he says. "But I'll no longer be principal of this school. I've taken a job at the college in Flagstaff."

"What happened?"

"It will be official on Monday, but it seems that Superintendent Menary has taken the Communist box seriously. Apparently, my name was in it several times. And he's given me the opportunity to leave—his words. But I suppose it's just as well with Cottonville closing, too, and all the surplus of teachers we'll have." Then Mr. Mackenzie takes out a piece of paper from his shirt pocket. "This is where I'll be," he says. "You call me if you need anything, you hear? Marilyn will stay until the end of next week to be with your mother."

He turns to face the trophies. "It's open, by the way," he whispers. "For some reason Charlie's forgotten to lock it, and he won't be making the rounds again until tomorrow morning." Mr. Mackenzie taps on the glass above the lock. "Remember, hope can never be taken away unless you let it," he says. "The future is yours, Felix. And you don't have to stay here either."

THE ARIZONA DOMINION
THE STATE'S BEST NEWSPAPER

Phoenix, Arizona   *Saturday, October 21, 1950*   *Five Cents*

GHOST TOWN BATTLES FOR STATE FOOTBALL TITLE

Clinging tenaciously to the side of the Black Mountains at the 5,000-foot level is a ghost town. Once the richest copper vein in the world, Hatley's ore has run out, and the days when 15,000 people filled the streets and 4,000 miners spent their paychecks in wild flings are only a memory. Now the old-timers and their families—some 500 of them waiting for the school to close—live in the collection of weather-beaten houses that hug the steep mountainside, the view from their porches extending 60 miles all the way to Flagstaff.

But immediately over their balconies is a gaping open pit run dry—a reminder of what their lives used to be.

Today at 3 p.m. the town's last football team, the Hatley Muckers, carrying a squad of only 12 and missing both their coach and the life of their town, will compete against the heavily favored power-house, Phoenix United, for the Yavapai Cup, on a type of field not seen in the southern parts of the state.

The little team known as the Mighty Mites is somehow unbeaten, for their size makes them the smallest team in Arizona. "We've been doing pretty well so far," Muckers assistant coach Hank Wallinger said. "And we know how to win on our field."

Their field, which is made up of the waste tailings dumped out by the mines, has no trace of grass on it, and that has Phoenix United, which is 6–0 against teams known as the best in the state, hopping mad. "It shouldn't be allowed, holding a state championship on a field akin to broken glass," Coach Pug Johnson insisted. "Forget about the championship. I'm risking my players' lives just going out there."

P.U. will also be playing a team that is unsegregated, as seems to be the case in the North, with the bulk of the roster made up of Mexicans led by an English-speaking quarterback named Felix O'Sullivan.

Chapter 26
HELL'S CORNER

SATURDAY, OCTOBER 21
1:46 P.M.

POP'S IN FRONT OF THE house wearing nothing but his unions when I head out for the game. He's got a mouth full of nails and doesn't look up when I pass him, so I guess that means he won't be going.

Cruz and Tony are at the corner waiting for me, fighting the wind. The air's cool and blustery for late October, and we shouldn't have to work this hard to get up the hill. The wind's carrying the sound of Pop's hammering so Tony looks back. "Your dad's nailing a FOR SALE sign on the house," he says.

Me and Cruz keep walking. There's no way I'm looking back at that sign. And I don't know where it leaves me, but Pop can haul that house all the way to Bisbee as far as I'm concerned. All I need is a win.

The company houses are boarded up below the H; they got shuttered yesterday. There's a flowerpot overturned on the steps of Mrs. Hollingworth's house—they left for Bisbee

232

more than a week ago. In the distance is the Cottonville smelter. Cruz and Tony are eyeing it, too, but none of us says anything. We've despised it all our lives and the sulfur that came with it. Now it's just a column of copper bricks left blackened by its own smoke, and it seems stupid that we ever hated it.

"They couldn't wait another month to close the mine?" Cruz says, spitting out a gnat. "So the town could see us play?"

"The new shifts already started in Ajo," Tony sniffs, holding his helmet tighter when we get to Upper Main. We look to our right, down into the Gulch.

You can hear the wind in the Barrio, nothing else. No kids laughing or clothes snapping in the breeze. And the burros have already staked their claims on the shanty porches, blinking back at us from their new homes.

The wind is still against us, blowing heavy by the time we reach the end of Main. "Coach liked it this way," Tony says.

"Cold and windy." Cruz nods.

Bobby did, too.

I thought a family was supposed to get bigger over time, and watch you on days like this with a pride so big you could just about see it bursting. And that the coach you played hard for stuck with you till the end of the season. But they're both gone and it's all because of war—the one before this one, though it doesn't matter which, it never lets up. Now Rabbit's in it, too. And I'm sick and tired of what a war and a mine can do to a family, whittling it down to nothing. Leaving you angry and broken like Pop.

"Somebody's playing the piano," Cruz says. It's Mrs. Featherhoff, sitting on a milk can behind her piano, which is still on the sidewalk. It's covered in Mucker pennants. "Here come our boys!" she shouts. "Rally sons of Hatley High!" She starts playing our fight song. And I don't know what to say, it's such a nice thing to do, so I shake her hand and she starts crying. "Now don't be doing that," I tell her. "We're gonna win."

"Then we'll come back and dance on your piano," Cruz says, taking the streamers with us and giving Mrs. Featherhoff a salute.

The icehouse is empty—Gibby went to Ajo last week—but we stop anyhow to take in the view.

"Would you look at those things?" Cruz says, pointing at the new bleachers. "I thought we were playing football, not going to the circus."

They're ten rows high and painted red and white—Phoenix colors—and only inches away from ours. Mr. Casillas built them. And I haven't a clue how he got them up here, but there's no way Tony helped. He won't even look at them and strokes his leathery brown forehead with his free hand.

Apparently, it's the rule to have seats for your opponents if you're hosting the state championship, and be real polite about it, too. Answering all sorts of questions that have nothing to do with football. Stupid ones, like why we chose to have Mexicans in our school instead of segregation, as if they shouldn't be here. That's what the reporter from Phoenix kept pestering me about on the telephone last night, wanting to know if "all those languages" got in the way. *In the way of what?*

They sure have a peculiar way of looking at things down in the South, figuring that we can't speak English because our folks weren't born here. Like we're not even American. But we didn't get this far because we're anything like Phoenix United, and we've gotten along just fine for thirty years without a grass field or a stadium full of seats for total

234

strangers or two separate schools. But the South never expected to play us when the North drew home field. They usually get Flag, which is just about as big as Phoenix United and more neighborly than we are, only we've got the better view.

Phoenix's coach doesn't seem to think so, or maybe he just doesn't care. All he's concerned about is our field. He's going off about it to the newspapermen scribbling notes beside him on the sideline. And he sure likes to talk, tossing that fancy red-and-white scarf across his shoulder like he's never met up with the cold before or felt the chill of an approaching winter.

I'm not sure what stung more, the newspaper calling us a bunch of ghosts or the fact that it might be true. I'm hoping there'll be enough people left to fill our side of the bleachers, but I don't really know for sure.

"Gonna need the blocking dummies to fill up our seats," Tony says, dumping his helmet in the first row.

"What, the two we scrimmage with?"

"Leroy's got his rocks," Cruz says. "I bet he aims one right at the noggin of that smart-ass Phoenix coach."

"We don't need to kill them." Tony fists up his hands. "Just pound them into the ground and beat 'em."

The sun takes cover under a ring of patchy clouds and there's no more warmth to give our freezing fingers, but Cruz and Tony start tossing the football anyway.

"Say, aren't you the starting quarterback for the Muckers?" one of the reporters asks me. "How does it feel to be playing the winningest team in all of Arizona?"

"We haven't played them yet."

"And you weren't expected to, were you? But beating Flagstaff, that's what got you here," he says, getting out a notebook.

"We're here because we haven't lost a game."

Cruz and Tony keep eyeing us between throws, and I want him to get back to the Phoenix side, but he doesn't.

"And your teammates," he says, looking sheepishly at Cruz and Tony. "How do you communicate with the immigrant players like the Mexicans?"

Cruz fires the ball at the guy's head, but I catch it before it hits him.

"Same as all the other players," I say. "We talk."

"So you know how to speak Spanish, then?"

Cruz smiles, coming up from behind. "Oh, he knows all the special words. Like *cabrón*."

I turn pink.

"What did he just say?" the reporter asks.

"He just called you a dumbass," Tony says with a laugh.

"When was the last time you were in the North, mister?" I ask. But he starts going on about Coach Hansen, wondering how Coach died, like he doesn't read his own paper, or never heard of him before.

"You seem to be doing just fine without him," he says.

Can you slug a reporter and still get to play? I wish I knew the rules on that one. "We're doing fine because of him," I say, then tell him I've got a game to get ready for and start throwing with Tony and Cruz.

We hear singing and cheering for Phoenix and watch a line of yellow buses winding past Hatley High, heading up to our field. And I'm not sure they built those bleachers big enough.

"I counted five," Tony says. He goes over to the bench and tightens the tape on his fingers.

"So what?" Cruz lobs a pass at me. "That means five buses full of nosebleeds and frostbitten Southerners. There's no way they can handle things this high or this cold. They'll be shivering so bad we won't understand a word they're saying."

I take the football and cradle it under my arm. I don't want to throw anymore, so I walk up a few rows to where Maw used to sit. If I could turn back time they'd all be here. Maw cheering two yards from the open pit, with smoke belching from that smelter, choking out the field. They'd be talking about *that* in the papers.

She'd be here, too . . . Angie . . . leaning by the columns of light, her soft brown eyes finding me, warming me, giving me strength. But I don't have any of that and I can't twist time around that way anymore.

"Here come the ghosts," Tony says. He points to the line of cars and trucks snaking up the hill behind those Phoenix buses. Some are loaded two stories high, hauling tables, ladder-backs, and trunks tied into place with binder twine. The Heydorn kids are perched on top of their stove, yelling and waving at us. And I didn't see this coming, either. They all should've been in Bisbee by now, and Ajo for sure, or at the very least getting out of town. But they're heading up to the field to watch us play.

Phoenix's coach isn't smiling anymore. And I suppose if you didn't know us, you'd be as surprised as he is, thinking there's no point in even showing up. That we may as well hand P.U. the game and follow that caravan right out of Hatley. P.U., with their fancy new uniforms and big-league tradition—those are the kind of folks who win state championships, not mongrel runts like us who play in hand-me-downs. But it's a funny thing about our town. We're used to getting cut up. And the one thing we know how to do is fight. And if I don't fight on that field this afternoon and win, we'll be forgotten. The memory of Hatley gone for good, too, with Coach and Maw and Bobby along with it. And that's not how it's going to be.

* * *

Their uniforms are white. There's barely a speck of red, except for the PU stuck square in the middle behind the angry face of a crazed coyote staring down on us as we line up on defense. Their star sprinter can clock 9.7 seconds for 100 yards. I read that in the paper, too.

He's big. They all are. Must outweigh us by fifty pounds apiece. They blow through our line on the first two plays like they could annihilate the U of A right now and win the Salad Bowl.

Don't buckle, I keep thinking. *Got to settle down. Stop them on the next play.*

I dig my shoulder into my opponent's and push hard, hearing Tony and Alonzo doing the same, but the Phoenix bench explodes into cheering. Their fullback has burst through the line and scored, with Rudy caught standing flatfooted.

The Phoenix coach looks smug on the sidelines, with his arms folded like it's a rout. Somebody hands him a bag of peanuts when his kicker makes the conversion, and he starts laughing.

The game's only two minutes old, and already it's 7–0.

"I don't like this," Cruz says, glaring at Rudy. "We can't let them get another or we'll be in too deep."

Then Diaz bobbles the kickoff and barely gets started before they tackle him deep in our end of the field.

"Muckers! Muckers!" our side calls out. They're kneeling on the hoods of their trucks and standing on the benches. Faye Miller and Samuel jump up and down in the front row, cheering like they don't know the score.

First play and I hand off to Quesada, who makes it to the line of scrimmage but no farther. On second down, we don't get anywhere either.

"We have to pass!" Cruz spits out the words at me in the huddle. "Stop calling runs; we're getting nowhere."

"Okay," I say. "Then get open."

The rush is quick and they're barreling toward me from both sides. I spot Cruz racing up the field, but he gets cut off and Torres hasn't made it through. That leaves Rudy on the wing. No choice but to get it to him or run. I throw it long and it should be an easy catch. All I can see before I get knocked to the slag is Rudy sidestepping to avoid getting pummeled. "Bye-bye, Hatley," the lineman says as he climbs off me. "You and your rocky field."

I ignore the jab and look up, hoping Rudy made the catch, but it looks like it slipped through his fingers. Now we're forced to punt. Quesada drops into our end zone and gets off a good one, with P.U. setting up near midfield.

Their offensive eleven are fresh, not winded like we are; they rested the whole time we had possession. We go after them as hard as we can, but they keep hammering out big gains, not even bothering to pass. I get in on a couple of tackles and just end up slicing my shins. I glance over at our bench but it's empty except for Tommy, the water boy. And Melvin. There isn't a sub who can help us, and we'll have to keep playing the whole game.

Finally, on third and four from our twelve-yard line, we catch a break. The quarterback rolls out and Casillas chases him, but he gets off a line-drive pass before Tony brings him down. Cruz leaps in front of the pass and intercepts it. He's got an open field ahead of him as he races along the sideline.

I start sprinting, too, closing in on the only man who has

a shot at catching Cruz. I reach him at midfield and crash into him, blocking him out-of-bounds and setting Cruz free.

The Muckers fans start honking their horns and hollering. Mr. Mackenzie grips Tuffy's shoulders as Cruz jumps up and smacks the goalpost.

"Are we in it? Oh, yeah!" Beebe yells. *"Are we gonna win it? Hell, yeah!"* She bounds onto the field, tossing her black-and-orange pom-poms in the air, yelling the cheer right in front of our faces, and I'm pretty sure that's illegal in the rule book. Francisco trots behind her on Paradiso, sprinkling the field with his holy water.

"You're all a bunch of crazy hicks," the Phoenix quarterback shouts. Cruz hoists Beebe up in the air and plants a kiss on her lips before she runs off the field. The refs hustle Francisco away.

"Damn wetback," the guy I knocked down says, eyeing Cruz. "How can you play with the likes of them?"

We've got them. I smile. Haven't smiled in a while. *They're intimidated. Scared, even. And on our field.*

Quesada misses the extra-point attempt, but maybe it won't matter.

We have the momentum now, I can feel it. Things have shifted. The whole team seems to feel it, too.

We stop Phoenix on three straight plays after the kickoff. They're still taunting us, calling us names. Stuff like greaser lover. That one made Rudy boiling mad and he grumbled that he wasn't one. Which only fueled the rest of us.

They manage a field goal just before halftime. There's a stiff wind and it's a wobbly kick, setting the ball off course, but it trickles over the crossbar for three points. We're trailing 10–6 at the half, but we all know we can win this game. As long as we get Rudy out of it.

"Keep it up," Wallinger says, clapping his hands as soon as we get to the sideline. His voice is raspy and breathless, but we're the ones who've been playing hard on both ends. "You're giving it your all," he tacks on. Then he doesn't know what else to say.

"Except Rudy," Cruz snaps, shaking his head. It's dripping with sweat and he's breathing heavy—we all are—too winded to take the water Tommy's offering us.

Tony walks over and faces Rudy. "I've had enough of you not trying." Tony puffs the words out at him, then jabs his fist into Rudy's chest. "And you can't touch me or my father," he says. "We're in lumber, not mining."

And I know what I have to do in order to win this game. "Take Rudy out," I tell Wallinger. "He hasn't got any fight."

"Rudy's no Mucker," Cruz echoes, folding his arms. "He's a frickin' Judas."

"You can't win without me." Rudy smirks. "I'm all you got."

"No you're not." It's Melvin's voice, high and squeaky like Rabbit's was when we were kids. He pokes his head in between Tony and Cruz and looks up at me all innocent, just like that lamb.

Rudy laughs.

"He's fresh, not winded like us, that's for sure," Lupe admits. He looks at Rudy. "If Rudy's in, then count me out."

Alonzo rests his elbows on top of Melvin's head. "He may be the size of half a man, but that's more than what Rudy's got on the field," he says. "I don't know where I'm gonna be next year, but I'm not sharing the field with Rudy anymore."

Wallinger keeps looking at Rudy, then back at Melvin. "You better get out there," he finally says.

Tommy hands Melvin a helmet.

"You're all loco," Rudy shouts, heading for the bench. "I'll have the best seat in the house when you choke."

Melvin smiles and runs for the field.

"Wait!" Cruz takes the nose guard off his helmet. He straps it onto Melvin's.

"Am I gonna die?" Melvin asks.

"We're all gonna die someday," Cruz says, "but not before we win."

"Remember—keep your eyes open," I tell Melvin as we line up. "Focus on the player with the ball. That's all you've gotta do. And don't let him get past you. You're just as tough as they are."

They call an easy fake and their star sprinter takes off like a rocket. Melvin jumps in the air, arms flailing, trying to stop him and getting mowed down like the rest of us.

"Nice try," I say to him. "Didn't know you could jump that high."

"Fight, Coyotes, fight!" the Phoenix majorettes yell, kicking up their calfskin boots to the beat of a dozen drummers. *"Break right through that line!"*

But we finally stop them.

"I can beat who's covering me every time," Cruz says as soon as we get possession. "We need to pass more."

"Whenever I drop back I get sacked or stomped on," I tell him. "Tony, Alonzo, you've got to hold them another second or two so I can throw a long pass."

I haven't connected with anything but a few short passes, so maybe we can catch them off guard.

I take the snap and hear the linemen stagger, the defenders groaning as they collide, then the butting of helmets as I drop straight back and search for Cruz. I catch a glimpse of his orange-and-black jersey a half step ahead of the defender.

He's pivoting left but I know Cruz. He's heading the other way and I send the ball there, watching it sail before I'm hit hard, landing face-first in the slag. I roll, scrambling to my knees, and hear the bleachers roar. *Our bleachers.* Cruz has the ball and he's past midfield. No way he'll get caught.

I should save my strength, but I can't help it. I race all the way up the field and grab Cruz after the touchdown, rubbing the top of his helmet.

"Told ya I'd get open. Think their Anglos know what that means?" he says, pointing to the scoreboard. "It's how we spell 'touchdown' in Hatley."

This time Quesada's extra-point kick is good and we take the lead. First time in the game. We're up 13–10.

I look across at the red-faced Phoenix coach. I guess that's what the paper means by hopping mad. He's got his defensive players huddled up around him on the sideline, chewing them out for getting burned like that.

They keep grinding out gains on every play. Nothing fancy. No passing. They take their time doing it, too, intent on eating up the clock and leaving us spent. It's grueling. I focus on that coyote, grunting my displeasure at him. But he shows us his teeth for eighteen plays, those ears pinned back like he might be rabid and could tear a decent chunk out of us. He does. They score, and Phoenix regains the lead, 17–13.

We get nowhere on our next possession, then it's like that for them, too. Nobody giving in.

Cruz keeps urging me to throw another long pass, but the wind's against us in the fourth quarter, and I call for an end-around instead, a lateral to Cruz as he circles behind me. P.U.'s big defensive end is right in his path and tackles him for a loss. Cruz comes back to the huddle rubbing his jaw. "Punched me as we were getting up," he says. "The refs aren't calling anything."

"Strangle the coach with that bloody scarf and win this thing!" somebody yells from the Muckers bench. It's Pop. And he's here. Cheering and slapping Manny on the back.

There's only three minutes left in the game when we get the ball back. We huddle up and a gust of wind comes through, breaking so strong it knocks Melvin unsteady. A lady's hat goes tumbling onto the field. Then the sky turns dark, pelting us with rain. No gradual buildup first, but an intense downpour, soaking our jerseys before we can even speak and puddling up the field.

Tony looks at the sky and smiles, rivers of raindrops splashing off his face like a hose.

"Mud," Cruz says, beaming.

I look up at Nefertiti Hill. I can barely see her through the teeming rain, but I know she's there. That she's given us this field. Our very existence. And that she's worth fighting for.

I need to move quickly.

Short handoffs, that's what I do. Forget trying to throw any kind of pass in this, with Lupe bulling forward for a few yards and Melvin clinging to the ankles of any P.U. player he can get to, just like a pesky terrier. Then Torres gaining a few more. On third down I keep the ball myself, cradling it like a tear-soaked baby, charging through the line and finding some running room.

The Phoenix players keep slipping, losing their grip on us, on the game, as we trudge forward heading for our target. Hell's Corner.

With every move there's a scramble. I burst through for another big gain, nearly breaking free before being brought down.

Twenty-seven seconds left and I call our final time-out, just inside the Phoenix fifteen-yard line.

"You have to pass, Red," Cruz tells me. "We can't stop the clock anymore. Get it to Hell's Corner," he says. "I'll be there."

"Hold that line," I say in the huddle.

Cruz fakes toward the sideline, then digs his foot along the chalk, into the only spot where the mud's clotted up and there's traction. He swerves, cutting across the center of the field. *Make it to the corner,* I'm thinking, but there's no time to wait. I focus on his number, soaked and blurred and clinging to his skin, then send a bullet directly at it. Cruz reaches for it, higher than I've ever seen—soaring across Hell's Corner. The P.U. players follow him, reaching as Cruz hauls the ball in. As soon as they set foot in the corner, their cleats give way and their bodies twist and roll before slipping into the muddy abyss. Another P.U. player climbs in, using his limp teammates as his very own carpet, trampling over them stuffed into that swampy pit. He catches Cruz's foot, mowing him down a body length away from the goal line.

"Line up!" I yell, splashing toward the pile of P.U. players, dazed and mud-soaked, forcing them apart with my clawing and screaming as the clock eats away at the time. I haul Cruz up, knowing it could end right here, as ghosts, swallowed up by time. *Forgotten.* Us. Bobby. Everything.

I won't let it. Got to get off another snap. I shove a Phoenix player to his side of the chalk as the referee places the ball at the two-yard line. No time to call a play. I can feel it: time slipping. "Hike!" I holler, both crowds cheering in echoing bursts through the downpour, each side aching for victory, a rush of Phoenix players packed tight, grabbing for me, furious and wild, their nostrils flaring like wild animals'.

There's a scramble of arms and legs and helmets, but

nothing can stop me. I surge, my whole body working in unison, one angry muscle exploding as I lunge forward, clawing over players, like I can walk on water. Then I float, crying out into the desert a piercing, primal scream that says everything I ever wanted to but never could. It's the same cry I made as a baby just out of the womb in the Gulch, only this time my eyes are wide open.

She's waiting for me on the other side, Nefertiti is, with her skin of slag and muddy loam. And Angie was right, the mountain still has plenty to give. The other players slip and fall but she's much kinder to me, catching my hurtling body a foot beyond the goal line and letting me slide gently along her skin, bathing in her brownness, in her mud, screaming, stretching, clinging to the football—my fingers forcing it further into my abdomen so there's no chance it'll come loose. Then I lie there, breathing in the mud, smelling its earthy smell, not wanting to move. I hear myself blowing hard, feel my heart tumbling against her skin, and taste the sweat and the mud and then something completely unfamiliar: the salt from my tears as I finally let go.

Chapter 27
MUCKER SUNDAES

CRUZ SAYS I KEPT LYING there, hollering, headfirst in the muck, clutching that football so tight until they told me the touchdown was good. And even then, the referee had to pry it out of my fingers. But I don't remember that. Or the faces in the crowd who got muddy, losing their shoes rushing to shake my hand because we'd won it. Just Pete Zolnich dancing in the field with Mrs. Featherhoff on his shoulders. Just the release—giving absolutely everything, then letting go and still being there. The slick ground supporting me and how satisfying that felt. How time had given me every second I'd needed. Then Cruz saying, "You gonna lie in the mud all night?", giving me his hand and knocking his helmet against mine and keeping it there.

We looked at each other eye to eye for a while, not saying anything, until he could hardly smile, his lips had gone so trembly. "So this is what it feels like to matter," he finally whispered. "We're champions. And no one will ever beat us again. Ever. Or tell me that I don't count."

* * *

They said it was a thunderstorm. The tail end of a blaster out of Phoenix that couldn't be stopped. It cut such a narrow swath that Cottonville never even saw it, but we did. It tore up the melons in Kellerman's field and left us nothing but mud. Victorious mud.

The town's covered in it and looks like it must've forty years ago, before they paved anything. There's cars everywhere, some abandoned in the field, stuck in the muck, others parked in front of the bars for the night since the owners are too drunk to make the trek out of Hatley until tomorrow.

The sidewalks are crowded, too, and everyone's wanting to buy me and Cruz a drink.

Benny wouldn't let us pay for supper either. They gave us a standing ovation when we walked into the diner. Faye Miller's boy, Samuel, stared at the trophy so long I had him sit beside me in the booth and hold it for a while. He kept hugging it like they were old friends. Then he up and stared at me, saying, "Can you show me how to throw?"

Now Benny's got the Yavapai Cup on top of the soda fountain and is making Mucker sundaes for the whole place without charging.

When they first handed me that Cup, I caught sight of Sims standing in front of the bleachers, smiling and clapping, and I didn't want to hurt him anymore. Him and that Commie box. Half the names in there must be in Ajo and Bisbee by now anyway, and Mr. Mackenzie's better off in Flag.

We've taken that trophy all around town. First to the Barrio, and we slid pretty good down Gulch Lane, where Francisco gave it a good dousing with his wand full of holy water. Tony's father built a bonfire out of the Phoenix bleachers, then we all ate tamales. There was so much singing and dancing going on you'd think it was Mexican Independence Day all over again, and I hardly thought of Angie.

Cruz can't stop smiling. He's stuffing his face with the crunchy brown bits of fries he found under the lettuce that was on his burger.

I wonder if she heard we won and how I'd been a part of it.

The rain's stopped, so we take the trophy up Main one more time, until we reach the edge of the field.

"How many you think are out there?" Cruz asks, aiming his toothpick at the cars.

"About fifty," I say, eyeballing the hoods and the cabs slick with rain, some buried halfway up to their hubs in the slop.

"He should be here," Cruz says. "Rabbit's part of this, too."

"I know it." I keep looking at the cars and picturing Rabbit stuck in the mud like they are, but still alive. Not missing in action like Buddy Ritz, but ready to come home.

Cruz holds the Cup above his head. "You should tell him about it," he says, resting the trophy on his shoulder. "In a letter."

"Why don't you?"

Cruz looks at me like I'm loco at first, then his expression changes, as if a thundercloud has lifted. "Maybe I will. . . . First thing in the morning." He tells me I've still got mud in my hair and that the cot's by the fireplace, same as it's always been, if I need a place to stay.

A light flickers above a tiered plateau in the open pit where a group of men in hard hats are trying to push a bulldozer knee-deep in mud onto a flatbed truck.

"May as well leave it there," Cruz says. "The way things change. Bet I won't even have to go to Ajo next year. Did you see those crowds? They'll find something. My father says there's more gold than copper down there anyway. Then he'll come back with my mother. Angie, too."

I don't say anything.

"You know," Cruz says. *"My sister?"*

"I know who she is."

"Don't give up on her," he whispers. "It broke her heart to leave you."

We're both quiet for a while, then Cruz hands me the Cup, tosses the toothpick in the mud, and rolls up his jeans.

"Where you going?" I ask.

"Tunnel number nine." He turns around and gives me a stupid-ass grin. "To meet Beebe."

I watch Cruz trot into the mud and wonder if he'll get bogged down by it, too. Those cars are staying put because they're stuck. And there's no way this town can come back now that the mine's closed. That's one thing the E.C. doesn't change their thinking on. The flatbed trucks have been hauling out houses and equipment all week. And if things really are changing, then why is Cruz still having to meet Beebe in the dark?

* * *

"Hey, Red!" Cussie's dad yells over to me, raising an invisible glass when I walk back into town. "You should see your pop. No one's happier than he is that you won. He's celebrating behind the theater."

The Cribs are back there, where Hatley folk go to gamble and drink and find company that you pay for. I've never been there when all those things go on, but tonight it doesn't feel so illegal. I won, and for the first time Pop's happy about it.

They've put up a tent because of the rain, and the

250

burly man guarding the opening smiles at me. I think he's Managlia's uncle. When he sees the Cup, he takes off his oilskin hat, rubs the trophy's belly with his nose, and raises the door flap to let me in. I have to blink a few times before I can see what's around me: men gathered in throngs, the lucky ones sitting on benches while the others lean over their shoulders, all eyes focused downward on a makeshift ring. Dozens of kegs form a circular wall separating the ring from the crowd, and I wonder if those kegs are full or empty. I scan the rows of sweaty faces until I find Pop. He's near the front, wiggling that squatty pink nose and laughing—I'd recognize that cackle blindfolded.

"There he is!" Pop says when he sees me. "The man of the hour. Here, come meet your namesake." His smile is wide and follows me as I press closer, fighting my way through the crowd. It's warm in here and my face flushes, but that's not it. Pop noticed me first off, and I don't think that's happened before. His grin gets bigger and I can tell he's proud.

"That's you," Pop says when I reach him, "in there." He aims his cigar at the sandy pit below and my knees buckle. Two roosters are in the ring and I know there's gonna be a cockfight. I've seen the plucked feathers left alongside the curb the day after from the one that goes into the soup.

"You're the red one," Pop says. I can only see part of its chubby neck, the tail feathers, russet and black, as the rooster struggles to break free of its handler. "All big and puffed up and proud."

He's weaving his hooded head back and forth, pecking blindly at the wind. The cover finally comes off and he shakes his neck, but the wattle's been cut off. The comb, too.

"You and he are gonna win again tonight." Pop winks, breathing his liquor on me. A bald head bobs up between us and lets out a loud *hork*. It's Wynn, the bookie. He snatches the money Pop's giving him and stuffs the bills in his belt.

"Five hundred says you will." Pop smiles. "He's desperate, too, that scrappy bird. 'Cause if you don't, that'll be the end of it. The last fight the town will ever see. And I know that won't suit ya, losin' that way."

"Is that all you care about?"

"Eh?" Pop mumbles. His attention's in the ring. I lean to grab his shoulder but somebody waves a Mexican flag and it gets in the way.

If Pop thinks I'm the one that gets stuffed in the soup pot he's dead wrong.

"Come closer," he calls. "Let me get at them lucky locks so the charm'll rub off."

I push his hand away. I want to leave, to run, even. But the crowds won't let me. They're lunging forward, three-deep, arms twisted, placing bets in Spanish, Croatian, and Chinese, yelling and pulling me in. A pint of beer gets tossed. The foam soaks my shoulder and I have to hoist the Cup above my head just to get a few inches to breathe and pry myself free.

"Would you look at him," Pop says, sniggering at me. "So chuffed up—all hundred twenty pounds of him, includin' that piece o' junk. Haulin' it high to put on a show and thinkin' he's bigger than us."

"No!" I shout. "That's not it." The men from his crew gawk as I hold the Cup closer.

Pop swerves to look at me, raising his bushy brows. "Well, I'm glad you brought it," he says. "I'll rub it, too. I knew you'd win. Didn't matter how small and beat up you all were. Desperate lads always make out better than even. That's why I bet on ya. 'Twas a good bet, that's for sure."

"So that's why you're here? To double the money you won on me?"

"It's just numbers," he scoffs, puffing at his cigar.

"No it's not." I jab my fist into his chest. "I'm your son. Family shouldn't bet on family."

"Do me a favor an' make your pop proud," he says, dumping the cigar in the Cup. "Hock it for a lunch."

I drag him down, catching a cheek with my fist.

"I got twenty on Junior!" somebody hollers.

The trophy nicks Pop's mouth, splitting open his lip. He goes to wipe off the blood but he misses. And I see that he's too drunk to counter with his fists, so I stop.

"Alastar's all liquored up," Wynn shouts. "All bets off."

My father takes a few snorts through his purple nose and wipes off the blood with his sleeve.

"Hah!" he spews. "The big hero, eh? You really think this means something?" He paws at the trophy, but I pull it out of reach. "Just gets you killed," he says, "on an island fulla Japs. A bloody waste o' time. But I know you'll keep it. You're the soppy one. Suppose you can piss in it when you get to Bisbee."

"I won't be going to Bisbee."

"Sure you won't."

The crowd groans, focused on what's happening in the ring. The cocks are dueling in midair, three feet above the sand, a flurry of feathers and knives. When the handlers finally separate them, the red one's lost an eye.

"He's down a blinker," Wynn says to my father.

"See?" he whines, still lying on the floor. "You lost your focus, Red. Do that for one minute and you get an eye gouged out. You got one more round. What's the score?" he yells.

"Up by one, boss," Wynn says.

"Ah, so you're left protectin' the lead. No matter. We're good with numbers, we O'Sullivans. Ten drinks to Bisbee, three eight-hour shifts gets you forty dollars, but a seven-an'-oh record got me half a grand. It's all numbers. Hours, games, wages. Me. You. Bobby. I got ten more years in the hole. What did he end up bein'? A ten-digit roll call in the marines. Win me that cockfight," he blubbers. "Squeeze out them numbers and win."

"You can have your numbers, Alastar." It's not natural to call him Pop anymore, the way he treats me. Or how a father ought to feel about his son.

I cradle the Cup like a football, not too tender, more like a solid hold with just enough room to give. Then I use my other arm as a block and find an opening.

He staggers toward me but I push him away. "I think they took her to Bisbee today," he says, landing on his wobbly knees.

I see a break in the tent. I lunge, stepping on his hand, and he lets out a howling scream. I keep sprinting, over bodies and bloodshot faces, until I land in the ring. I jump over the bloodied birds and out of the tent, where I can finally breathe.

"See ya in Bisbee!" He laughs. They all do. "He's a real cracker that one, isn't he?" I hear him bellow. "Broke my feckin' thumb."

* * *

I sprint up Main. She can't be gone. They told me that I had a week before they took them all to Bisbee.

I'm beat up from the game but I know my legs can go faster up this hill. They have to go faster.

The misty air's cold up top and a crisp slice shivers down my throat, cutting into my ribs. Still, I force my legs to pump higher, ignoring the sting, until the incline stops me at Company Ridge. The Yavapai Cup weighs twenty pounds, but it's another limb as far as I'm concerned. And she ought to see it.

I earned it. Not like a stupid bet. How long does that last? This is for always. After he's gone and I'm gone and she's gone, but not yet. Make him wrong about that, too.

I reach the landing of the hospital. Someone turned on the light above the door, but when? My heart's tumbling and just about ready to rush through my skin. But the hospital's dark inside and it's cold and hollow.

I feel my way around the stairwell, anxious for a whisper or a moan. Even a desperate sigh to prove him wrong.

I suck back sweat and phlegm, stumbling, not wanting to be the only one gasping for breath. I smell coffee. Slightly burnt, but a pot's been on sometime today. My forehead hits the wall so I know I can't climb any higher. I turn right, into the moon's milky stillness streaming through the window above the corridor, and run to her room.

"Maw!" I call into the silence. I push the door open, my eyes searching for the bed, her silhouette.

She's there. Lying in it. Thank God, she's there.

"Maw," I whisper, kneeling beside her. I reach for her hand, then bury my wet face in her shoulder.

"I did it, Maw." I show her the trophy, resting it on the bed. "I won it. We're champions. The very last ones."

There's a whinny in her throat and her eyes sparkle then search, diving and darting about like a nervous bird, frantically probing my face. *She's about to know me.* Her cheeks turn pink and then the glint comes. The glint of recognition. She squeezes my hand, then the whinny gets stronger and her mouth opens.

"Bah-bee!" she calls out.

She's glowing. Happier than I've seen her in years, beaming up at me, and won't let go of my hand. She's so happy thinking I'm Bobby that I have to smile. I reach for his letters, giving her one to take hold of, and wrestle my fingers free. Then I take the Cup, hugging it close to my chest, and follow the purple shaft of light out the door.

THE VERDE MINER

Twice-Weekly News of the Mountain

HATLEY, ARIZONA   SUNDAY, OCTOBER 22, 1950   FIVE CENTS A COPY

SPECIAL CHAMPIONSHIP EDITION

Muckers Upset Phoenix Before Record Crowd

Ending the football season in a blaze of glory, the Hatley Muckers hoisted themselves to the top of the heap in the entire state Saturday by upsetting heavily favored Phoenix United, 19–17, before a mud-soaked crowd. An estimated 1,600 watched amazed as the Mighty Mites cut their rugged opponents down to size to win the Yavapai Cup.

It wasn't the breaks that won it for the Mucker eleven, though they took full advantage of the few they created, somehow finding traction on the muddy field. Nor was it because the Coyotes let down. P.U. looked and was formidable with their rugged line and powerful backs. It was heads-up, inspired football that was the deciding factor in the game.

It was the cool passing of Felix O'Sullivan, the sticky fingers and quick breaking of Cruz Villanueva and Lupe Diaz. It was the hard charging of the whole Muckers forward wall, including unknown junior Melvin Sneep—who had never seen first-string action before, in a game that frequently saw All-State guard Tony Casillas breaking through to spill a play before it started.

O'Sullivan scored the decisive touchdown on the game's final play, charging into pay dirt after catapulting over the entire Phoenix team from the two-yard line. In winning the game, the Muckers have won the admiration and respect of the entire state.

WANT ADS

FOR SALE—1940 Ford Deluxe. Never driven past Cottonville. Call Cruz at Copper Star.

WANTED—Sewing of all types. Buttonholes a specialty. Hand- or machine-made. Mrs. Ben Hansen. E.C. Apartments. Phone 133-H.

HOUSE FOR SALE— Everything in it. Move in next week or haul away. A. O'Sullivan. The Hogback. 869-H.

FREE PIANO—Situated under a tarpaulin on the sidewalk of Upper Main. Kindly use care when moving. Go softly on the middle C, harder on the soft pedal when playing.

Chapter 28
AFTER

THE CHEVY ISN'T MUCH. IT'S been under a tarp most of the year because of all his drunk-driving infractions. I pretended to be asleep last night when he came into my room and put the keys on the washstand. I know how to treat this old car. That if you bring it back real gentle till the needle hits fifty, it won't give up on you.

I turn off the engine, gliding it under the oak on top of Gulch Lane, and take the duffel bag with me.

It won't be easy to hide because of the moonlight, but I figure I've got an hour of stillness. The night animals are done feeding—they've already taken cover—and it's much too cold for any belly crawler to venture out and hunt.

I crouch low, inching through the switchgrass, but by the time I reach the Villanuevas' house my Levis are all wet— the Barrio's covered in mud.

I come to the shanty from behind, dipping under the broken shutters so the moon's glow won't cast a shadow and

258

wake up Cruz. Then I suck in my breath—there can't be more than two feet between us—and tread lightly onto the porch. What I'm holding belongs to him, not in that trophy case collecting rust. I take the letter from my boot and put it on our Northern Crown trophy. Then I rest the '41 trophy that Manny and Bobby won next to it, looking at that kicker a last time before walking away.

I'm shaking—it's already winter cold—and I hope Cruz won't be sore. It's just that I couldn't think of any other way of doing this that didn't involve me staying.

The moon is hanging low above the open pit. There's a good amount of blue around it instead of the usual gray, now that the blasting's stopped. It's strange not seeing any lights or digging down there. Just a ring of dew lining the ledge where they left the dozer. Even the wind passes it by, and when the breeze finally reaches me, I've made it to the cemetery. I start to breathe normal again.

Bobby's empty coffin is buried several yards away in a spot that's all wrong. Father Pierre chose it and it's the farthest you could be from the football field, on a cliff without any shelter.

I look for some high growth that might give Bobby relief from the wind and the heat and the cold (at least the memory of him, locked up in this memento I'm holding). Just a spot—not a big one—where there's cover. He never had that on the island. You couldn't even build a decent foxhole on Iwo Jima. It's time for him to come home and I think this spot would suit him just fine.

There's enough dirt between a chalky white monument and a thornbush with a clear shot of the field. They call it a crucifixion tree, and its thorns are growing in all directions along branches too thick to give in to the wind. The limestone ledge of the headstone has a chunky silver heart on it—a *milagro*. It's the same color as the Eagle Scout medal and has a ribbon around it, too. The heart isn't shiny but has a weighty presence to it, like if you cupped it in your palms, it would feel solid and ripe as stone fruit. There are wings on either side of it and I like that, too. And the heart puffed out to bursting with little suns all over it. I suppose it's to thank a patron saint for making a prayer or some sort of wish— maybe even a miracle—come true.

With Bobby it wasn't about miracles. He did things. Earned things like that medal and the Northern Crown. Now I've earned something, too, and it's time to start thinking about after. That's not getting too far ahead. I know I can't stay. And the mountain's already given me plenty.

There's a rustle in the grass behind me, so I turn and see Francisco standing there.

"You need a shovel," he says.

He's got one in his hand and tells me to take it. The handle's warm and my chilled fingers loosen. The soil is moist, too, and gives way without a struggle. Francisco's praying while I dig, and it's as proper a burial as you can get, I suppose, with him being a minister, self-ordained.

I tuck the cigar box with Bobby's Eagle Scout medal in the hole while Francisco's got his eyes shut, murmuring things in Spanish. I haven't a clue what he's saying until he gets to the *corazón* part. I know that means "heart," but it's more than that, beyond the simple beating of it. I think it's one of those words that get lost in translation, because whenever a Mexican says it, they get all weepy or quit talking and start clearing their throat, the way Francisco's doing now.

I think about all the people in my life—the ones who are

lost to me, like Bobby and Coach; those I'm not sure about, with Maw living inside her head and Pop broken and hard as those rocks in the mines; and the ones I consider real family, Cruz and Rabbit. I know I'll see them again. Angie, too.

Francisco waits until I've covered the box with sandy loam. He spits on his hands and shows me what's between them: a seed, then points to the paradise trees behind us angling over his rugged garage, makes a cross in the dirt, and buries the seed in the crux with his thumb.

Taking hold of my shoulder, Francisco tucks a photograph in my shirt pocket. I don't have much time, but I let him lead me to his trees. He opens the gate and I follow as he scurries past the garage.

Paradiso nuzzles up to me. I keep stroking the burro's neck, since I don't know what to say—the sight before me is so remarkable. Even though it's barely dawn, I know what I'm seeing is real.

He did it. Francisco built a church. Not just a miniature version of something you hope to build someday, but a *real* church. Thousands upon thousands of dynamite boxes that we'd cut up for him as kids make up the walls, a steeple, and a nave.

Francisco smiles and points to the sky. He tells me he's going to get an airplane, fill it with seeds, and shake them loose over Hatley so the mountain can become green again. I watch him standing against the horizon, his fedora over his *corazón* and his eyes closed, head raised to the sky as the dawn breaks. *Praying.* Maybe even for me.

* * *

The sun's holding steady above the horizon and playing tricks on the dewy macadam. It'll be like that for another hour, I'd imagine, till I pass Oak Creek. Cruz will have read the letter by then and found the money that I'd saved for Bobby's pew. That Ford Deluxe doesn't belong to anyone except Cruz. The money will make sure he keeps it.

The H is gone from my rearview mirror. It hung there for a long time. Now there's nothing but green, a hundred miles of it stretching out in front of me across the horizon to Flagstaff. That's where I'm headed. I'll be staying with the Mackenzies while I figure things out—start thinking about the future. I've got options. Maybe I'll finish school up there. Maybe someday I'll coach.

The ponderosas are so thick in Flagstaff that the sun can barely get through them. I bet it's the same green in Antrim. And maybe in Hatley someday, a dozen years from now, after those paradise seeds take hold. I guess people can start over. Shed their skin. Even a snake gets a shot at it every year.

I stop the Chevy on a wide spot of dirt beside the road and take out the picture Francisco gave me. It's of Faye Miller sitting in the Gulch with her boy when he was a baby. He's wearing a baptism dress and is holding Francisco's wand like it's a rattle. But the best part is what's written on the other side: *July 18, 1943. The Baptism of Samuel Robert O'Sullivan.*

I should have known the first time I saw him. He's got Bobby's smile and that forehead with all those freckles. *Our* freckles.

I tuck the photograph in the kimono next to the Yavapai Cup with the pearls. The material's red like Angie's lips and not too shiny. Just perfect, actually. It's a couple of hundred miles from Flagstaff to Ajo and it's no place for someone who isn't a miner, but that won't stop me from seeing Angie.

I get back on the road and head for those peaks. I just might climb them when I get to Flag. I'll have plenty of time to go fishing, too. Catch me a trout. I know what I'll do. I'll eat it while I'm waiting for the sunset. I've never seen one from that side before. Then I'll look in the opposite direction toward Hatley, and think of all the miracles that have already happened.

Author's Note

WHILE THE FIRST YEAR OF the Korean War, and the Communist scare it ignited, are the backdrop of my novel, the story itself is inspired by Jerome, Arizona, a mountain town that was once a billion-dollar copper camp in the rugged north of the state a hundred years ago.

You can still see the entire community defying gravity as you drive through it today. Looping past the gulches where the old-timers are buried below the hulking bones of a swimming pool built for "foreigners," you first come to the old high school—its burnished copper doors now shuttered. Jerome High closed in 1951, the year the mines tapered off production, spurring a mass exodus that left the town practically deserted. But like the houses that seem impossibly placed up the thirty-degree incline of Cleopatra Hill, the people of Jerome seemed to defy logic, too. During that final year of decline, they accomplished an incredible sports victory.

I first found out about the Muckers football team while living in Sedona, Arizona, about a twenty-minute drive from Jerome. I was working as an announcer for ESPN, covering the WNBA and the X Games, but the truth is, all I wanted to do was write.

I'd been researching a different story about Jerome and had reached a dead end. Still, the town had a hold on me (once you visit you'll see what I mean), and I think Alene Alder Rangel, archivist of the Jerome Historical Society at the time, felt sorry for me that morning as I sat staring at microfilm. She pointed to a cardboard box that had recently arrived and asked if I wanted to take a look. Inside were the typical memorabilia a historical society would kindly accept—things like yearbooks, school newspapers, and photographs of people picnicking in the Gulch eating watermelon a century ago. But then the letters tumbled out—dozens of them—addressed to Mr. Lewis McDonald, who was the longtime principal of Jerome High (and later, a Northern Arizona University administrator). It was Mr. McDonald's request that these mementos be given to the historical society after his death. The precious notes—some handwritten, others typed from the bunks of battleships— were all from young men who had gone to Jerome High, and spanned nearly three decades' worth of correspondence, beginning in the 1930s. (Nearly half of the 1950 Muckers starters served in the Korean War, which escalated and continued until 1953. All survived.)

Flushed with excitement, yet not quite knowing what I would find, I photocopied everything in the box, then went home and read into the night. By morning I'd learned what history books could never reveal: about separate swimming pools and young soldiers eager to share what they'd gone through. I connected the letters with faces in the yearbooks and became a witness to the anguish of forbidden love, final notes from those who would perish at Iwo Jima, and glimpses of Coach Homer Brown, writing from his sickbed about the head wounds that would later kill him.

But what kept me up all these years was an article in *Arizona Football*—and likely the only one ever written about the

Jerome Muckers' incredible story. It described their valiant history and the football team's final season, when they managed to win a title in herculean fashion without their long-time coach. This was my story.

They were a ragtag team of diminutive players with a mountain of odds against them: the smallest team in the state, a football field made of slag instead of grass, and a coach who would die of his war wounds before the season even began.

One of the few racially mixed teams in Arizona, the Jerome Muckers often played against high schools that were either all-black or all-white, but not Mexican and white like they were. Not only did the Muckers win the 1950 Northern Arizona Conference title, they went undefeated, trouncing teams from big cities like Phoenix and Flagstaff who were double their size. The remarkable feat earned the Muckers bragging rights for the mythic state championship. (Play-offs were not held back then, so the state title was determined by merit and led to plenty of arguments.)

It was a spectacular story that never made national or even state headlines. Prejudice, under the guise of the Communist red scare, had seeped into every part of American society—including newsrooms.

The story would have remained buried in the hearts of the few Mucker players who are still alive and scattered like tumbleweed across desert towns if I hadn't opened that box.

Interviewing some of those Muckers about their story (how else would I have known about the school-bus drills, the bitter rivalries, or even where the football field really was?), I became certain I could create a novel that echoed their spirit. But it was in the letters that my characters took shape, allowing me to write in the voices of young men.

I wrote much of the novel on location, sitting in Coach Brown's office at the abandoned gymnasium, or on the metal fire escape where that crazy tree really did grow, reading 1950 editions of the *Verde Independent*. Even now, you can go into the high school and visit artists who rent studio space amid the khaki-colored lockers, the staff john, and the empty trophy case. And if you walk down North Drive to the cemetery, you'll find clusters of paradise trees by a tall house that used to be the Mexican Methodist Church (built with powder boxes by Sabino Gonzales, who inspired my character Francisco). But the shanties in El Barrio Chicano (Mexican Town) are gone, except for a few foundations. And the slag football field has become a parking lot beyond the fire hall, where the long-abandoned open pit continues to dominate the view.

I think the best view of the pit, though, is from the first pew on the left-hand side of the Holy Family Church, which still has its tin ceiling, the organist's mirror, and that ill-fated lamb across the altar. The parish and its former priests (one left the church after making a fortune in mining stocks and married; the other was known to collect hundreds of women's left shoes and to hide thousands in offertory money in coffee cans) helped me create the Sacred Heart of Mary and the character of Father Pierre.

I've watched that gaping pit (and the forty-foot-high J painted on the hill above it) slowly disappear from my rearview mirror a hundred times while driving home. But I'll never forget how Jerome looked the night I left it after interviewing former Muckers quarterback Rusty Winslow. Watching the town prepare for the night as I looped around the old high school, I saw the lights from the old mining hospital (now the Grand Hotel) turn on first, starting up the birthday-candle glow. By the time I'd reached Cottonwood, the illumination had grown wider and brighter, and I imagined the whole town celebrating a spectacular achievement that had gone unnoticed for too many years.

Acknowledgments

A STORY BECOMES A NOVEL because so many people work hard to make it so. In my case, that's especially true, since I'd discovered the spark of this story more than a dozen years ago, right before the trajectory of my life made several dramatic turns that could have derailed it.

By the time the final draft of *Muckers* had been written, I'd lived in two different countries and three states, and gone from being an ESPN announcer—single and travel-bound—to being married and a stepmom, and writing from home in (very fashionable) sweatpants.

Before all that, though, I'd collected my own boxes full of material. They would be the first items on the U-Haul trucks. I'd also written fifty pages of *Muckers*, sitting on the fire escape of Jerome High (which had long been abandoned) or in the auditorium next to a few chatty squatters who often gave me Dunkin' Donuts napkins to write on when I'd run out of paper.

During that time, I was most thankful for meeting Rusty Winslow, a Jerome Mucker quarterback who became a football coach. Unassuming and courteous, Rusty kept calling me "ma'am," his wavy hair looking like it must have in 1950, and walking with the gait of a man still proud of his town and what they'd achieved. Standing on the old field as Rusty told me about Coach Brown and pushing that school bus around or about those Wolves was the highlight of gathering golden nuggets for my novel. I'm thankful for Rusty's stories about playing Muckers football and grateful to his wife, Barbara (Hollingshead) Winslow—they were Jerome High School classmates—for her recollections about living in Jerome.

Of course, when it came to crafting the novel, I have several people to thank for supporting me through the writing process and keeping me grounded to the finish.

Nancy Hinkel is one of those editors who authors hope to have for their entire careers. I'm told that notion is very old-school and that it rarely happens anymore, but then again, I'm married to an editor, so I do have a reference point. And I suppose with a novel set in 1950 and featuring old-time football, it's obvious how much I value tradition and maintaining treasured relationships. I'd like to thank Nancy for gently nudging me to let go of what I had to in order to make the story better. Nancy also helped me strive for that elusive balance in historical fiction—between what really happened in the town I'd grown so attached to and what was best for my characters. Thanks also to the watchful eye of Nancy's editorial assistants, Jeremy Medina and Stephen Brown. Is there anyone left in publishing who returns emails immediately? They do, and that means so much. Special thanks to the extraordinary copy editors Iris Broudy and Artie Bennett and to the jacket designer Sarah Hoy.

To my husband, Rich Wallace. I keep reminding myself that I've known this story longer than I've known you. But I have *Muckers* to thank for bringing us together. When we met in Prescott at that writers' conference, I was trying to compose rhymes, but we talked sports and about *Muckers* and it felt like I'd always known you. Thank you for making sure that Red's voice and the essence of *Muckers* never shifted when the stress of moving and life sometimes clouded my reference point, and for always being as excited about this story as any of yours. No one writes sports action like you do, so I appreciate how you watched over mine.

Research can be a tricky thing. It was Alene Alder Rangel, then the archivist of the Jerome Historical Society, who allowed full access to reporters like me. Without Alene, I would have never known about Mr. McDonald's box, had access to photographs and alumni, or been able to listen to dozens of taped interviews of Jerome old-timers to get a sense of language, history, and personality. This is how I was able to put flesh on the bones of my characters, and I'm so grateful to Alene.

Getting the additional information I needed once I'd moved to New Hampshire could have been tricky also. But thanks to an archival swap program, I was able to have every 1950 edition of the *Verde Independent* and the *Arizona Republic* brought to the Keene Public Library from the Arizona State Library, Archives, and Public Records—five microfilm reels at a time. Thanks to the staff at the Keene library for never "shushing" me whenever I gasped at discovering new headlines or want ads that took my breath away. These fascinating tidbits found their way into the novel, creating their own story parallel to the main one.

To Judy Goldman, the wonderful Mexican children's book author who breathed language into my characters Cruz and Angie, making sure that they spoke "Mexican" Spanish and that their voices and traditions rang true to their ancestry. Mexico City seemed so close, and I thank you for always responding so quickly and enthusiastically. And to Kathy Cannon Wiechman for your watchful eye when it came to continuity.

Some things just fall your way, and finding the late Barry

Sollenberger's article on the history of Jerome Muckers football was my lucky break, and how I knew I had a sports story. I never got the chance to meet Barry but am so grateful for his commitment to chronicling the history of Arizona high school football. Without Barry, much of that state's sports history would have been lost.

And finally, and perhaps most of all, to the late Mr. Lewis McDonald, Jerome High principal and chief secret keeper of his students' hopes and dreams. You defined the course of their lives by standing up for civil rights at a time when teachers could be fired for it. If I could, I'd write and tell you that I found it—that precious box—and cherished every letter. And that I keep copies of them close by, next to a handful of rocks I pilfered from the schoolyard. And that because of them, the Jerome Muckers won't be forgotten.

SANDRA NEIL WALLACE,

a former ESPN sportscaster, may have snagged her greatest lead yet in uncovering the inspirational achievements of the Jerome Muckers football team. She discovered the story while sifting through a box of letters and other memorabilia. The trail of letters led her to write *Muckers*.

Wallace was named an outstanding newcomer to the children's literature scene by the *Horn Book* following the publication of her first novel, *Little Joe*. The book was a finalist for the South Carolina Children's Book Award and a U.S. Department of Agriculture selection for its Ag in the Classroom program. *Muckers* is her first book for young adults. She lives in New Hampshire with her husband, author Rich Wallace.

Visit Sandra Neil Wallace at sandraneilwallace.com.
#gomuckers